THE
BACHELOR

USA *TODAY* BESTSELLING AUTHOR
MARNI MANN

ISBN-13: 979-8-9871060-4-4

To my ladies who fantasize.
Who dream about all the places and positions and appetites a man can satisfy.
Who want to be ravaged.
Worshipped.
Devoured.
Camden is for you.

PLAYLIST

"Me & My Demons"—Omido x Silent Child
"Not Enough"—Elvis Drew x AVIVIAN
"PLEASE"—Omido, Ex Habit
"Cravin' "—Stileto, featuring Kendyle Paige
"I Want You"—Reignwolf
"A Closeness"—Dermot Kennedy
"I Can't Go on Without You"—KALEO
"Chainsmoking"—Jacob Banks
"Her Life"—Two Feet
"VANISH (INTERLUDE)."—SUNDERWORLD
"SUMMER RENAISSANCE"—Beyoncé
"Haunted"—Beyoncé

You can find the playlist on Spotify

PROLOGUE

Camden

Nine Years Ago

Oaklyn fucking Rose, I thought as I walked into my sister's bedroom after having just seen Hannah's best friend in a bikini for the last hour, a bunch of us hanging out in our hot tub. *Holy shit, that girl gets hotter by the day.*

Tight body.

Nice rack.

At this age, I was sure she was a virgin—most of the girls in our sophomore class were.

And that was the reason I'd come into my sister's room after the little party we had. Everyone had already gone home, Mom and Dad were due back any minute, the empty beer bottles were hidden in the trash, and buried beneath those was a jar of water with all the cigarette butts swimming inside. We hoped the bath would drown out the smell of ash.

My sister and I were always careful, hiding all the evidence.

Except for now, apparently. Her drunk ass had a beer and was sipping on it while she sat on her bed, still in her wet bathing suit.

"Wanna share that?" I took a seat next to her in my soaked swim trunks and held out my hand.

If she didn't care about getting her bed wet, then neither did I.

She handed me the bottle. "Tonight was the best time ever." She had a solid buzz—I could hear it in her voice.

"Good time, for sure."

And the perfect opportunity to bring up her best friend.

"Hey, you know your girl, Oaklyn? She's really turned into quite a hottie."

She laughed. "She's always been a hottie. Maybe you need glasses. When was the last time Mom took you to the eye doctor?"

"Hannah, that's not what I mean." I took a drink and handed the beer back to her. "What I mean is, what do you think about me asking her out?"

She tapped my arm like it was the top of our golden retriever's head. "You're funny."

"I'm serious."

"No. No. *Nooo.*"

"Why not?"

She faced me, crossing her legs, her hair clinging to her cheeks, which she eventually tucked behind her ears. "You'd crush her. I can't let that happen." She wiped her mouth after she took another drink. "Oaklyn can't handle someone like you."

I pointed at my bare chest. "Someone like me?"

She nodded. "My brother is the ultimate heartbreaker. I can't lose my best friend because of a shattered heart."

It was almost like I wasn't even in the room and she was talking about me, not to me.

My brows rose as I stared at her. "Are you being serious?"

She gave me the beer back. "Heck yeah, I am." She then held out her pinkie. "Make me a promise, Camden Dalton, that my friends are forever and ever off-limits."

Shit, she was being serious.

But just to confirm, I said, "All of your friends?"

"Just my super-close ones, like Oaklyn, Suz, Tracy, and Justine."

Fuck.

When my sister gave me her pinkie, that was our solemn promise to each other. We didn't do it often, but when we did, nothing could break that promise.

Therefore, I had no choice.

I couldn't fight her on this.

I had to fold.

And that meant I could never touch Oaklyn Rose.

Damn, that sucks.

I locked our pinkies together and gave her the words she wanted to hear. "I promise."

ONE

Camden

There was no way in hell that my twin sister, Hannah, should leave me alone with her best friend in their apartment.

That was rule number one.

Rule number two was that I shouldn't be mentally stripping the jeans and sweatshirt off Oaklyn's perfect, tight, lean body. I shouldn't be fantasizing about wrapping those gorgeous legs around my waist and slowly burying my dick into her pussy. I shouldn't have this desire to make her scream so fucking loud that the neighbors on both sides would come banging on the door.

But that was what I was doing.

Because, *goddamn it*, she was so fucking hot.

So enticing.

So sweet. I just wanted to twist her long brown hair around my wrist and dirty her up a little.

Oaklyn Rose was the one girl I'd always wanted and the one girl who had always been off-limits.

The twin brother couldn't touch the twin sister's best friend.

And normally, I didn't break rules.

But rule number two had been shattered a few hours ago when I came over to their place for dinner and immediately caught sight of Oaklyn bending over to take a pizza out of the oven, showing me that spicy, heart-shaped ass. And rule number one was about to be broken since my sister had just been called into work.

"Shit!" Hannah shouted as she got off the phone with her boss, sprinting into her room to get changed. "Have I mentioned how much I hate him? Because I do. With a passion I can't even describe."

My sister was bitching about Declan Shaw, her boss at The Dalton Group and the top litigator in the state of California. After meeting him this past weekend, I'd learned he wasn't just a pit bull, but also one that fucking snarled. You would think that when you interned for your family's law firm, like Hannah, you would get to choose your mentor. Not at The Dalton Group. They didn't play that way. But there was an advantage to working under someone as skilled as Declan, which Hannah would eventually realize, and I hoped once I graduated law school this spring and moved back to the West Coast, I would become a clerk on his team.

After what sounded like a mini tornado erupting in her room, my sister returned to where Oaklyn and I were standing.

Oaklyn placed a soft-sided cooler in Hannah's hands. "Take this."

"What's in it?" Hannah asked.

"Brownies. Fruit. The leftover pizza we had for dinner."

Oaklyn knew Hannah could be at the office all night and didn't want my sister to go hungry.

Man, that girl was caring and motherly.

Nurturing.

My dick was fucking throbbing.

Hannah wrapped her arms around Oaklyn. "I love you."

"Go kick his ass," Oaklyn replied. "Or better yet, show him why you're an ass-kicker."

Hannah released her and moved over to me. "If you want to stay and hang instead of going back to Mom and Dad's, just crash in my bed. If I'm lucky enough to come home before morning, I'll climb in with Oaklyn." She hugged me. "I don't know if I'll see you before you leave, and I hate that. Hard."

What I hated was that I'd only come home for a long weekend, I was flying back to Boston tomorrow, and this was the first time I'd seen Hannah. The previous evenings, she'd been too slammed with work and babysitting our cousin Ford's daughter to get together with me.

I set my hand on top of her baseball hat, lifting the brim to see more of her face. "Hang in there. You're going to get through this."

She gave me the smallest of nods. "See you at spring break?"

"I might go to Mexico with some friends."

Where Hannah had opted to do her internship her final semester, I'd chosen the fall semester, so that freed up my spring break, and now, I only had to focus on school and prepping for the bar.

She sighed. "You mean, you might come home and hang with your sister because she's your fave."

I smiled.

As much as I loved her, that wasn't going to happen.

She knew that, and she returned my expression with a

7

frown. "See you guys later."

I watched her leave, and the second the door clicked, I turned to Oaklyn. She was in front of the couch, less than ten feet away, eating a Nutella brownie my sister had baked, a full plate of them on the coffee table.

I pointed at the door. "Should I get out of here too?"

She covered her mouth, a chunk of fudgy brownie at the tip of one of her fingers. "No. Stay. I'm just going to eat the rest of these and finish drinking the rest of that. You can join me."

These were the brownies.

That was the wine, and there were several more bottles in addition to the one sitting on the table.

I took a seat on the opposite side of the couch, catching a glimpse of her licking the gooey dough off her nail.

The way her tongue scooped.

The way her teeth nipped her flesh.

The way her cheeks sank in as she sucked the remainder of the dessert off her skin.

Fuck.

Me.

Oaklyn and my sister had been friends for as long as I could remember, so she was a girl I'd grown up with. A girl I'd seen grow through every physical stage, starting with the adorable, pigtailed princess, morphing into the sultry twenty-four-year-old woman she was now.

She finished chewing, and her piercing blue gaze connected with mine. "Just a little bit longer, and you'll be moving back here." She grabbed her wine from the table and tucked her legs beneath her. "Hannah will be so happy. All she talks about is how much she misses you."

And I missed her.

But I'd chosen Boston for my undergraduate degree and New York for law school because I knew, ultimately, I would be joining The Dalton Group as soon as I graduated, so I just wanted to get away for a handful of years and have some fun outside of LA and the usual crowd we hung around with.

Besides, choosing Harvard and NYU had meant I could pave my way with a reputation I earned all on my own.

And I'd certainly done that—with the ladies and my professors, neither of whom would ever forget my name, although for entirely different reasons.

"I'm ready to come back," I admitted, reaching for my vodka. "Ready to get a place of my own and take the bar and start work. Declan's not going to hold the title of the top litigator for long."

"Oh, yeah?" She laughed. "Well, you're going to have to fight your sister on that. She's after the same title, and she would like nothing more than to rip it away from that dick."

That fucking word.

I wanted to hear her moan it.

"It's been a while since we've caught up. Tell me about you, Oaklyn. How's the marketing world? And your dating life? Seeing anyone serious?" I settled into the corner, fixing the pillow to give me a better angle to view her.

And what a view it was.

Oaklyn had this natural look about her—creamy skin and the most arresting sapphire eyes, puffy pink lips that she constantly licked, the wetness she left behind always making them glossy. There weren't many women who could pull off a clean, makeup-free face and still look fucking breathtaking.

But that was her.

I'd seen her in the morning when she just crawled out of bed, after a full day of skiing when she was soaked in sweat, in a bikini following hours of being in the ocean. I'd also seen her in a gown at prom when her lids were painted and her cheeks were glowing and her lips were red.

Tonight was the way I preferred her.

Raw, unpainted.

Innocent.

She let out a huff of air, her cheeks beginning to flush.

Something told me it wasn't from the wine.

"Marketing is going great. I just got promoted to senior account manager, and my book of business is triple from when I first started with the company. I'm working with the dreamiest brands, and within a year or two, I should have enough to buy my first condo."

"Impressive."

She drew in a deep breath. "My dating life ... not so impressive."

"Why is that?"

She held the glass near her chin, watching me, but not drinking. After several seconds passed, she tilted the opening, allowing some of the wine to trickle in between those invitingly plump lips. "Are you sure you want to hear this?" She let out a small giggle. "This is my second glass of wine. I don't know what's going to come out of my mouth at this point."

Now, wasn't that an interesting question?

And description.

"I don't see why I wouldn't," I told her.

"My last boyfriend, Trevor, he recently ended things for the stupidest of reasons." Her hand moved to her hair, running her fingers through a curl. When she reached the end, she started over, this time going much slower. "At least, I think it's stupid."

"Let me be the judge of that."

"It's because ..." She looked away, her skin turning even more flushed, her teeth grinding across her lip before she continued, "I wouldn't sleep with him." She locked our stares. "Lame of him, right?"

"You mean, you didn't want to do it every day? Or weekly? I ... don't understand. It's not like you're a virgin."

The corner of the couch hugged her so tightly that she looked half-swallowed, and so did her face while she stayed completely silent. Blinking. Looking at me like a deer in fucking headlights.

"Wait, you're a virgin? Oaklyn, how is that even possible?"

Her chest rose, staying high as she said, "Oh, it's possible."

A fucking ... virgin?

That response vibrated across my throat as I repeated it silently in my head.

How the hell can this woman, one of the most beautiful I've ever seen, still be a virgin?

"I don't believe it," I replied.

We'd gone to the same private school. Many of my friends had tried to hit it, and I knew she'd graduated without sleeping with any of them. But the fact that she'd held out through college and beyond was fucking mind-blowing.

She gazed at me through her long, thick lashes. "Camden, I am."

That confirmation took my brain on a journey. One that began with re-breaking rule number two—imagining peeling those jeans off her legs and dipping my tip into that snug, untapped pussy.

What that would feel like.

What that would sound like.

Shit.

My cock wasn't just throbbing. It was dying to burst through my zipper and soak into that wetness—wetness no one had ever felt before.

Still, I didn't get it.

"Are you saving yourself for marriage?"

"No." She tucked the curl behind her ear. "I'm saving myself for someone worth having sex with."

"And the ex wasn't worth it?"

"When we first got together, I hoped he would be. I mean, I wanted him to be." She drained the rest of her wine. "But it quickly turned into one disappointment after another, and then he dumped me after he didn't get what he wanted."

She glanced at her empty glass. "I'm not looking for Prince Charming. I'm just looking for a man who isn't going to constantly fib to me. Or when he invites me away, he doesn't get his credit card declined, so I have to pay for the weekend he planned for me. Who follows through with the things he promises."

She refilled her glass and snuggled back into the couch. "I'm not looking for a man who's rich or model hot. Looks and money, honestly, don't really mean much to me. I just want a guy who's going to treat me with respect and kindness."

She sipped from her full glass and then continued, "That's part one. Now, for part two." Her face winced. "I'm terrified I've hyped up losing my virginity to the point where I'm worried I won't be good at it. Camden"—her eyes widened—"I can't be bad in bed. That would be the biggest tragedy ever."

A woman who cared about her performance.

God, she was fucking adorable.

"Oaklyn, you're good at everything you do. Sex won't be any different."

"Says the expert." She wiggled even deeper into the corner. "Neither of us knows if that'll be true or not."

My mind couldn't stop reeling from this news.

Twenty-four years old, drop-dead stunning, and she'd never had her cherry popped.

Never experienced mind-bending sex.

Never dug her nails so hard into a man's back that she

struck blood.

I swished some vodka around in my mouth before I said, "You want me to read the verdict?"

She nodded. "Please."

"Sounds to me like you haven't picked a dude who's even worthy of dating you, never mind being your first."

"But, Camden, I want to experience that first." As she sighed, her head tilted back to stare at the ceiling. "I want to feel intimacy. Pleasure. All the things that are exchanged when you share something like that with a man."

"You will. I fucking promise you that."

"But when?" Her head straightened, and she twisted the stem of her wineglass, the dark burgundy liquid sloshing against the sides of the glass. "I've waited this long, and it hasn't happened. At this point, it feels like it never will." She held up her hand. "I don't expect you to have an answer for that." She moved those same fingers to her mouth. "I can't even believe I told you all this."

"Listen, if this were an NFL game and the spread was a year, I'd take the under."

Her stare intensified. "You really think it's going to happen within the next twelve months?"

"Yes."

"And if it doesn't?"

I sucked an ice cube into my mouth, smashing it between my molars. "I'd be shocked."

Silence ticked, and then, "I'm going to put something out into the universe, and I'll possibly regret it later, but the wine has certainly taken over everything I'm saying now."

"You have my full attention."

"Good, because I have a proposition for you, Camden Dalton."

The way she'd said my last name made my dick clutch

hard.

I kicked my feet onto the table and set my tumbler on my lap. "Just what I'm good at. Hit me with it."

"I've seen the movie, and I refuse to become that main star —in other words, I will not be the forty-year-old virgin. I also don't want to give myself to just anyone and, at the end of it, be regretful because it was dismal at best. I want my first time to be amazing."

"What are you saying, Oaklyn?"

"I'm saying"—she untucked her legs and crossed them in front of her, leaning forward to bring us closer—"if I'm in the same situation a year from now, I want my first time to be with you. And I want you to teach me all the things I need to know, so I can be good at it."

A full laugh wasn't what came out of my mouth. This was more of a half, followed by me chugging the remaining vodka in my glass. "Let me get this straight. You want me to take your virginity and teach you how to please a man? That's what you're asking me?"

A series of images instantly played in my head—the tasting of that beautiful body, how wet I could make her pussy. The hugging of my dick, a type of virgin tightness that I hadn't felt in a long time.

The fucking moaning.

Jesus Christ.

"Yes," she responded.

My feet dropped to the floor. "Oaklyn, do you know what my sister would do to me if she found out? We shouldn't even be having this conversation right now."

"Camden—"

"No." I shook my head. "You're so fucking off-limits."

She reached across the space, her hand gently touching my thigh. "Please listen to me, okay?"

It was just fingers casually resting on my leg, but something about them felt so good.

Too fucking good.

"I've heard you out." I moved her hand away, assuming that feeling would leave with it. But it didn't. "And what you don't know—or maybe you do—is that I made Hannah a promise in high school that I wouldn't go anywhere near you or any of her close friends. Even though that promise was a long time ago, it's good for a lifetime."

Back then, I had gotten around as much as I did now.

The bachelor, the ultimate player—Hannah rotated between titles, depending on the day, but they meant the same thing. I was the guy who had no plans on settling down, and my sister didn't want me to fuck her friends and then leave them right after, which was what I was known for.

"Camden, Hannah doesn't have to know." Her voice was a little above a whisper. "And what I'll get out of this will most likely be the best sex I'll ever have in my life."

My face tilted to the side; my brows rose. "What would give you that assumption?"

"You're forgetting we grew up together. Hannah's room was directly next to yours; you guys shared a wall. I heard"—she smiled—"everything."

"That was years and years ago."

She leaned back against the cushions, putting distance between us. "And I'm sure you've only gotten better."

Praising my manhood.

I liked her style.

But this proposition was risky.

Did I want to taste her?

Fuck yes.

Did I want to feel her virgin pussy pulse around my dick?

Fucking yes.

But doing that would come with consequences.

Oaklyn was practically family. Given that she'd never done anything like this before, that could make her extra emotional and clingy. Needy even.

I didn't handle any of those well.

"What do you say, Camden?" As she repositioned herself again, her sweatshirt fell off her shoulder, showing the dip of her neck, her jutted-out collarbone—both incredibly sexy. "In one year, if I'm still in the same place, are you going to swoop in and rescue me?"

There was nothing rescuing about the way I liked to fucked.

I was naughty.

Insatiable.

Animalistic.

I wanted sweat and pain and shouting at the top of our fucking lungs.

I jiggled the remaining ice cubes. "When the time comes, how will I know you're still a virgin?"

Where did that question come from?

What the hell has gotten into me?

Why am I even teasing myself when I know how dangerous this is?

"I'll tell you." She grinned. "It's not like I haven't had your cell number for a million years."

Oaklyn was wrong; she did in fact want a prince, one who would ensure her first time was like a fairy tale. Where she'd be kissed. Loved. Desired with soft, tender embraces.

But I was no fucking savior.

Nor was I soft. Tender. Loving.

I was a man who focused on orgasms, not commitments.

I didn't just want my power to break the bed. I wanted my stroke to send the headboard straight through the wall.

There was a big difference.

And because one of us needed to act with something other than what was between our legs, I said, "Oaklyn ..." My voice faded as her expression began to captivate me in a way I couldn't fight, so I got up and went into the kitchen, adding more ice and vodka to my glass before I returned to the couch. I thought the break would make this easier, but my dick was even harder now. "You do know what you're asking from me, don't you?"

She bit her lip, those deep blue eyes fucking twinkling. "I'm not asking you to strip me naked right now." She allowed that thought to simmer. "It's a year away."

She had a point.

So much shit could happen in twelve months.

Hell, she could be married by then.

"I'm also not going to beg you to take my virginity—"

"You don't have to beg me," I growled.

Fuck, that wasn't the appropriate response.

I needed to be stronger.

I needed to say no.

I needed to show her that I was unaffected by this request.

But I couldn't.

There was plenty of pussy I'd turned down over the years. Women who had done nothing for me or couldn't handle a one-night stand.

But Oaklyn Rose wasn't a woman I could ever deny.

She held out her fingers. "Should we shake on it?"

The moment our hands locked, rule number three formed in my head.

You don't fuck your sister's best friend when you promised her you wouldn't.

And, goddamn it, I had a feeling that one would be broken too.

17

TWO

Camden

One Year Later

The text came through my phone as Declan and I were walking out of the downtown Boston office of Hooked, a dating app that had been founded by three Harvard graduates. They were several years older than me and all part of Harvard Business School, which was why we'd never crossed paths on campus. They were currently in litigation with Faceframe, a social media giant, along with one of Faceframe's employees.

That was where we came in.

Easton, Grayson, and Holden, the partners of Hooked, wanted to take those motherfuckers down, and Declan and I were going to do everything in our power to make sure that happened.

The second my feet hit the sidewalk, on my way to the

SUV that was parked outside, I caught a glimpse of the message on my screen.

"We need to discuss Hooked," Declan said.

The sound of him dragged my attention away from the text. Before I could even register the words I'd just read, I shoved my phone into my pocket and slid into the backseat, and the SUV immediately took off for the airport.

"I thought the meeting went well," I told him. "They're ready to go to war, and there's no question in my mind that we're going to destroy the opposition in the courtroom."

"Is that what you think?" His brow furrowed, his tone as condescending as usual.

After passing the bar several months ago, I'd been placed on Declan's team. Since his relationship with my sister was now common knowledge—accepted by my aunt and uncle, the owners of The Dalton Group, and their three sons, Dominick, Jenner, and Ford, who ran the whole show—she worked under a different litigator at the firm, my cousins' attempt to keep their personal lives out of the office. That made me the only Dalton on Declan's team, and during the short time I'd been employed under him, one thing had become apparent.

When it came to law, Declan Shaw was a fucking animal.

And I loved every second of it.

Even the ones that tested me, like he was doing now.

I loosened the tie from my neck and adjusted my cuff links. "No, that's what I know."

"Then, you do know who they've hired for the opposition, I assume?"

"Declan, you're fucking kidding me, right?" I chuckled. "I don't give a shit who we're about to face. We're going to destroy them. End of story."

"Cocky bastard. I've taught you well."

"Nah." I shook my head. "I just know how good we are, and I'm not afraid to say it."

"We've got a lot of work ahead of us."

He clasped my shoulder with one hand, holding a thumb drive with his other, which contained every bit of data we would need for this case. Declan didn't trust the mail or a courier to handle confidential information, so that tiny drive that was tucked under his fingers was the whole reason we'd flown to Boston.

"And I know very little about tech," I confessed.

But in preparation for this case, I'd been studying, reading up on the terms, the process of developing an app, and the roles within Hooked. I needed to understand what I was really looking at and what had happened within the inner layers of their company.

"I can't say I know a lot more than you, but after this, we're going to be experts," he replied.

"I don't know if it's because we share an alma mater or because they're from Boston or what, but I feel like I've got a personal investment in this one." I glanced out the windshield as the driver turned onto the tarmac. "I want these Hooked guys to get the justice they deserve."

"They will, but it's going to take a hell of a lot of billable hours to get us there."

I placed the strap of my briefcase over my arm. "We have a huge team. We can handle it."

"Tomorrow morning, I'm going into Dominick's office to tell him I want another paralegal and three more associates."

Even though each of the brothers had equal roles, Dominick was the oldest, and with that came a bit of hierarchy.

But adding four team members? That surprised me.

"You really think we need that many more to help?" I asked.

He placed the thumb drive into his suit pocket and lifted his briefcase onto his lap. "I don't expect you to know this— you're too fresh—but we have two tech monopolies going to war. There's been mishandled information, stolen designs, and the breach of an ironclad noncompete. This isn't Pop's coffee shop we're talking about, Camden. This is the largest dating app in the world, suiting up against the largest social media site. Shit is going to get fucking ugly."

"Was that supposed to make me shiver?"

His brow loosened from its furrow and rose. "It doesn't?"

I rubbed my hands together. "I'm ready to fight."

"Just the answer I wanted." He took out the thumb drive and handed it to me. "Start poring through some of what's on there during this cross-country flight. When I leave Dominick's office in the morning, I'm coming straight to you for a recap." He opened the door as the SUV came to a stop and walked up the steps of the jet.

I followed behind him, and once I took a seat, I opened my laptop and inserted the drive, transferring the data to my hard drive. As the information began to load, I took out my cell and clicked on Messages.

There were several unread texts.

Only one got my focus.

OAKLYN

Heeeeey, it's time to talk. Can you believe it's been a whole year? Come over tonight … if you can.

"For the long flight," the flight attendant said, setting a vodka on the rocks beside me.

I thanked her and brought the glass up to my lips, swallowing the cold, burning liquor as I scanned Oaklyn's message again.

I knew how much time had passed since she'd propositioned me. I didn't have a countdown going on my Calendar
app, but every month, a mental check mark would swish across
my brain, letting me know I was one step closer to potentially
tasting her.

A thought that was still so fucking wild.

Dangerous.

Something I still shouldn't even consider.

But, hell, I knew the temptation was far out of my control.

I wanted her.

I wanted to be inside her.

I wanted to be the man she compared all others to. Even
when her future husband was pounding her pussy, I wanted
her to remember me.

And every time I saw her, I was reminded of that fact. Like
when I'd first moved back to LA and my parents threw a gradu-
ation party. Then, there were the times I'd stopped by their
shared place to see my sister and when Hannah had brought
Oaklyn to the gathering I'd put together when I got my condo.

Every time, she was there.

Always taking me in, locking eyes, silent words passing
between us.

But there were spoken ones too. Ones that she would
subtly say in front of me, so I knew what was happening in her
life. A way to keep me updated without reaching out to me
directly.

A year.

Shit, I had been positive things were going to change for
her during that time, but the dates she'd gone on were nothing
more than a few dinners, a concert, and a trip to the movies—
details I'd heard about when I was in her presence.

None of those outings had amounted to anything more,
which dropped Oaklyn straight into my hands.

Hands that were fucking dying to touch that perfect body.

Still, there was a *but*.

A realization that had come to me over the last several weeks as the one-year anniversary sprinted closer.

As my sister's best friend, a woman who was off-limits and someone I cared about and wanted to protect, I was going to do her a favor.

That favor would show her exactly who I was and why I wasn't the right man to take her virginity.

Not that I didn't want to—fuck, I wanted nothing more.

But she needed someone soft.

Someone tender.

Someone who ... wasn't me.

And once I made her aware of that, I was sure she'd be too terrified to follow through with her proposition, and this whole fantasy would be over.

THREE

Oaklyn

E xactly one year ago, I'd told Camden I wanted him to take my virginity. The next morning, when my eyes flicked open and Hannah was curled up next to me in my bed, the urge to speak to Camden was far stronger than the guilt I was already feeling about my best friend.

I loved Hannah more than anyone in this world. She was like a sister to me and had been since we were twelve years old.

And every feeling that churned through my stomach, every alarm that went off in my chest, told me she would hate the idea of her brother and me sleeping together.

But I wanted this.

I wanted this for me.

Even though I knew how wrong it was, I silently slipped out of my bed and hurried to her room with all intentions of sneaking inside and waking him up to talk.

But the door was already open, and her bed was empty.

Camden was gone.

He'd left before I got the chance to tell him I didn't want to wait a year.

I wanted him to take my virginity now.

When I crawled back into my bed, I took my phone off the nightstand, my thumb hovering over his name in my Contacts, debating on whether I should text him or call him later, once Hannah went to work.

But I hadn't.

Nor had I talked to him about my new plan during any of the times I saw him following that initial night.

Maybe I'd lost my nerve. Maybe I was reminding myself that Hannah would go nuts if she found out. Maybe I was taking that time to really ask myself if I had the courage to give my virginity to the sexiest man alive.

Because, the truth was, I'd been crushing on Camden since the day I'd met him all those years ago.

Of course, I knew us becoming a couple would never be a possibility. I wasn't foolish enough to think he was into girls like me—girls who wouldn't immediately spread their legs, who actually wanted a relationship, who were looking for love.

Besides, as kids, Hannah had told me on more than one occasion that it would be gross if one of her friends hooked up with her brother. As we had gotten older, gross had changed to disgusting, and she'd emphasize that she'd murder him if he ever got near one of us, especially because Camden had earned himself quite the reputation.

There was a reason I'd called him an expert.

Which was why I'd been so nervous when I finally sent him the text today, telling him it was time to talk. Sure, I wanted a professional to show me the ropes. Someone who spoke the language of pleasure much more fluently than me.

But, *my God*, that thought was intimidating.

So was the idea of having his experienced hands and seasoned lips on my body.

What if I disappoint him?

What if I turn him off?

What if he turns me down and never writes me back?

I kept checking my phone to see if I'd missed a notification and that his reply was waiting for me in my Messages. But there was no response from him, no little bubbles on his side of the text box anytime I looked. I even wondered if the *Delivered* that appeared under my words was misleading, that the message was actually stuck somewhere in cyberland and hadn't gone through.

I took another sip of my wine, a bottle I had opened after work when the nerves got the best of me. I didn't usually drink during the week unless Hannah and I were having a girls' night, but the hurricane storming through my head was becoming far too much.

It had been hours since I'd sent that text.

How can he not write me back?

Will he really just ignore me?

Not even having the decency to tell me he was no longer interested—

My brain silenced the second I heard the knock at my door.

A knock that I hadn't expected.

I hadn't ordered food. Hannah had moved in with Declan a few months ago at the renewal of our lease and never popped in, unannounced.

Could it be Camden?

I set down my wine and stood from the couch, taking a quick glance down my body to make sure I had something appropriate on. A sports bra. Yoga pants. My bright red toenails gleaming from the chandelier Hannah had installed during one of her sleepless nights.

I was about to dart into my bedroom to grab a sweatshirt when I heard another knock.

Impatient and demanding.

It had to be him.

I rushed over to the door and quickly checked the peephole, unable to hide the smile on my face when my guess was confirmed.

Hello, beautiful man.

He couldn't reply to a text, but he could find his way to my apartment, and the small circle I was looking through showed me he was still dressed for work.

Why is it so difficult to breathe?

I slowly opened the door and was completely unprepared for the sexiness on the other side. The peephole had acted as a filter; it certainly hadn't shown me the depth of this hot, sizzling Dalton steam.

Camden was in a navy suit and white shirt, his gold tie loose at his throat. He was holding the doorframe with both hands, putting his weight into his arms, leaning as close to me as he could get. But his head was down, like he was deep in thought. His face was hidden, his messy, short, dark, gelled hair the only thing that was pointed at me.

"Camden ..."

His head gradually lifted, and his ocean-blue eyes connected with mine.

His perfect, soft, thick lips parted.

His small, sloped nose and angular cheeks and square jaw and heavy scruff were now all facing me.

Oh God.

A wave of tingles blasted through my entire body.

In a way that I hadn't expected.

In a way that made it even harder for me to breathe.

His gaze stayed on my face for several seconds and then

began to travel down my body at a speed that was achingly slow. He stalled at my chest and stomach before going all the way to my feet.

Silence continued to tick between us.

But in that moment—the period where I felt like I was naked and on full display, his watchful eyes taking in every inch of my body—I wrapped my arms around my navel and said, "Hi." I paused, waiting, receiving nothing but a heavier gaze. "You never replied, so I didn't think you were going to show up."

"Surprise." He licked across both lips. "Unless you don't like surprises?"

My foot was holding the door, and I dropped an arm from my waist to open the door a bit wider. "This was a good one." My smile hadn't faded at all. "Do you want to come in?"

"I want to know something first." His head still low, he looked at me through his lashes, an expression on his face, like he hadn't eaten in days.

"Sure." My throat was heavy and tight. "Anything."

"Me. This." He stalled. "Is that really what you want?"

I didn't have to think.

I'd already done plenty of that over the last year.

"Yes, Camden, it's what I want."

His hand left the wooden frame and moved to his face, where he rubbed his fingers down the side of his short, trimmed beard. "Then, we're going to do it my way."

"What does that mean?"

He nodded toward me. "What do you have in there to drink?"

I moved out of the doorway to allow him inside, and he walked into my kitchen. Since this was the same apartment I'd shared with his sister, he was already familiar with where everything was located. He opened the cabinet next to the stove and took out the bottle of vodka, pouring some into a glass before adding ice.

With the open concept, I was able to see him from the couch in the living room, where he eventually joined me. That was when I got a whiff of his cologne. An aroma that was as captivating as his eyes and his presence—a strong wind of citrus with a robust blend of woods.

I was positive I'd smelled it before, but it was more prominent tonight.

Or maybe I was just soaking in every detail since this was the evening when everything was going to change.

An evening I was never going to forget.

"Oaklyn ..." He traced the lip of the glass with the inside of his thumb. God, even his regular, simple movements reeked of lust. "You've put me on this sexual pedestal, and I promise to fulfill every need you have." He rested his forearms on his thighs, holding the drink between his spread legs. "But I want to make something very clear. I'm not Prince Charming. Hell, I'm probably no better than any guy you've dated." He wet his lips, licking across the top of them. "Oaklyn, you've known me forever, so you know I don't do emotions or relationships. I don't do soft or tender or any of that kind of shit you might be looking for. I'll give you whatever you want physically, but that's where it ends."

Every time he mentioned my needs, there was a twinge in *that* spot.

A tightening.

A dampening.

And it wasn't soft and tender, the way he had described.

This feeling was vicious.

"I understand," I told him.

"Have you changed your mind?"

I lifted my wine off the table, holding it with both hands as I raised it to my lips. I sipped and swallowed. "No."

"You're not afraid of me ..."

He hadn't phrased it like a question. More like he was shocked to discover this.

"Why would I be afraid of you?"

"Because you think I wouldn't hurt you, but you're wrong. I would." He turned the drink in his hands, the ice rattling, but he kept his eyes on me. "When I walk away from this, it could crush you. I don't want to hurt you. I want you to know that, going in. I just won't want more, Oaklyn. More isn't me. And we'll forever be tied to each other through Hannah, so I'll continue being in your life after this. I want you to be prepared for how that might feel."

Even if I wanted him to, I didn't expect my best friend's twin brother to fall in love with me.

Even if I wanted more, I didn't expect this to extend beyond our one night together.

I was naive, but not that naive.

I knew what I'd asked for and was fully prepared to take it and watch him walk away.

"You're assuming I'm looking for more. I'm not. This is about you taking my virginity and showing me all the ways to please a man, nothing else."

His eyes narrowed, and he swirled some vodka around in his mouth, his Adam's apple bobbing as it went down his throat. "You're going to have to prove that to me, which is why we're going slow and doing things my way. I'm going to show you how I'm the opposite of Prince Charming, and you're going to show me you can handle that."

"How?"

"First, you're going to do a little homework. You're going to watch some porn, talk to friends—not my sister. You're going to

30

recall every fantasy you've ever had. You do whatever you have to do to come up with a list of three things you want to try. Not sex. They can be anything but sex, and we're going to turn those three fantasies into lessons. The fifth lesson, which I'm pretty positive we won't make it to, is when I'll take your virginity."

I did some quick math in my head. "Five lessons? But you asked me to come up with three?"

"That's because lesson one will be my pick, not yours."

My skin was on fire.

My heart was pounding so hard that I was convinced he could hear it.

"But, Oaklyn, all of this is under one condition, and if I get a feeling that condition has been broken, we're done."

Now, even my ears were burning. "What's the condition?"

"You can't fall in love with me."

Love.

Something my best friend would shoot me for.

But something I could certainly see being possible if we were going to share so many intimate moments together.

And that was when I realized the whole point of drawing this out.

Each lesson was a test. A way for me to prove that I wasn't falling for him. But if I couldn't do that, if he sensed my emotions were coming into play, we were over.

Camden didn't think I was up for this kind of challenge.

I was going to show him how wrong he was.

"All right." I took another drink.

"You and my sister are hopeless romantics. That shit isn't happening here."

"Fine, but I have a condition of my own."

"You think you're in a position to negotiate?" He winked. "I don't think so."

31

I ignored his cuteness and said, "My condition is that you have to teach me how to be the best lover. How to use my mouth and my hands and my body, so the next guy I date, I can blow his mind with my sexy skills."

"Isn't that what lessons are for?"

I took one more drink and returned the glass to the table. "And—"

"Fuck no. There is no *and* in this conversation."

"Camden," I gasped. His relentlessness made him the best litigator, but impossibly difficult to bargain with. "I'm giving you all my firsts. The fantasies I'm going to come up with are things I've never done before—I mean, I've done things, but not much. I want one of your firsts. I want something that you've never experienced with another woman."

He leaned against the cushions, extending his arm across the back of the couch, a single eyebrow rising. "You do know there's very little—if anything—that I haven't done with a woman."

"Now, that's something that doesn't surprise me." I laughed.

He was quiet for a moment. "How about I promise to come up with something you won't ever forget? Does that work?"

"I like that idea." I stuck my hand toward him. "So, we have a deal?"

He stayed still for what felt like an excruciatingly long time, and then he set down his drink and used his arms to lift himself off the couch. Placing a knee on the cushion between us, he moved toward me.

It happened so fast that I didn't have time to react.

To think.

To process what he was actually doing.

But he gripped my cheek, aiming my face toward his, and leaned my back into the couch, moving on top of me.

Muscles I'd seen and known he had but never touched were now pressed into me.

His scent completely enveloping me.

A combination that was setting me on fire.

As he hovered above me, his stare was animalistic, his thumb running over my top lip and then my bottom. His face was a foot away, but he closed that distance, and as I drew in air, I anticipated our lips to lock.

But they didn't.

He brushed his beard across my neck.

The feeling was rough.

Almost painful.

But there was something else, this pleasure that I hadn't expected.

When I felt it again, this time on my cheek, my lips parted, and a moan escaped from between them. My back arched so deeply into the cushions that my chest aligned with his as he worked his way to the other side, dragging his whiskers. The feel of his hand, the strength of his fingers, the way his flesh rubbed into mine were scorching.

Until it all stopped.

And his lips were above me, and we were only breaths apart.

I waited.

I inhaled.

I felt my eyes close.

And when he finally kissed me, it wasn't an embrace that was soft and tender even though he'd told me it wouldn't be.

It was as coarse as his beard.

As ravenous as his grip.

As powerful as the cars I could hear on the road outside my apartment.

The moment he pulled away, he scanned my eyes while he licked me off his lips.

I wanted to know what he was looking for.

I wanted to know what he saw.

I wanted to know how I tasted.

Just as I was about to ask, I heard, "We have a deal."

FOUR

Camden

I'd arrived at the office an hour earlier than normal so I could finish scrolling through all the data from the thumb drive we'd collected yesterday in Boston. Declan would be walking in here within the next thirty minutes, following his meeting with Dominick. In order to answer all his questions, which I knew would come at me in rapid-fire, I needed to make sure I understood everything I was looking at.

I picked up my office phone and dialed the number to Easton's direct line. Even though Hooked had three equal partners, Easton was the CEO and my main point of contact.

"Easton Jones," he said as the call connected.

"It's Camden Dalton."

"Camden, I hope you and Declan had a safe flight back to LA?"

My hand returned to the mouse, and I began to scroll through the documents that I'd transferred over from my laptop. "We did."

"Excellent. What can I do for you?"

I flipped through one of the spreadsheets before pulling up several side-by-side images. "Within the next hour, our team is going to start plowing through all the information you provided. Before that happens, I want to confirm that the forensic data analyst who Hooked hired was able to detect that files were actually stolen from your network. I can't seem to locate their findings or contact info."

"We never hired one," he replied. "We conducted an in-house investigation to rule out other possible suspects, and our lead developer was in charge of that. At the time of the investigation, that was all the proof we needed. Now that new evidence has come into play, I know that changes things tremendously."

I closed out the files and opened my email. "Our firm employs a full-time forensic data analyst who's incredible. If information exists, I assure you, she'll find it. I can send her your way sometime this week and have her run her own investigation, if you're open to that?"

"Absolutely. We'd welcome it," he confirmed. "I'm extremely interested to see what she finds and if it'll help our case."

"I'll set that up, and I'll reach out if we have any further questions. As we dig deeper, we'll be talking daily—quite possibly, even hourly."

"It's a good thing I like you, Camden." He laughed. "Honestly, it's almost a relief to have a fellow Harvard grad on our legal team. I know you and Declan are going to do great things for us."

"We are," I promised. "I'll be in touch."

I hung up and lifted my cell off my desk, swiping through the latest round of notifications on the screen. Now that I had a little more of a handle on the Hooked data, I could focus on the other issue that had been haunting me.

Oaklyn Rose.

I'd had no intention of kissing her last night.

Or touching her face.

Or thinking about her from the moment I'd left her apartment to right now.

But I couldn't get her out of my fucking head.

When I'd shown up at her place, I'd expected her to be open to the three fantasies she wanted to try and how I'd kick things off with a pick of my own. What I hadn't expected was the moan that came from her mouth as I brushed my beard across her face and down her neck, even going as low as the top of her chest.

I knew that kind of sensation wasn't always pleasant and it could be painful to some.

That had been the point.

She needed a warning that I really wasn't soft and I most definitely wasn't tender.

But Oaklyn seemed to enjoy it. So much so that she pressed her chest against mine and tightened her legs around me. Movements that told me she wanted more.

That she couldn't get enough.

That she was accepting the little I gave her.

But once I had kissed her, I'd pulled back, quickly ending what I had started. If she wanted more, she was going to have to wait.

The thing was, I didn't want to fucking wait.

ME

8 p.m. Tonight. My place.

OAKLYN

Ohhh. That must mean it's time for lesson 1.

> **ME**
> Did you think I was inviting you over for dinner?

> **OAKLYN**
> Ha! Dick ...
>
> Should I bring anything?

> **ME**
> Your body.

> **OAKLYN**
> Obviously. Anything else?

"Someone's talking to a woman."

I glanced up and saw my sister leaning into the doorway of my office.

"Why the hell would you think that?" I opened my top drawer and placed my phone inside, hiding the screen from Hannah's watchful, wandering eyes.

"You're smiling." She came in and took a seat in front of my desk.

"Hannah, women don't make me smile. They make me scream. Huge fucking difference."

"Gag."

I lifted my orange juice off the desk and pounded a few sips. "What's going on?"

She shrugged. "I just had a few minutes before my next meeting, so I wanted to pop in and see how Boston went."

"Declan didn't tell you?"

"He gave me the highlights."

I rested my arms on the desk. "Now that I've pored through some of the info, I don't think I can even comprehend the magnitude of this case. The two companies going to war against each other, the evidence that's been presented, the lies, the data we're going to have to sift through—it's going to get interesting."

"Declan mentioned that. He even said he needs to add more people to the team—he doesn't think he has enough to cover what he needs."

I nodded, linking my fingers together. "He's meeting with Dominick right now to discuss that."

"You lucky little shit." She grinned.

"Hey, I didn't tell you to go bang your boss and start a relationship with him so you'd have to get assigned to a different team. That decision was all on you."

She laughed. "So out of character, I know. Let's just say, I pulled a you."

"If you had pulled a me, you would have ended things with him before they began; you wouldn't be living with the dude, talking about how many babies you're going to have."

She tucked her hair back. "Babies aren't going to happen until I'm at least thirty."

"And you just proved my point."

Even so, this conversation had me feeling guilty over last night, and another heavy dose of regret hit my chest when I thought about what was going to go down this evening.

I shouldn't be going behind Hannah's back to pleasure her best friend's pussy.

I couldn't even imagine what my sister's reaction would be.

But Hannah certainly wasn't going to hear about it from me.

Once we hit lesson five—if we even got that far, which I highly doubted since I didn't think Oaklyn would even be able to handle lesson one—Oaklyn and I would be done.

Still, I didn't know if Oaklyn could hide what was happening from my sister, who was one of the best people readers in the world. If I was giving her endless amounts of orgasms—something I planned to do during each lesson—then

39

Hannah would know the moment the two of them got together, reading it from Oaklyn's expression.

That was something I needed to discuss with Oaklyn before I got anywhere near her again.

"Are you going barhopping with the guys tonight?" she asked.

I shook my head. "I have too much work to do."

"Lamest excuse ever," Ford said from my doorway, who must have heard our conversation as he was walking by. "I've even got a sitter for Everly tonight. You're going out with us even if I have to drag you there."

I laughed at my cousin.

Usually, he was the one bailing on our outings because he didn't want to leave his daughter or he didn't have anyone to watch her since his nanny had become his girlfriend.

"I'm not going," I told him. "I've got hours and hours of work to do on this case, and I get dick done at the office because people like you two"—I nodded at them—"keep coming in and disrupting me."

"You know Jenner and Dominick are going to give you endless jabs for not being there," he muttered.

Once my other two cousins found out, my phone would be blowing up with texts from them, where they'd remind me that they were actually my bosses, not Declan, and that I needed to put my work down and meet up with them.

"That's why I'm not telling them until later," I said. "And neither are you two. Mouths shut, got it?"

Ford put his hands in the air. "We never had this conversation—but let it be known, I'm pissed you're not going to be there."

"You know I'm a vault," Hannah added before her eyes narrowed. "But I still can't believe you're choosing work over a night out. Who are you? And what have you done with my brother? You live for guy time."

I was thinking with my cock.

Even if I shouldn't have been.

"And there will be plenty more of it in the future," I told her. "Missing one hangout isn't the end of the world. Besides, your boyfriend is a fucking hard-ass, and he's going to ride me to hell and back if I don't start weeding through this case."

She crossed her arms over her chest, glancing at Ford and then back at me. "So, that's the reason you're giving us?"

I focused on Ford and said, "Do you have any work to pass off to Hannah? She obviously has too light of a day if she's wasting all this time arguing with me."

She stood, holding the edge of my desk, leaning toward me. "For the record, if I were really arguing, you'd end up going out with them. Because I always win. We both know that." She winked.

I chuckled. "Good fucking God."

Her smile grew as she asked, "Drinks this week? I need twin time."

"Yes."

"What about me?" Ford asked. "Where's my invite?"

I looked around Hannah and replied, "Are you a twin?" to Ford.

"I wouldn't have survived the womb with the way you two go at it."

"It's all out of love," Hannah responded, and then her attention shifted to me. "How's Friday? Or will you have to work?"

"Get out," I groaned.

She laughed as she joined Ford in the doorway, both of them disappearing down the hall.

41

Once I was sure she was gone, I removed my phone from the drawer, opened Oaklyn's last message where she'd asked what she should bring, and I started to type.

ME

An appetite. Not for food.

FIVE

Oaklyn

E ven though Camden's doorman had alerted him of my arrival, he still looked a bit surprised when he opened the door to greet me. Of course, I was dressed a lot differently than I had been last night. Rather than the loungewear that had shown every inch of me, I'd chosen a pair of skinny jeans and a cream tube top that sat at the lowest part of my chest and ended just above my belly button, a navy blazer to go over it, and sky-high heels.

He said nothing as his gaze lowered to my feet and rose to my face, but his expression gave away his approval. I could tell he wasn't just pleased; he found what I had on extremely sexy.

I was a novice at all things physical, but when it came to clothes and putting myself together, I certainly had the upper hand.

I was sure my expression was revealing how handsome I found him, how sexy he looked tonight, even if I was trying to mask those thoughts. He had wet, tousled hair, as though he'd just gotten out of the shower, wearing a pair of gray sweatpants and a T-shirt that didn't hide the hard, corded muscles underneath. His signature thin leather bracelets circled his wrist, and his beard was even thicker than it had been when he dragged it over my skin.

A memory that made my thighs clench.

Hell yes.

Even in athletic wear, Camden looked achingly hot.

A type of attraction where I wanted to wrap my legs around his waist and run my hands through his wet locks and cover his lips with mine.

"Are you going to invite me in?" I asked.

He chuckled, like he was taken aback by what I'd asked, and he glanced over his shoulder at the inside of his apartment before connecting eyes with me again. "It's a lion's den in there. Are you sure you want to be invited in?"

I'd been thinking about this moment since he'd texted me this morning.

My body was still reeling from the evening before.

His question was a no-brainer.

"Yes, with zero doubts in my mind," I admitted.

He moved to the side, giving me enough space to slip between him and the door. "Then, enter at your own risk."

I smiled as I passed him, stalling for the briefest of seconds to take a deep inhale of his cologne, and continued to the kitchen.

I'd been here with Hannah once before, when he first moved in, attending the party he'd put together. In the time that had passed, there were changes. More decor hung on the walls, additional furniture was in the living room, a bar had been set up against the far wall. The tall, wide glass windowpanes were now framed in sheer curtains to emphasize the expansive view of the Hollywood Hills. And to add to the vibe, music played in the background, a tune that was more instrumental than singing, giving my ears the perfect kind of massage.

A pad that had been designed for the bachelor.

He made his way over to the bar. "Before we get into the details of tonight, I want to talk to you about something."

I leaned my back against the corner of the island, watching him pour vodka into a short glass and some red wine from a bottle that was already open. "Okay."

He knew what I drank and didn't have to ask.

Another surprise.

One that I loved.

He came into the kitchen and handed me the wine. "It's about my sister."

"What about her?"

"Unless you want her to know about us, I need you to play it cool when you're around her. If she brings me up, you can't get all smiley and obvious."

I didn't clink my glass against his. I just took a sip. "Hold on. You're giving yourself an awful lot of credit here. You think I'd get smiley if she mentioned your name?"

"After tonight, fuck yes."

I shook my head, sighing, "Go on."

"You also can't act any differently if the three of us are around each other, or she'll know in a second."

Besides the nature of this conversation, nothing had changed between us.

Camden had forever been the guy who smiled as he spoke, adding that additional layer of charm into every discussion. He was the guy who teetered the line of friend and flirt. The guy who turned comments into sexual innuendos.

The same guy who was standing before me now.

Hannah might not trust her brother's decisions, but she

would never think I would hook up with him or have him take my virginity.

But as that thought hit me, my God, the betrayal really sank in.

Would Hannah hate me for this if she ever found out?

I couldn't put my mind there. I needed to focus on why I was here.

What I needed.

What I wanted.

I studied his face. "Why are you telling me all this?"

"My sister's a goddamn PI. If you point the slightest grin in my direction, I promise you, she'll know."

"Camden ..." I ground my teeth over my lip. "Don't worry; we're in the clear. She'd never think I'd date you or want to date you."

"Why do you say that?"

I twirled my glass of wine before taking a sip. "Hannah knows you're not my type."

Except he was.

I seemed to be attracted to the impatient assholes, and Camden Dalton was definitely one of those.

He set down his vodka and closed the distance between us, one hand going to my waist, the other to my chin, where he traced his finger across my lips. "And what makes you think that?" Before I could respond, he continued, "You've told me about your ex. Aside from the fact that he had no money and his credit card was declined—something that wouldn't ever happen to me—we sound pretty similar." He leaned into my ear, his mouth so close that I could feel it. "He was a dick ... I like to think with my dick."

Goose bumps rose over every part of my skin.

And when they did, I tingled.

Everywhere.

I cleared my throat, searching for my voice. "It doesn't matter if you were like him or not; she wouldn't think I'd go after you. It's not a thought that would even enter her brain."

He pulled at my lip. "You think you know her better than me?"

I wanted to laugh, but I couldn't.

I was too turned on to push that puff of air through my lungs.

"As well as you," I replied. "But you've just got to trust me on this. Like earlier tonight, when we FaceTimed and she asked if I wanted to hang out with her, Sydney, Jo, and Kendall, I told her I was slammed with work and couldn't. She didn't question me or come up with some sneaky conclusion that I'd made other plans and wasn't telling her about them. See, we're good."

His brows lifted. "Wait a sec. You told her you were slammed with work?"

"Yeah. What's wrong with that?"

His hands left me, and he took a step back, picking up his drink and bringing it to his mouth. "That's the same excuse I gave her when she asked why I wasn't going out with the guys."

"So?"

"So ..." He glanced away. "You don't think that's obvious?"

"Why would Hannah ever think the two of us would be together? I think you're paranoid and trying to make this into something it's not."

He looked at me again.

Really looked at me.

"I hope you're right about that, Oaklyn."

"I am."

He took several sips and wiped his lips, still staring at me as he said, "Since you have it all figured out"—he stopped to chuckle—"then it's time for lesson one."

A burst of nerves shot through my body, and I began to guzzle the remainder of my wine.

I was only a few swallows in when he gripped the glass and gently pulled it away from me. "You don't need any more of that right now."

"But I think I do."

He set the wine on the other side of the counter and went over to the bar to refill his glass. "You'll resume the drinking once we're done."

Professor and alcohol-intake controller. This was already getting interesting.

Still, I stayed pressed against the island and waited for his next command.

Watching.

Completely frozen.

I had no idea what was about to go down.

What he was going to do to me.

Because this lesson wasn't my fantasy; it was his, and even if my life depended on it, I couldn't begin to guess what Camden would want.

After returning to the kitchen, he clasped my hand and said, "Come with me," and he brought me into the living room.

The couch was a large sectional, shaped as a U, outlining the whole room. He placed me on one side of the horseshoe, and he took the other side, so we faced each other. That gave me the impression that he was not only going to watch; he was going to have a front-row seat.

But of what?

"The only thing I know about you sexually is how your lips taste." His legs spread as he settled over the cushion, his drink resting on one of his thighs. "I don't know what you like. What makes your pussy wet. What makes you come." His hand lifted his glass and paused midair. "You have made yourself come, haven't you?"

The embarrassment swept in, and it took me a moment to respond. "Yes." But the previous statement, the one about my likes and wetness, I couldn't tell if he wanted answers to those. "Do you want me to tell you what I like?"

"No." He shook his head, thumbing his lips to dry them after he took a drink. "I want you to show me."

I felt the redness move over my cheeks; the tingles slid into my chest and pulsed like electricity. "Show you?"

He rested further into the couch, like he was at the movies, and at any second, he was going to extend his legs and recline. "Yes."

"I'm not sure I understand."

He slipped his phone out of his pocket, and after pressing the screen several times, I realized he was adjusting the lights. The ones in the kitchen dimmed; only the pendants that hung above the island were now aglow. The lamps in the living room were also turned down, but the brightness he did increase was from the lights built into the tray ceiling above.

That was when I really processed this whole setup. With the ceiling lights acting like a spotlight, my reflection could be seen on the windows to the right of me, giving him a whole other angle to watch.

"You want me to do this right here?" I asked.

"Yes."

I glanced toward the tall panes of glass. "Can anyone see in?"

His stare intensified, something I could still see since he was under the lit-up tray. "Would that stop you?"

"Everything is threatening to stop me," I said honestly.

I'd never done anything like this before. The thought of him seeing me come was completely overwhelming.

"I thought you could handle this, Oaklyn."

There it was—his motive.

Every bit of this was a test.

And I had a feeling he didn't just want to see if I'd complete his request; he also wanted to see how I'd react when it was over. If I would need that soft tenderness that we'd talked about, if I would be clingy and needy and wanting more of him emotionally, or if I could be the strong woman who needed absolutely nothing from him.

"I can," I whispered.

"Prove that to me."

I took a deep breath. "Let me make sure I get what you're asking. You want me to masturbate on this couch, in front of you, and come."

"Naked."

Naked.

That meant I had to strip off my clothes, like I was putting on a show for him, giving a full view of my body and the spot no man had ever been inside of.

"But if you can't do it," he said, "we can stop now and forget you ever propositioned me—"

"I can do it."

Except, deep down, I wanted to die.

I wanted to bury myself in more clothes to hide every part of me.

The idea of his eyes on me while I unveiled my body, while I slid a finger between my legs, while I came ... it was too much.

"What are you waiting for, Oaklyn?" He kicked his legs onto the ottoman, even crossing them, one arm going behind his head as though it were a pillow.

Damn him.

He knew how hard this was going to be for me—that was why he wanted it.

He thought I was going to fail.

I wished more than anything that I had three more glasses of wine in me, but he'd taken away the first, and I knew he'd done that on purpose too.

Such a little shit.

He glanced at his watch before he took a drink. "I'm waiting."

Regardless of how challenging this would be, I wasn't going to fail.

If he wanted me naked and coming, then that was exactly what I'd give him.

I tried to fill my lungs as best I could and stood, figuring that would be the easiest way to take off my clothes.

There was no reason to rush at this point, so I found the beat in the music. Trying to get lost in the rhythm, I slowly slipped off my blazer and heels, dropping the jacket beside me, and left on the tube top while I unbuttoned my jeans, lowered the zipper, and peeled them off my legs. Since the shirt was tight enough to act like a bra, I had nothing on underneath, and below was just a lacy light-pink thong.

As I took everything off, I didn't look at him. I didn't have the courage. He was too beautiful, too experienced, too honest in his assessment—things I didn't want to see.

But I looked now.

And what stared back was a heat.

A fire in his eyes.

In his cheeks.

Lips.

I took a seat on the couch and pushed all the way back into the deepest part of the cushion. While I gazed at him, I dug for that bravery I used during work whenever I presented a new concept to one of my large clients.

I knew my body, my own touch.

I didn't know what it was capable of when it came to a man, but I knew what I liked.

What I could do to myself.

So, I ran my fingers down my chest, pulling the material with me as I dipped, gradually revealing my cleavage and nipples, and as the hem lowered to my ribs, I finally freed my breasts.

Now that I was topless, his stare warmed even more.

Does he like what he sees?

Is he turned on?

I tried not to get too far into my head as I pulled the wrap down my torso, hooked my fingers into the sides of my thong, and brought it with me as I traveled past my thighs and knees and over my toes.

I spread my legs, showing him what was between them, except my palm was there, gently tapping that sensitive spot at the very top.

"Fuck me, Oaklyn."

Those three words told me he wanted to take me in.

He wanted to see what this proposition really looked like.

And even though that thought made my entire body blush, made me want to jump behind the couch, I moved my hand, revealing the rest of me. I then separated my legs even more, pressing my heels into the edge of the cushions beside me.

Now that he had the sight he was after, I expected more words.

More of an expression.

What I didn't expect was for him to get up and sit on the ottoman in front of me, lowering his face so it was eye-level with my pussy.

"You're perfect. Every fucking bit of you." He then growled, "*Fuuuck.*" He drained the rest of his vodka and set the glass on the floor, and that was when he circled my ankles, pulling me down the cushion so my ass was on the end, my feet on the ottoman on either side of him. "Show me how you play with that pretty pussy."

He was so close.

His lips were a foot—maybe two—from my entrance.

This wasn't a front-row seat.

This was standing on the stage, like he was in a chair and I was straddling his face.

The quick movement had taken away my breath.

I searched for it again.

That bravery—even if it was impossible to find under the passion of his gaze.

After several deep inhales, I trickled my fingertips down my chest and stomach and stopped at that place I normally touched when I was alone in my bed. The highest part of my clit. The place that throbbed the moment I circled it.

"Oh God," I moaned.

The pads of my fingers were gentle, and I used just enough pressure until a wave passed through me, causing my head to grind into the fluff behind it.

I didn't realize my eyes had closed.

But when I opened them, his were on me.

His lips parted.

I couldn't exactly read the expression on his face, but it reminded me of anger and frustration and hunger.

Does he want to touch me?

Is that driving him mad?

But he wouldn't touch me because this wasn't about what he liked, what he needed, what he wanted.

This lesson was for me.

I was the star.

The only thing was, I wasn't acting.

The sounds that swished out of my lips, the strain I was using to keep my legs open—that was all real.

Especially as my pointer finger began to circle my entrance. "Fuck yes," he roared.

My breathing turned heavy as my palm moved to my clit, giving my finger more freedom to dive in.

I didn't go in far—I never did—just the distance of a tampon, stopping when I reached my middle knuckle, and that was when I pulled out.

"Let me see your finger."

His demand almost startled me, his voice ringing in my ears.

I lifted my hand, completely abandoning what I had been doing, and I held it out to him.

"You're so fucking wet," he hissed.

I thought the next order was going to be to return to those same spots I had been in before, but that didn't come. What came instead were his lips, opening around my nail and sucking the wetness off of it. He then lowered to my knuckle and lapped up the wetness that was there.

When he finally left my finger, he leaned back, almost like he no longer trusted himself to be so close. "Oaklyn, goddamn it. That taste ... it's fucking amazing."

I leaned up on my elbow, pleased with the glare in his eyes. "Shall I continue?"

"Yes. Now. Quickly."

With skin that was dampened from his spit, I went back to that place, focusing on the top of my clit and my entrance, giving friction to both. That second intrusion caused another moan to leak from my mouth and, "*Ahhh*," to follow.

I didn't know if it was his presence.

If it was the fact that I had an audience.

Or if it was that it had been several days since I'd had an

orgasm and I was starving for one, but the intensity was already flaring.

Threatening.

Erupting.

"Oh fuck." I reached up behind me, grasping the first thing I came into contact with, which seemed like the corner of a pillow, and I squeezed it in my hand. "Yes!"

My back lifted, my weight going into the heels of my feet.

And my hand moved faster.

I wasn't watching him; my eyes were closed again while I rode toward the peak of this roller coaster.

But as I got nearer to the top, there were so many other aches in my body.

More needs.

Rippling fires that needed to be extinguished.

"Oh, yes," I cried out and released the pillow to clutch my breast, thumbing that hardened bud in the middle.

I rubbed back and forth against it, pressing harder, swiping faster, giving myself just enough that it added to what was already ablaze inside me.

"Fuck," I heard in a low, raspy breath.

A breath that wasn't mine.

But I still didn't open my eyes.

I centered my attention on the feeling that was rising, a feeling that was like a bullet, firing from my legs and darting toward my pussy and up through my stomach.

"Oh God!" With that shot came a vibration. One that ricocheted across my navel, over and over, causing a shudder to move through me. "Fuck!"

My eyes opened.

My head leaned back.

My legs caved, my ass lowering to the couch since it had

lifted off, and I rubbed out the rest of the desire since it had already reached its highest point.

This was the comedown.

The period where I turned into a pool of mush, where there was nothing left, not even a breath.

"That was ..." I swallowed. "Wow." My finger very slowly slid out, my palm moved off my clit, and my feet dropped to the floor, the coldness from the wood below shaking me awake.

As I connected our gazes, I almost couldn't fathom what was looking back at me.

His untamed eyes.

His feral mouth.

How his hands were wringing together, like he was stopping himself from reaching for me.

This was a side of Camden I hadn't seen.

I quietly searched for a blanket, a throw pillow, anything to cover myself up and not feel as exposed.

But there was nothing.

"Oaklyn ..."

"Yes?"

It took him a while to respond. "I didn't see that coming."

"No?" I filled my lungs. "What did you think was going to happen?"

His eyelids narrowed, his hands releasing the lock they had been in, and he briefly traced the inside of my knee. "Not *that*."

Because *that*, his eyes told me, had impressed him.

Because *that*, his mouth showed me, had proven to him that I could handle this.

Even silently, the honesty on his face radiated in a way I'd never experienced from him before.

But there was something else behind that gaze.

Something that made me say, "Is this the end of the lesson?"

Air came out of him as though he were blowing through a straw. "Unless you want to do that all over again, which I have no objection to."

"No." I laughed, the thought ridiculous. I couldn't come again—there was no way. "I was asking for a different reason."

"Which is?"

I sat up a little taller, moving my hair to one side in case it was looking a bit wild. "I want to make you feel the same way I just felt." My arms wrapped around my stomach, the shyness creeping back in as I nodded toward the extremely large tent in his sweats. "You know, I could try and take care of that. With your direction, of course."

SIX

Camden

Oaklyn was perked up tall and completely naked on my couch, her creamy skin a bit sweaty and flushed, looking absolutely fucking gorgeous. She always appeared exceptional in clothes, that heart-shaped ass the kind I wanted to constantly grab and squeeze, tits that would fit so well in my hands, nipples that liked to taunt me as they hardened under her clothes.

She had the kind of body that deserved to be worshipped.

But naked was an entirely different story.

She was perfect, to the point where I couldn't stay away, where underneath my T-shirt and sweats, I was just as damp and heated as her.

And turned the fuck on.

No part of me had expected this sexually timid woman to strip and finger-fuck her pussy. To rub one out in front of me, using the flat heaviness of her palm and half her finger—the only amount her virgin cunt could handle, I assumed.

But it was the sexiest sight I'd ever seen.

So much so that I'd had to get closer while she was doing it. I had to be within range to get a whiff, to see the wetness on her skin and not have to strain when I leaned forward and sucked it off her finger.

I'd just needed a taste.

I'd needed to know if she was as sweet as I thought she would be.

And she was.

Fuck.

Now that it was over, she'd handled the lesson just fine.

But this was the after. The part I questioned as much as the actual act itself. Because once I told her we were done for tonight and pointed at the door, her reaction would be extremely telling.

Can she handle the emotionless side of hooking up?

Before I got that answer, I needed to address her offer.

The one that involved her lips around my cock.

While she'd gotten herself off, she had gazed at me with a pulsing passion. That was how I had known how badly she wanted to come.

As she stared at me now, waiting for a response, she looked no different.

I picked up my empty glass from the floor and went over to the bar. I took the opportunity to adjust my hard-on, tucking it under the elastic waist of my sweats, and I refilled the tumbler before I joined her on the couch.

"Tell me something, Oaklyn. Is sucking my dick your fantasy for lesson two?"

She played with the ends of her hair, the dark strands so long that they hid her tit. "I haven't finalized the list yet."

"That's not an answer."

Her thumb went into her mouth, chewing the side of her nail. "It's not going to make the list, no."

I hadn't thought so.

She just wanted to please me.

And, goddamn it, I wanted nothing more.

But this proposition wasn't about my pleasure or fucking her mouth, like I dreamed about thrusting into her pussy or shooting my cum into her throat, like I wanted to fill her ass. It was about accomplishing each of the lessons that would lead to taking her virginity and teaching her how to be an expert in bed while making sure she didn't break down emotionally.

The second I made this about me, everything would change.

We'd change.

I couldn't let that happen.

I reached forward, tracing the outline of her lips, teasing myself with what those plump beauties could potentially do. How hard they could suck. How low her tongue could reach. And when I couldn't take a second more, I whispered, "Maybe another time," and pulled my hand away.

"I owe you, then. Consider it an offer that never expires."

I tilted my head, thinking of the possibilities. "I'll keep that in mind."

She was quiet for several moments and then, "I think I've earned myself the rest of that wine."

Although the idea of her walking naked across my living room was a vision I would fucking love, she'd already fulfilled every obligation this evening, so I got up and retrieved the drink for her. When I returned, she was putting her clothes back on— a sad scene as she covered that beautiful body.

I waited until she buttoned her jeans and slid on her top, stretching her arms through the blazer before I handed her the wine.

"Cheers," she said, clinking her glass to mine.

We both took sips.

"I've got plans this weekend," I told her, "but sometime early next week, I'm thinking we knock out lesson two. You do know what that means, right?"

She shook her head. "No."

"I need your fantasy list."

She licked the wine off her bottom lip and smiled. "I can do that, no problem."

"I have to say, Oaklyn, you're an extremely studious student so far."

"Maybe you're just a good teacher."

I chuckled. "What exactly have I taught you?"

She swallowed the rest of her wine and went into the kitchen to place the glass in the sink. When she came back to the living room, she didn't sit. She stood halfway between the couch and my front door. "More than you think," she finally replied.

There was a lightness to her expression.

A happiness.

A look that showed full contentment.

"I'll text you my list."

I nodded.

"Good night, Camden." She raised her hand to her mouth and blew me a kiss. "See you later."

I watched her walk out, and as I heard the door click closed, that only reinforced that she'd passed lesson one.

But whatever she chose for lesson two and beyond, I didn't think it would go as well.

It couldn't.

Because I had a feeling Oaklyn was going to need more from me. More security. More of a promise that this wasn't just physical. Most women weren't like men in that way. Sex was just an endgame to us, but for most of them, they couldn't disconnect their pussy from their heart—the two were joined, running simultaneously. When that happened, when she realized she needed assurance and I couldn't give it to her, she'd snap.

She'd pull back on the proposition.

And we'd be done.

That still didn't solve the problem I had right now, which was my ass on this couch with a raging fucking hard-on in my pants.

Sure, there were plenty of women I could call, chicks who had more than enough experience to do whatever I wanted.

But something had become extremely apparent tonight.

Something I didn't want to even admit to myself.

Not a single one of those women—or any I'd ever been with —could compare to Oaklyn Rose.

"To twin time," my sister said in her seat across from me at the round table positioned in the corner of the bar. She aligned our glasses and tapped them together before she took a sip of her wine. "Man, I've needed this. It has felt like the longest week ever."

I adjusted my ass on the small barstool and swallowed the vodka in my mouth. "You're not kidding. Shit is out of control with Hooked. HR has already reassigned a bunch of team members to join us. Not to mention, the weight of our current caseload and how much time those clients need from us in addition to the Hooked dudes. The past two nights, I haven't left the office before midnight."

"And this is why we love Fridays, amiright?"

Even though I'd only taken a sip, I connected eyes with our

waiter and pointed at my glass, letting him know I was already ready for a refill.

I then turned to Hannah and said, "Except Declan mentioned something about going in this Sunday. Do me a favor; work your magic and make sure that doesn't happen."

She laughed. "I don't have that much power."

"But you do." I swished the tumbler around, mixing the splash of dirty with the vodka. "That man doesn't fold to anyone but you."

"All right, I'll see what I can accomplish, but I make no promises. It's all about timing with him, so I'll have to plan this one out."

"I know when the perfect time would be, but please don't make me tell you." I made a gagging face. "The last thing I want to think about is you and my boss together."

She squeezed my arm that rested on the table, giggling. "I'm on it."

I glanced around the bar, looking for the guys, surprised as hell that I didn't see one of them. "You know, Jenner, Dominick, and Ford were trying hard to get in on tonight. They wanted to come. Bad."

"And you wouldn't let them?"

I shook my head. "You said you wanted it to be twin time."

"Oh boy."

"What?" My brow furrowed as I stared at her, trying to figure out what was on her mind. "Should I have let them come?"

She dragged her nail across the top of the table, like she was picking something off. "No, it's not that. It's ..." She paused to look at her watch. "It doesn't matter. Anyway, tell me all the things. I feel like I have no idea what's going on in your life right now."

"You see me multiple times a day. We text constantly. What the hell are you talking about?"

"Girls. Who's the newest one in the picture?"

I guzzled half my booze, hoping the waiter didn't take too long with my refill. "You already know the answer to that, Hannah."

"Then, who was making you smile the other day when I popped into your office?"

I leaned my arms on the table. "The other day, the other day," I repeated, acting dumbfounded even though I knew exactly what she was referring to. "I think it was probably Jenner, sending me some fucking meme that made me laugh."

"*Hmm.*" She shook her head. "I don't think so."

"Why do you feel the need to play PI with me? Meddling away, like usual, when there's nothing to investigate."

She flipped her hair off her shoulder. "First off, our cousins are all taken, so I can't get up in their business and play match-maker. But you have to admit, I did a wicked job with Ford. I literally set him up with Sydney. I mean, I mostly did despite the fact that she'd already slept with him, which is a minor, unimportant detail."

I dipped the straw into the clear liquid, like I was fishing. "Don't tell me your next conquest is me."

She gripped my forearm. "I don't want you to be single forever."

"Why? My sex life and who I date—if you can even call it that—shouldn't be a thought in your mind."

"But it is." Her other hand gripped the stem of her wine. "I want nieces and nephews and a sister-in-law who's going to become my new bestie."

"Must I remind you that we're twenty-five years old? Kids aren't on my radar; they shouldn't be on yours either." I drained the rest of my vodka. "Besides, you already have a bestie. Her name is Oaklyn."

"True." She nodded, smiling. "But I have room in my life for another one, just like, despite Macon being your best friend, you still have room for Declan, and he's become more than just your mentor."

Out of all the cousins, Jenner and I had always been the closest, and when things had become more serious between him and Jo, it'd happened to be one hell of a coincidence that I knew her cousin Macon and was good friends with him. He was just a few years older than me, and we'd played soccer together. Macon had two older brothers, Cooper and Brady, but they had graduated before I got to high school. Now that Jenner and Jo were engaged, the two families merged for most holidays, and we spent a lot of time with the Spades. I liked them all, but the dude I had the most in common with was Macon, for sure.

I groaned, "Declan's a serious pain in my fucking ass—that's what he's become to me."

She released my arm to slap it.

"Once I have my own team, maybe I'll feel less of an urge to constantly strangle the motherfucker. The only thing that's kept him alive is that you're in love with him and you'd hate me for life if I offed the man."

She gazed up at the ceiling, her eyes practically fucking hearts. "Every bit of the asshole I fell in love with." She looked at me again. "I get the *wanting to strangle him* part. When it comes to being a boss, he's the absolute worst. But he's also a genius—you can't deny that."

I rolled my eyes. "There's something wrong with you."

"No, there's something wrong with *you*. What will it take for you to settle down?"

"A miracle."

"Which I believe in."

I sighed. "Well, you shouldn't when it comes to me. When was the last time I even had a relationship anyway? High school? And that lasted, what, a whole week?"

Her hands went to her chest, holding her heart. "Dana Wade. I'll never forget her."

I was mid-chew and almost spit out a chunk of ice. "How in the hell do you remember her name?"

"I was so jealous of the way she curled her hair. She had these long, bouncy ringlets that fell down her back. I couldn't ever—"

"Stop."

She shook her head, grinning. "My God, that feels like a lifetime ago, doesn't it?"

"Which is why you shouldn't get your hopes up about me settling down anytime soon. It's not going to happen, Hannah."

Even if something were to grow with Oaklyn—it wouldn't; I was sure of that—it couldn't go down because of my sister.

Hannah wanted me to get locked into a relationship; she wanted to welcome that woman into her life.

She just didn't want that woman to already be in her life.

"I'm not giving up," she voiced.

The waiter delivered our next round, and I held the full glass in my hand. "You're wasting your time, but you do you, sis."

Her eyes narrowed. "I don't know about that." She took a drink, and her attention moved toward the center of the bar, her face lighting up as though she'd spotted someone. She set down her wine, taking a quick peek at me. "Don't kill me, but I invited Oaklyn."

"You two can't stay apart, can you?"

"We can; we just hate to."

Hannah held out her arms, and Oaklyn immediately fell into them, the two girls laughing as they embraced in a hug.

But that wasn't the same sound that came out of my mouth.

Because I was bullshit.

A chill night with my sister was now turning into an evening of acting, trying my hardest to hide what had gone down between Oaklyn and me, attempting not to stare at her, revealing my attraction.

Since I found her so fucking irresistible, this challenge was going to be impossibly hard.

Fuck me.

If I pulled her against my body and hugged her hello, I'd have a raging erection that everyone would be able to see. Since that hard-on was already threatening to mount, I got up from the stool and moved over to the girls, angling myself so only my mouth got near her.

"Good to see you, Oaklyn," I said, and I gave her the fastest kiss on the cheek. I stepped away and added, "I'm going to go grab a shot," before heading for the bar.

SEVEN

Oaklyn

"What, did I drive him to drink?" I asked Hannah as I watched Camden walk to the bar. "That was the quickest hello he's ever given me." I took a seat next to my best friend.

"He's probably a little grumpy." She rolled her eyes. "First, the guys wanted to come out with us, and he told them they couldn't, and then I went and invited my bestie—*oops*." She laughed as she pulled a piece of hair off my lip and tucked it behind my ear. "And *theeen*, we were talking about girls before you got here, and I was giving him a little shit, so he's probably extra salty about that part since that isn't his favorite topic to discuss with me."

Oh man, but it was just the topic I wanted to hear about.

"What kind of shit were you giving him?" I asked since she hadn't been specific enough in her description.

"Do you happen to remember when he dated Dana Wade in high school?"

"How could I forget? You were completely obsessed with that girl's hair," I said. "You came over to my house and sat in front of my mirror with a curling iron, trying for hours to do your hair like hers."

"Yes! Her!"

"Didn't they date for, like, five minutes? And the entire school was talking about it the whole time?" I questioned.

"But that's longer than he's ever dated anyone." She handed me her wine, and I took a sip. "I just don't want him to be a bachelor forever. He needs to find love and give me nieces and nephews." She put her hand on my arm as I tried to chime in. "Not today. I mean, we're young—I get it—but I just need to know it's going to happen."

"I hate to tell you this, Hannah, but it's also okay if that doesn't happen."

"No, no, *nooo*." She took her wine back. "Now, you're sounding like him. I need you on my side."

I took a quick glance toward Camden, where he was standing at the bar, talking to the bartender. She was tall with long, dark hair, wearing a corset with cleavage triple the size of mine. What made it even worse was that she was gorgeous.

He'd probably go home with her tonight.

Ugh.

I shouldn't care.

But I did.

The whole thought of it made me feel sick to my stomach.

I needed to get my mind and my focus off Camden.

I looked back at Hannah and said, "You're acting like he's forty and still a virgin. Which will be my story, by the way, not his."

"We both know that's not even close to being true. You're going to lose your virginity; it's only a matter of time."

"Except I can't seem to find a nice enough guy to woo it

from me."

She laughed so hard that she snorted. "That's because you don't like nice guys. You're into bad boys who can't be tamed or transformed." She set both hands on my shoulders. "You're the angel in our friendship and the type of girl who wouldn't even kill a mosquito if it landed on you. When it comes to dudes, you're the same way. They sting you, and you let them. It's like they smell you out, and you're too sweet to swat them away." She smiled. "You need to be attracted to guys like yourself. Who will welcome you with open arms and woo the hell out of you."

"Says the girl who's dating the ultimate asshole."

She pulled her hands back and surrounded her wine. "Hey, I can handle an asshole. I can be one myself—let's not forget that."

"Then, why can't I?"

"Oh, my Oaklyn, because you don't have an asshole-ish bone in your body. You're, like, this innocent, sweet, gentle unicorn who deserves to be treated like a princess."

"Nonsense." I waved my hand across the air. "You tamed Declan, so anything is possible."

She sighed. "I don't think I tamed him. I think I molded him. Huge difference."

"And how did you do that?"

Her eyes narrowed as she stared at me. "I made him want me so badly that he couldn't breathe, and then I made him realize his life wouldn't be the same unless I was in it permanently." She paused, still gazing at me. "You'll know exactly what I mean once you're there."

Before I could reply, there was movement at the table, and as I glanced away from Hannah, I saw Camden taking a seat beside me.

Within a few seconds, his scent wafted toward me, and I

briefly closed my eyes as I took in that amber and woodsy and citrus smell.

An aroma that brought back memories of the night I'd stripped for him.

I'd touched myself for him.

There was a heat building between my legs, and I glanced down, as though I could see it.

As I looked back up, I felt Camden's eyes on me, and a smoldering expression crossed his face, like he knew exactly what I was thinking.

"Decided to finally join us, Mr. Grumpy?"

"Grumpy?" He huffed, his stare shifting to his sister. "I needed another drink. Don't make this into something it's not."

"Then, thanks for the refill ... dick."

He chuckled at his sister, a sound so sinister and sexy. "The waiter will be by; don't you worry."

"You could have at least grabbed me something," I said softly. Because of the way I was positioned at the round table, Hannah couldn't see my wink.

But Camden did.

Without pause, he said, "How would I know what you like to drink?"

He'd known the other night at his place, pouring me a glass of wine almost immediately without any prompting.

But he still had a point.

If nothing was going on between us, it was a detail he wouldn't bother noticing.

I had to be careful when constructing my response. "Wine would be a solid guess, given that's what your sister drinks and we're basically the same person."

He called the server over and ordered wine for the both of us. "Is everyone happy now?"

"That's a start," Hannah replied.

"What were you guys talking about when I came back to the table?" he asked. "I heard something about taming?"

"Oh, Oaklyn asked how I tamed Declan. I told her I didn't; I just molded him." She smiled again. "And now, he's Mr. Perfect."

Camden shook his head. "I'm not even going to comment."

"How about you do something better? You give my girl, Oaklyn, some advice on how she can tame the man of her dreams. And just to give you some backstory, she likes bad boys. I told her she needs to stop looking for assholes and start focusing on good guys. Since I know she won't, maybe it'll help if she gets some advice from someone like you."

His brows rose. "Someone like me?"

"Yeah, you know, you're, like, the ringleader of the whole bad-boy club."

I wanted to crawl under the table and die.

This wasn't a conversation I wanted to have with him or in front of him.

Camden rested his arms on the tabletop, briefly grazing mine in the process, and linked his hands together.

That small touch, just the tiniest brush of skin against skin, and I was already feeling a blaze within my stomach.

"You're fucking kidding me, right?" he asked.

"On which part?" Hannah inquired. "The advice part? No. The kind of guys Oaklyn likes? No on that too."

"Jesus." He took a drink, his gaze slowly shifting to me. "Stay away from them. That's the best advice I can give you."

But his eyes told me differently.

In fact, the story unfolding in his stare was enticing.

Addictive even.

Enough so that I took my phone out, trying to be as inconspicuous as possible as I pulled up Camden's last text and began to type.

ME

I just want to make sure I understand things correctly. Is a bad boy the best kind of guy to teach me how to be a good lover? Or should I find myself someone who's a little more giving?

CAMDEN

Texting in front of my sister. You've got balls.

ME

Avoiding the question. You've got balls.

I slipped my phone back into my pocket just as the server brought us our wine. Hannah polished off the rest of her glass before she handed him the empty.

"He's not the best advice giver, I see," I said to my bestie, ignoring that Camden was still on his phone, appearing to be typing.

She clinked her glass against mine. "But you've got me, and that's what I'm good at." She eyed up her brother. "*Ohhh,* Camden, something just came to me. I think I have a wicked idea." She waited for Camden to look up before she continued, "Why don't we set Oaklyn up with Macon?"

His brow furrowed. "My Macon?"

Hannah laughed. "You say that like the two of you are together—which is fine, but I know that's not the case. Yes, brother, *your* Macon."

He set his phone down, the screen facing the table, and took a long drink. "Oaklyn wouldn't like him."

"How do you know that?" Hannah asked.

I used that moment to look at my phone.

CAMDEN

Don't question if I'm giving, Oaklyn. I assure you, you'll never leave my presence unsatisfied.

> **ME**
>
> But if I'm going to use my own fingers, I might as well do that at home.

"It's just a hunch I have." Camden shrugged.

"Hold on a sec." I returned my phone to the top of my back pocket. "Macon, Macon ... I know him. He was at your apartment the night of your housewarming party, right?" I said to Camden.

Camden nodded, but his eyes had changed since the mention of his best friend's name.

They'd darkened.

Almost like he was giving me a warning.

And then he lifted his phone and read my text, his thumbs hitting the screen to type his reply.

"Did you find him cute?" Hannah asked me.

I smiled at Hannah. "Cute? More like incredibly handsome. He was tall with dark hair and these striking green eyes, if I remember correctly."

I knew I couldn't make Camden jealous; he wasn't into me at all—at least not in the way where he'd care if I found another guy attractive. Plus, I wasn't trying to make him jealous. I was just speaking the obvious.

Macon Spade was a really good-looking man.

"He fits your physical criteria—that's for damn sure," Hannah said.

"I think when we met, he was telling me about some exotic vacation he'd just gone on," I told her. "A guy who enjoys traveling—that's definitely a bonus."

"His job is another bonus. He's one of the top executives at Spade Hotels." Hannah put her arm around my shoulders, turned her face in the same direction as mine so we were both looking out toward the crowded bar, and pressed our cheeks together. "Can you imagine the perks? Let's envision them, shall we? Dreamy, five-star hotels all over the world. The best room service ever. Fuzzy slippers. Spa days."

"Sign. Me. Up." I giggled.

"You two are ridiculous," Camden said. "You don't need an executive at a hotel brand to provide those perks. You just need to date someone who can afford to take you on that kind of trip. Like Declan."

"And Macon," Hannah offered.

She released my arm, and I carefully snuck into my pocket and checked out his text.

CAMDEN

> That was a lesson for me. I made that clear.

ME

> When I could have simply just told you what I liked—something I made clear.

"Excuse me," I quickly butted in. "I actually don't need a man to provide those perks. I can certainly afford to take myself on one of those trips."

Hannah shook my shoulder. "Heck yeah, you can, girl. You're a badass—there's no doubt about that. But still, wouldn't it be fun if you had someone delicious lying in bed next to you?"

She reached across me and pinched her brother's arm even though Camden was back on his phone, probably replying to me. "Let's set them up anyway. It'll be a great match. They're both dedicated to their jobs. They like to travel. They're both beautiful. It'll be a home run."

There was no way I could complete these sexual lessons with Camden and then go out on a date with his best friend. I just wouldn't feel right about it. And ending things with Camden wasn't an option.

He was the man I wanted to give my virginity to.

There were zero doubts in my mind about that.

But that meant I had to get Hannah off this track, and to do that, I had to bring up the obvious.

Before I did that, I checked my phone.

CAMDEN

What makes you think that the lesson was only about learning what you liked? How do you know it wasn't for another reason? Something I didn't tell you?

ME

So, tell me.

I faced my bestie and said, "Han, we have a bit of a problem that I think you're forgetting."

"Problem?" she mirrored. "Huh?"

I kept my phone in my lap, holding it close to read the screen.

CAMDEN

What's far more important is you telling me what your next three fantasies are, so we can get started on this little proposition of yours.

"Must I really say it?" I pleaded with her.

"*Hmm*," Hannah groaned. "Yes. That."

"What's *that*?" Camden smirked.

Dick.

He knew exactly what *that* was.

And he loved putting me in the position where I had to talk about it.

But there was no reason why I should be ashamed of my situation, so I turned to him and immediately realized the confession wasn't coming out as easy the second time around.

Maybe that was because Hannah was here, watching, listening, analyzing.

"I don't have a lot of experience with men," I voiced, hoping that would satisfy him.

"What do you mean, Oaklyn?"

I should have known he would keep pushing until I said the word.

I took a deep breath, feeling the sudden sweatiness on my palms. "I just don't have a lot of experience with men—that's all."

"Does that mean you've only been with a couple of dudes? One? Or ..."

Why is he doing this to me?

What point is he trying to make?

"Oaklyn, just tell him," Hannah said.

I'd avoided looking at her during this entire conversation, but I stole a quick peek. "He's your brother."

"But he won't care, and he certainly won't judge you for it," she replied.

If Hannah only knew what her brother had witnessed on the couch at his condo ...

Why did I put myself in this situation?

"Come on, Oaklyn. What do you mean?" Camden urged.

"Oh my God," I groaned. My desire to just get this over with was at its peak. "I haven't had sex with anyone. Ever. I'm a virgin." I looked around the table. "Now, is everyone happy?"

His lips pulled into a grin. "You don't say?"

I returned the expression, making sure my smile was wider than his. "And that sometimes causes a little bit of a problem. I don't put out on the first date. Or the third. Or even the tenth."

"Yeah, that's definitely going to be a problem with Macon."

Hannah craned her neck so our faces were close again while we both gazed at her brother. "Why? He can't woo her a little first?" She paused, like she was waiting for a response, but didn't get one. "Camden, not every guy in this world is like you and expects to get laid on day one."

He laughed and pointed at us. "This little duo you've got going on here is similar to my friendship with Macon. I know what the dude wants, and waiting to fuck—or woo, or whatever the hell you called it—isn't going to work for him."

"I don't believe it," Hannah said, and she leaned back.

That gave me a chance to reply to his text.

ME

I want to get off in a public place. You know, in front of people, where they don't know what's going on and I have to kinda hide what's happening and how I'm feeling.

"Believe it," he replied to her. "He's got about as much patience as me when it comes to chicks." He held his phone while he went on, "He's not looking to settle down. Macon Spade isn't going to be your Prince Charming."

CAMDEN

You're into voyeurism? Nice. I can do that. What's lesson three?

ME

I want to use a toy.

"Who says she's looking for Prince Charming?" Hannah countered. "She just needs a guy who's nice, who isn't after the one thing she's not ready to give away. Who will treat her with respect and—"

"That's not Macon." He typed and glanced up. "Didn't you hear me? The dude isn't looking for a relationship. He's a player. You're not really going to hand your best friend over to a guy who's a wolf, like me, are you?"

Except I was ready to hand myself over to Camden.

In fact, I already had.

Oh God.

> **CAMDEN**
>
> Do you buy your toys at a sex shop? Or have you only bought them online?

> **ME**
>
> Don't laugh ... I don't own any sex toys.

Hannah froze. "I see your point. That would be tragic."

"You can say that again," I whispered, and I gazed at the screen of my phone.

> **CAMDEN**
>
> What do you use at home?

> **ME**
>
> My fingers.

"But I'm not sure I believe that about Macon," Hannah said. "I've hung out with him countless times. Sure, he's a player. I can tell that by the way he smiles—he's got that mischievous grin that girls completely die over—and the man is the definition of charming. But I get the sense that, like you, he just hasn't found the right girl. Maybe neither of you is looking for that girl, but if she happens to fall in your lap, you'll turn into everything she wants and more. That's my guess."

I was drowning in thoughts.

And they were coming from both sides—the secret conversation I was having with Camden and the one he was having with Hannah about Macon.

And how all of this was about me.

But his refusal to set me up with his best friend was definitely something I found interesting. Not that I wanted a chance with Macon. I didn't—at all. I just didn't know why

Camden cared so much. Why it seemed like he was trying to protect me. Why he wouldn't offer to play matchmaker, especially given that, very soon, my virginity would be a thing of the past.

CAMDEN

Your fingers ... fuck me.

What about lesson four?

ME

You know when I said that I'm giving you all my firsts and I want one of yours? Something you've never experienced with another woman? That's what I want for that lesson.

"Who's to say the right girl hasn't already fallen into my lap and I didn't bite?" Even though he was staring at his sister, I could feel the penetration of his gaze. "Well, shit, maybe I bit, just not in the permanent sense."

"You're that opposed to a relationship?" Hannah pressed.

"Maybe." He brought the drink up to his lips, glancing at me for several seconds and then at his sister. "Or maybe I just like fucking with you."

"If I had a straw"—she searched the table—"or anything for that matter, I'd throw it at you right now."

He took a long drink and set the glass down.

CAMDEN

Hold on. I asked you to come up with three fantasies, and you're putting one of those on me? That wasn't the deal.

ME

I'm not exactly putting it on you. It's more like telling you that I'm open to anything and I want you to surprise me with something that's going to blow my mind.

CAMDEN

I want to fuck your ass. Does that blow your mind?

"That still doesn't answer the question about Macon," Hannah said. "Just because you're allergic to permanently having someone in your life—or so you say—doesn't mean he is. I think we should put the two of them together and see what happens."

ME

Blow my mind? No. Surprise me since it's you? No. Freak me out? Yes. Worry like hell about it? Yesss. Camden, I'm a virgin, so you're saying you want to do anal before you even take my virginity? That's kind of a major step, no?

CAMDEN

You asked. I gave you my answer.

ME

But I'm trusting you to lead me, Camden. Is that really the right direction to take me in?

CAMDEN

Are you sure you should have that kind of trust in me? The conversation I've been having with my sister tonight has shown you a lot more about me. Enough to make you rethink this whole plan.

ME

I've learned nothing I didn't already know.

CAMDEN

So, you're telling me you haven't changed your mind?

ME

No.

CAMDEN

Even if I'm telling you I want anal?

ME

Shit ... no, I guess.

CAMDEN

Fearless. I didn't know that about you.

ME

I'm not asking you to fall in love with me, Camden. I'm asking you to give me an experience I'll never forget. That doesn't make me fearless. It makes me hungry to learn more about my body.

"Hello?" Hannah sang, her eyes on Camden. "Are you going to answer me? Or at least put your phone down and pretend you're listening to what I'm saying?"

"Sorry," Camden replied. "What did you ask?"

"Unbelievable." Hannah shook her head, clearly annoyed. "Who are you texting with?"

My heart began to beat so fast that my throat was vibrating.

His eyes lit up, and he traced the inside of his lip with his tongue. "The girl I'm going to fuck tonight."

I couldn't be sure he was only texting with me at this table, but the thought of him having conversations with other women at the same time didn't sit well with me.

Hannah crossed her arms over her chest. "The bartender?"

"Maybe."

Ouch.

Why does hearing that hurt so much?

It wasn't just because she was gorgeous and she was here, which made it so easy for her to leave with him at the end of her shift.

It was because I didn't want him touching any other woman while this proposition was in motion.

That was stupid of me to even think that was possible. That he would only want to be with me when he wasn't getting anything out of this.

Lesson one, I'd only had an orgasm, not him.

Lesson two and three would be the same.

And maybe it was selfish to want Camden all to myself, but I did.

And, gosh, that thought was heavy.

"What about you?" Hannah said to me. "You've been on your phone half the night too. Who are you chatting away with, girl?"

She couldn't see my screen, but that didn't mean I hadn't been completely obvious.

I'd just been so wrapped up in my conversation with Camden. So curious to what his replies would be. So drawn to him in a way I hadn't expected that I was being careless in front of my best friend.

"My dad," I blurted out, my family the first excuse that had come to me since it was a conversation I'd had with my father several hours earlier. "He's trying to buy a gift for my mom, and he needs my help."

"A tennis bracelet. Done. Tell Dad you're welcome." She smiled, and then her lids narrowed again as she looked at Camden. "Back to Macon. Let's pursue this and see what happens."

"You're not going to let it go, are you?" Camden asked.

"Unless you want to introduce Oaklyn to another one of your single friends. I mean, there's also Cooper and Brady, if you think they'd be better fits."

"Nah."

"Why *nah*?" Hannah mocked.

Camden thumbed his screen for a few more seconds and

tucked his phone under his arm. "They're not right for her either."

> CAMDEN
>
> When I take your ass, I assure you, that's something you won't forget.

> ME
>
> Are you telling me that'll be your first time doing that? That is what I requested.

"Why aren't they right for her?" Hannah pushed. "It seems like whoever I suggest isn't good enough for our Oaklyn. I need to understand your reasoning."

> CAMDEN
>
> I can't tell you that.

> ME
>
> I figured.

> CAMDEN
>
> But I can tell you that I'll be gentle ... and that's not something I've done before.

> ME
>
> Isn't that nice of you?
>
> You know what? On second thought, I don't need one of your firsts. This is about me. Not you. The man I fall in love with can give me one of his firsts. I need nothing more from you other than these lessons. And don't worry, I'll come up with something for the fourth one.

I slowly looked up at him.

His lips wet and parted, he took me in before he said to his sister, "Hannah, my friends aren't the kind of guys you're looking for. They're all like me. Every one of them. Wild. Uncommitted. Fucking dominants who aren't looking to be soft and tender with a virgin. Macon and I aren't the only players of the group. They all are."

Soft and tender. Camden's favorite words when describing what I needed.

Yet the other night, hints of both had shown through.

He didn't touch me, he didn't even direct me, but he could have bitten my finger when he put it in his mouth to lick off my wetness, and he didn't. He could have skipped straight to lesson five when I was straddling the cushions of his couch, and he didn't do that either.

For a wild, dominant wolf of a player, he had certainly shown patience with me.

Except for tonight.

Tonight, he was living up to everything he had said he was.

"You're telling me you literally know no one?" Hannah asked him.

"That's what I'm telling you."

CAMDEN

I'm sure I can get you to change your mind.

As I processed the thought of Camden being gentle with my ass, of him conquering not one, but two of my firsts, of him owning literally every single part of my body, a thought came to me. A thought that involved my mouth. A thought that caused a tingling between my legs, forcing me to push my thighs together, shifting them back and forth to add friction. My nipples ached as they pressed into my bra.

What's happening to me?

How is he doing this to me?

And who am I turning into?

ME

Doubtful.

85

> And don't try to claim that blow job tonight unless you're into pain.

I turned to my best friend, the desire to kill this conversation stronger than ever. "Han, I really don't need you finding me someone. When I meet the guy I'm supposed to be with, I'll know it, and it'll happen naturally." I squeezed her arm. "It won't be because my best friend is trying to play Cupid—even though I love you dearly for that."

"And if the natural plan doesn't work out, we can always put you on Hooked."

> **CAMDEN**
>
> You said I could have it whenever I wanted.

> **ME**
>
> And I'm telling you, tonight, I'll bite.

> **CAMDEN**
>
> But the fact that you're even thinking about sucking my dick in the same bar that my sister's in? Now, that's fucking hot.

"Whatever," Hannah sighed. "I'm not giving up. Next time I see Macon, I'm totally weighing the situation and playing matchmaker if I get a good feeling about him."

> **ME**
>
> It's only hot if you like teeth.

Camden stood, draining the rest of his drink. "You do that," he replied, and then he moved around to his sister's side of the table and gave her a hug.

"Are you leaving?" she asked him.

He released her and came over to me. "Yeah, I've got to go." He held me in a hug for the briefest of seconds, just long enough for me to feel his strength and to inhale his scent.

86

Both making the ache inside me pulse even harder.

When he pulled away, he reached into his pocket and took out his wallet and dropped some cash onto the table. "Drinks are on me. Good night, ladies," he said before he left.

I counted the three crisp hundred-dollar bills and looked at Hannah. "We can have some fun with that tonight." I laughed.

But inside, I was a mess of emotions.

I didn't want to see Camden's back as he walked out of the bar.

I had been enjoying ... this.

Whatever this was.

But I also worried that, even though he was gone, I could still feel him in my lower half, even more so in my chest.

"I'm ordering us a bottle of champagne." She searched the crowd for our server and called him over, putting in her request. The moment the waiter was gone from our table, she said, "Thanks for tomorrow's hangover, Camden." She wiggled her wineglass in the air, laughing. "While he's off, doing who knows what with who knows who, we're going to have a blast."

I lifted my glass and tapped it against hers, my throat tight, my chest now slightly achy. "Yes. To that."

I glanced down as I felt my phone vibrate.

CAMDEN

You will be sucking my dick without your teeth. Very soon.

EIGHT

Camden

I'd needed to get out of the bar. Away from Oaklyn and the temptation that had been fucking haunting me. Not only had she given me two fantasies that were hot as hell—scenarios that I couldn't wait to enact, screams that would fill my ears in a way I was dying to hear—but she had also pleaded with me to come up with an idea of my own.

Anal.

Was there anything better?

When I presented the idea, I knew it was a long shot. I knew she would have reservations, but what I liked even better than her immediately agreeing was that she fought back.

A little spiciness that had come out of nowhere.

That I'd never seen from her before, making me want her ass even more.

Somehow, I was going to find a way in there before making my way into her pussy even if I only used a finger.

But the real highlight of this evening was that after learning more about me, she hadn't changed her mind, and that told me she was a woman who had a lot of trust in me.

Who was willing to do anything for pleasure.

Who believed me when I told her she would never leave my presence unsatisfied.

Words that I meant wholeheartedly.

And then, like I was living in a goddamn fairy tale, the conversation shifted to her biting my dick—something I knew she wouldn't do, but, dammit, I enjoyed the threat. It was as though our conversation had triggered her to think about giving me head, as though she couldn't get my cock out of her mind.

Her desire to get me off so incredibly fierce that she couldn't help but mention it.

Man, I appreciated that.

I wanted that.

I would fucking do almost anything to make that happen.

Was there a purer, more innocent, perfect woman than Oaklyn Rose?

That was why I'd needed to leave. To escape these two women who were choking me for entirely different reasons. To be around my boy, Macon, and listen to him talk about the chick he'd fucked last night to distract me.

Because these thoughts—the ones swirling, the ones marinating, the ones fucking owning me—weren't me, nor were they making sense.

So, I'd texted Macon and told him where to meet me, and I'd hidden my hard-on as I got up from the table that I shared with the perfect girl and my PI of a sister. I rushed a block down the street, where Macon was already waiting for me.

"My boy," he said, clasping my back when I leaned in for a man hug. "I was surprised to hear from you. Weren't you supposed to be out with Hannah tonight?"

I took a seat and lifted his tumbler off the table, downing all the liquid that was inside.

He laughed as he watched me. "It turned into that kind of night, huh?"

I wiped my lips. "Shit." And then I shook my head. "The past hour has been interesting as fuck, to say the least."

A waiter happened to be walking by, and Macon stopped him, requesting a drink for each of us.

My best friend then eyed me down, that bright green stare feeling like it was hitting straight through my chest. "What's going on?"

He was safe.

A vault.

Still, for some reason, I didn't want to get into all the details.

"Do you remember Oaklyn, my sister's best friend?"

"Oaklyn ..." he repeated, using both hands to pull at his gelled hair. "The hottie with the best ass in LA? Long, dark hair, icy-blue eyes—"

"Yeah, her," I said, cutting him off, his description sending a feeling into my chest that I didn't like.

He was right; her ass was a fucking trophy.

Any guy at my party that night would have noticed.

Still, there was something about his portrayal that rubbed me the wrong way.

"She's a virgin," I continued. "And she wants me to take her virginity." I reached for his drink again before remembering there was nothing left, so I poured some of the ice into my mouth and chomped. "I put it off for a whole year."

He rested his arms on the table, leaning forward, bringing us even closer. "She's a virgin? Damn, I never would have guessed that." He took the toothpick out of the empty glass and sucked the olives into his mouth. "Second, why the fuck did you put it off for a year and not tap that immediately? Dude, that's not like you. The Camden I know would have popped that cherry the second she asked."

I ground my teeth together.

He didn't understand the difference between her and all the other girls. She wasn't like them. She was a part of my family. I'd have to see her and endure her expression every time she was with my sister.

"Oaklyn is Hannah's best friend. The two of them are like sisters and have been since we were kids."

He loosened his black-striped silk tie, telling me he'd just come here from work, and unbuttoned the top of his crisp light-blue shirt. "And?"

I went to respond, but I chuckled first.

This motherfucker didn't get it at all.

But it didn't matter.

I wasn't going to waste my time explaining it to him.

His brow furrowed. "You've already touched her, haven't you?"

"What would make you think that?"

"I can see it all over your goddamn face."

I wasn't going to tell him about what had gone down at my condo. I wasn't going to tell him about the lessons. Those were just for me.

"Nah, man"—I glanced down—"I haven't."

He laughed, the sound loud enough that it made me look up. "Who the fuck are you? And what have you turned into?"

"What are you talking about?"

"Going all silent on me. Refusing to speak about her. That isn't like you. Normally, you can't shut the fuck up about all the juicy details."

"You don't know what you're talking about."

His grin was wide and telling. "Right. Sure I don't." He

91

crossed his arms over his chest. "So, she showed up at the bar tonight while you were there with Hannah, I assume?"

I nodded.

"And what made it so *interesting as fuck?* At least, that's the way you described it."

"The three of us were sitting at a table, and Oaklyn was texting me about shit that we're planning. That was when it turned interesting." The drinks got delivered, and I lifted the booze straight to my lips, chugging down several sips. "She's a good girl. That's all I'm saying. Far too fucking good for me."

"Why would that matter? It's not like you want to date her" —his stare turned even more serious—"or maybe you do."

I laughed. "No, nothing like that."

"Are you positive?"

"Yeah"—I took a deep breath—"I'm fucking positive."

"How are you going to tackle this situation, player?"

"I'm not tackling it." I huffed air between my lips. "I'm sitting here, about to drink my face off, and ignoring it."

"I'm curious about something." He gazed toward the crowd, inconspicuously nodding toward a blonde with a huge rack, who was standing with a couple of friends near the bar. "If she came over here and offered to suck your dick, would you take her into the restroom, guide her to her knees, and drop your load down her throat?" He looked back at me. "Right now?"

"Until I'm hit with that offer, I can't give you an answer."

"You know what the old Camden would have said? He would have said, *The restroom is too far away. My car is right out here.*" He pointed at the wall behind us. "And you would have had her in the passenger seat in seconds."

"There is no old Camden. There's me. I haven't changed a fucking bit."

"If that's really what you think, well, that's just sad." He traced his bottom lip with the inside of his thumb. "Why are things with Oaklyn so different? It's not because she's your sister's best friend—I don't buy that. There's another reason you're acting this way."

My head shook back and forth. "There isn't another reason. That's the truth."

"All right, if you want to tell yourself that, I'll let you live in that bullshit world for a little while. And maybe, in a few weeks, we'll have this chat again, and I'll see if you're still in denial."

What the fuck?

He had no idea what he was talking about.

Even if I did have feelings for Oaklyn—I didn't; I couldn't—it wouldn't matter.

Hannah would have my ass, and it wouldn't be pretty.

So, whatever my friend was referring to, I wasn't going to address it. I was moving on and forgetting this part of the conversation ever existed.

"The funny part is," I said to him, "Hannah mentioned setting Oaklyn up with you. Next time you see my sister, don't be surprised if she pushes that on you and tries to set up a date."

"*Hmm.*" He rubbed his large hands together, his cuff links clinking each time his palms passed. "A virgin. Now, what the fuck would I do with one of those?"

"She won't be for long."

And, damn it, that was another set of thoughts that haunted me.

The sounds of her untapped pussy when I slid my way inside.

The tightness I would feel as her cunt pulsed around me.

The slowness I would have to give her at first.

Half of a finger—that was all she'd been able to handle. I didn't know how the hell she was going to fit me.

"Ah, but we can change that, my friend." His eyes narrowed as he looked at me. "You can hand her over to me, and I'll take care of her."

My jaw felt tight as I clenched it.

"Or maybe I'll just taste her when you're done," he added. "You wouldn't mind, would you, brother?"

This wouldn't be the first time Macon and I had slept with the same woman.

Fuck, we'd done threesomes together.

But I didn't want his hands anywhere near Oaklyn.

I wasn't going to tell him that.

I wasn't going to feed into this obsession he currently had, thinking I was whipped and in love.

But the truth was, Oaklyn wasn't mine. I really had no right to stop him.

But I also wasn't going to serve her to him on a goddamn platter.

Hell fucking no to that.

I blew air out of my lungs and held the tumbler between both palms.

"What?" he inquired. "You don't have an answer for me?" He paused, waiting. "I didn't think so." He pounded my chest lightly with his fist. "Why don't you stay in Oaklyn-land? See what happens. Don't pull yourself out until you need to. Then, who the fuck knows? Maybe you won't want to be pulled out, and you'll find a home there."

"I have no fucking idea what you're talking about."

His head bounced. It could have been to the music. It could have been a nod to me.

But he said, chuckling, "Man, you're something else."

"Can we move on to you now? I didn't come here to talk about myself. I came here to escape or some shit like that."

"Says the dude who sat down and immediately spilled his guts."

I drained the rest of my drink, calling the waiter over for another round, losing count of how much alcohol I'd had tonight. All I knew was that it wasn't enough. "Macon, do me a favor, and start talking."

He laughed as he looked at the blonde again, his attention eventually returning to me. "You know I was in Maui last week, touring different pieces of land where we could potentially build a new hotel. But I don't think I told you about the real estate agent who was giving me that tour." He whistled as he exhaled. "Fuck me, she was something else."

"Did you have to fight Cooper and Brady for her? Or did your brothers play nice and there wasn't any competition?"

That was one thing about the Spade brothers—they all liked the same kind of women.

Beautiful. Sensual. Sexual women.

If this chick was as hot as I assumed, then I was sure all three of them were frothing for a bite.

"Nah, man, my brothers didn't go on this trip. It was just me, scouting out locations. Jenner flew out a few days later once I narrowed down the search. He wanted to make sure the land would work logistically and legally if we ended up moving forward." He mashed his lips together. "But those first couple of days, it was just Kalea and me, fucking at each of the show-ings. *Mmm*," he moaned. "Once Jenner was there and Jo came out, it turned to all business, and we made an offer on the land. But, shit"—he chewed his bottom lip—"Kalea gave me a taste of that island that I'll never forget."

My cousin Jenner represented the Spade brand in all of their transactions. And if the trip involved a real estate offer, I wasn't surprised to hear that Jo, Jenner's fiancée, had tagged along, considering she was now the Chief Marketing Officer of Spade Hotels.

"So, when are you going back out to Hawaii to see her?"

He stared at me like I had something on my face, and then he clasped my shoulder and squeezed it. "I'm going back to Hawaii before we break ground, but not to see her." He tilted his head. "You got a whiff of Oaklyn's pussy, and now, you're suddenly going soft on me?" He released me and picked up his glass. "There are thousands of other women on that island, and I plan to fuck as many as I can while I'm there."

"Did it sound like I was insinuating that you were going to fucking marry the girl? Jesus, give me a little credit here."

He extended his arm, wrapping it around my shoulders. "It's all good." He nodded toward the group of girls. "What do you think of the blonde? And the two brunettes?"

I gave each one a quick glance. "They're all right."

"Just all right?"

"Dude, what do you want me to say? They're the hottest chicks I've ever seen? I can't tell you that."

Not a single one compared to Oaklyn. I didn't know if that was just shitty luck or if there was something wrong with my eyes or if there was something wrong with me.

"Because Oaklyn is hotter," he mocked.

"I didn't say that either."

"You didn't have to." His arm dropped, and he grinned at me. "I'm going to go buy them a drink. You should join me." He drained the rest of his and stood.

I reached into my pocket and pulled out my phone. "I'll be there in a minute."

"I won't hold my breath," he said, laughing again before he joined the girls.

I watched him flirt with them for just a second, and then I scanned the notifications that had come through on my phone.

Aside from a lot of social media bullshit, there was a reply from Oaklyn. She was responding to the text I'd sent her that told her she would be sucking my dick without teeth soon.

OAKLYN

I'll be ready ...

Damn it, that girl.

The mere mention of her offer had a hard-on working its way to my tip.

How did she have that fucking power?

What would it actually feel like to see her on her knees, sucking my crown, palming my sac?

It was tempting to claim that offer tonight.

But I'd had a lot to drink. I was sure, at this point, she probably had, too, and I didn't want it to go down that way. I wanted the details of her mouth and hands and throat to be fresh.

Still, I wanted something.

ME

Are you with my sister?

OAKLYN

Yes, we're still at the same bar, and we're half a bottle of champagne deep. Thanks for that, by the way.

ME

Don't get too drunk tonight. I need you functional for tomorrow.

OAKLYN

What's tomorrow?

ME

Lesson two.

OAKLYN

Ohhh.

ME

Are you free?

OAKLYN

I can make myself free.

ME

Good, because tomorrow's lesson is all about coming in public. You're going to do it quietly and on command with lots of eyes on you.

OAKLYN

Are you actually going to touch me this time? Or are you going to make me touch myself?

ME

You're going to get me. Not all of me ... but enough.

OAKLYN

And you think you can make me come by simply saying the word?

ME

I'm not just going to say it. I'm going to build the orgasm inside you, I'm going to let it hang there while you're in agony, and then I'm going to let you shudder so fucking hard that it's going to be almost impossible for you not to scream.

OAKLYN

When?

ME

I'll text you the time and place in the morning.

And, Oaklyn, wear something easily accessible. I need full access to your pussy tomorrow night.

NINE

Oaklyn

T his isn't a date. That was what I had to keep reminding myself of.

I was just meeting up with Camden at a restaurant about twenty minutes from my apartment, like it was any other night —minus the fact that Camden and I had never eaten alone together—and I was taking my own car and had every intention of splitting the bill with him.

But even though I continued to repeat that over and over in my head, I couldn't stop the jitters from exploding in my stomach. They were there while I got ready and left my apartment, strengthening as I drove to the restaurant. At each red light, I lowered my visor and checked myself in the mirror, making sure there wasn't any gloss on my teeth or that there wasn't any eye shadow fallout on my cheeks. That my hair had stayed curled.

That I didn't look like a woman who was about to get fingered at a restaurant.

Oh God.

What's happening to me?

Is this a mistake?

Am I going to end up screaming in the middle of the dining room, and the whole scene will be captured on social media, where it will undoubtedly go viral and cause me to lose my job?

And my best friend?

Before I even lose my virginity?

Those were the thoughts nagging at me as I pulled into the parking lot at a painfully slow speed before idling in the parking spot for several minutes.

I was already five minutes late even though punctuality was one of my strongest suits. I just couldn't shake the nerves. I couldn't stop thinking about what Camden was going to do to me tonight.

He was a guy I'd known most of my life and one I'd been crushing on for almost as long. He'd already seen me naked, already watched me touch myself. Already seen me scream out an orgasm.

So, why did this suddenly feel so different?

Unlike the other evening, he was going to be the reason I came.

And in my head, that would change everything.

This was, without question, going to bring us closer.

But he'd warned me, challenged me that I wouldn't be able to handle the emotional aspects of a physical relationship.

I needed to keep that in mind. I needed to just concentrate on the sexual acts. Once this evening was over, I couldn't get myself wrapped up in the feelings.

Because if not, I was for sure going to get my heart broken.

Even if I sensed that was going to happen anyway.

And that was what I repeated in my head as I turned off my car and grabbed my purse and headed up to the restaurant entrance. I was greeted by the hostess the moment I stepped inside.

"Hi," I said to her. "I'm meeting Camden Dalton. I'm not sure if he's arrived yet."

She glanced at her tablet. "Oh, yes, he's here. Follow me."

Nerves continued to shoot through my stomach as she led me into the main dining room and over to the side, where there were small booths that aligned the wall of windows.

There were two things I noticed immediately.

The first was Camden's eyes and how quickly they found me. How they stayed on me. How they were unquestionably taking me in and devouring me.

A look that made all the thoughts in my head swirl even faster.

The other was that this dining room was packed with people. A full audience to watch what was about to go down. Camden obviously knew this restaurant and had chosen it for that reason.

I wondered what would happen if I failed a lesson.

Or if my silence the moment I came would be considered passing.

I attempted to fill my lungs, my feet feeling extremely heavy as I took the remaining steps to the table, the hostess shifting out of the way to give me room to sit.

"Is there anything I can get either of you before the waitress comes?"

Courage, I wanted to reply.

But I shook my head, as did Camden, and I set my purse on the corner of my chair before regaining eye contact with him. "Hi."

He looked incredibly handsome, wearing a button-down shirt in a bright blue—the exact same color as his eyes. His sleeves were rolled up, showing the dark hair on his arms and leather bracelets that bound his wrist, balancing his Breitling with a little edge. There was an extra thickness to his scruff, and as he rubbed his palm over those whiskers, the scent of his cologne came wafting over. So did his long legs as he extended them far beyond the center of the table, and when I crossed mine, my bare calf grazed his jeans.

That brief bit of contact caused a flutter.

One that, once ignited, didn't let up.

"You're late," he responded, his gaze narrowing as he stared at me. "Traffic or nerves?"

I laughed, waiting for a lightness to enter my chest.

But it never came.

"What would make you think I'm nervous?"

He placed his arms on the table and leaned into them. "In the next hour, I'm going to reach underneath this table and touch your clit. That's where I'm going to start. Rubbing it in every direction, feeling it harden, making it so fucking wet. And then I'm going to give you one of these"—he stretched out his fingers, emphasizing their length—"which are far longer than yours, and I'm going to make you feel so good that you're going to stop breathing. You're going to do everything in your power not to scream while every man in this room is looking at you. Do you know why?"

I gasped when his shoe touched my ankle, the sensation so unexpected, especially as he lifted the brushed leather up the back of my calf.

"Because you're the most gorgeous woman in here, Oaklyn. That's why."

His compliment soared right through my chest.

I pressed myself for a response. For a way to express the way he'd just made me feel.

Anything.

But I had nothing.

Except for wetness.

There was already so much of that.

"I know you've been thinking about how you're going to stop yourself from reacting in front of everyone in here and what it's going to be like to look me in the eyes while I finger-fuck your pussy." He scraped his teeth over his bottom lip. "Do you know how I know that?" As he took a breath, his stare intensified. "I'm reading the way you're breathing, your eye contact, the movement in your hands, shoulders, your back, like you're on the stand and I'm cross-examining you." His gaze lowered down my chest, stopping at the edge of the table, where he couldn't see any further, and rose back up. "You can tell me it was traffic. You can say your nonexistent dog stole your car keys or you got lost on your way here even though you followed your Maps app, but you're as timely as me, and I can see the nerves all over you."

"Welcome. I'm Kimmy. What can I get you to drink?"

To drink?

What's even happening right now?

From the moment Camden had started talking, he'd sucked me into a cloud of scorching heat, and I'd forgotten everything, including that we were even in a restaurant.

I quickly glanced to my right, seeing the server, smiling, waiting for an answer to her question.

I cleared my throat. "Vodka on the rocks. Make that a double, please."

"Nice choice," Camden replied, and I could still feel the warmth from his stare even though I was no longer looking at him. "I'll have the same."

One more of those, and I'd be taking a rideshare home.

I didn't care.

Something told me I was going to need a second round.

And possibly a third.

"Great. I'll get those ordered for you," Kimmy said. "Do you have any questions about the menu, or would you like to put in any appetizers?"

"Let me ask you something," Camden voiced to her. "Are there any starters on the menu that Kimmy just can't live without?"

She pointed at her chest, her cheeks reddening. "Me?"

"Yes. You."

Camden had this unbelievable talent to make you feel like you were the only woman in the room. That he was whispering the question directly in your ear. Even his tone was tantalizing.

Her smile widened, and she reached for a chunk of her hair, holding it, curling it around her finger. "I have two faves. I eat them almost every shift."

"Bring them."

She giggled. "But I haven't told you what they are."

"You don't need to." He traced his lips with his thumb and pointer finger. "I trust you."

"Wow, okay. You're definitely going to be my favorite table of the night." She didn't glance at me at all when she added, "I'll be right back with the drinks."

Once we were alone, I asked, "What if I'm a picky eater?"

"You're not."

I tried to find the answer in his stare and couldn't. "How do you know that?"

"Oaklyn, come on. You're forgetting we're friends on social media, and you've been in my life for how long?"

Details I was surprised he'd picked up on.

Shocked actually.

But I wasn't going to focus on that. I was going to change the subject.

"You know, you have such a way with women. I don't know if I've ever seen anything like it before."

"What do you mean?"

I searched his eyes. "How can you possibly not know what I'm talking about? You just made Kimmy want to straddle you in a matter of seconds."

His head cocked to the side. "Does that make you jealous, Oaklyn?"

This time, when I laughed, it was the most honest sound even if the reply wasn't. "No."

"No?"

"There are zero feelings involved here; therefore, there's no jealousy." And because I felt like he needed a little dig for even thinking that, I added, "Don't flatter yourself, Camden."

With his arms still resting on the table, his thumbs rubbed together. "With this being the first major lesson, I needed to make sure."

"Fair enough." To try and throw him off from reading me even more, I glanced around the large, open space and asked, "Why here? And why a restaurant and not a bar?"

"There are three reasons. For one ..." His voice faded out until I met his eyes again. "I'm fucking hungry."

"Bars have food."

"But they're loud and filled with chatter and music. You can hide in a bar, sort of fall into the background and no one will notice. Which brings me to reason number two—restaurants are more transparent, and it's a setting that will really test you."

"Are you trying to set me up to fail?"

He licked across the same lip that he'd scraped earlier. "Now, wouldn't I be a stupid man if I did something like that? You've promised me your ass, Oaklyn, and that's something I want so fucking badly. If I haven't already told you, your ass is perfect." He shook his head. "Shit, it's one of the best I've ever seen, and I get to slide my dick inside its tight little hole. And then I get your pussy—another territory that no one's ever been inside of before." He leaned even closer to me. "You picked the lesson. You told me you wanted it to happen in public. So, tell me, why would I want you to fail?"

I knew I had to answer his question, but I was drowning in what he'd just said.

I wasn't sure I was even capable of forming words at this point.

That was how hard his words had hit me.

I'd known long before tonight why he was the king of one-night stands, but the more time I spent with him, the more I realized why.

That statement, that description—if we were back at his condo and not at this restaurant, I would probably tell him to forget all the lessons and just take my virginity now.

That was how turned on I was.

He smiled. "Nerves got your tongue?"

"You would like that to be the case, wouldn't you?"

I paused to get my brain straight and focused again.

"Why would I want you to fail?"

Because maybe he was afraid he was going to fall in love with me and wanted to end my proposition before it even started.

That was a long shot, but it was still an option.

One I wasn't sure I could even wrap my head around.

Or maybe he was having second thoughts about all of this, and he wanted to make lesson number two so extremely difficult that he was hoping I'd quit, and he wouldn't have to be responsible for taking my virginity.

Or maybe he really just wanted to see me come at a table inside a restaurant.

The problem was, I couldn't read Camden like he could with me.

And something told me he'd never tell me the truth.

"I don't know," I whispered. "It's just a little hunch I had. It looks like I was wrong though."

Kimmy returned with both glasses of vodka in her hands, and she set them down in front of us. "The appetizers should be right out. Have you decided on your main courses?"

I hadn't even opened the menu. "No—"

"I think we're just going to start with apps," he said, cutting me off. "We'll see where that takes us."

She gazed at him as she replied, "Sounds like a good plan to me."

When it was just us again, I asked, "What's reason number three?"

He gave me a sly grin. "I didn't think it would hurt for us to have a little conversation before the lesson went down. Like I said, bars can be loud. This atmosphere almost forces us to talk."

I couldn't believe that was what he wanted. This proposition was physical, nothing more. Conversation opened up avenues I was positive he didn't want to explore.

But if that was what he wanted, I'd give it to him, so I said, "Am I allowed to ask about the Hooked case?" I held up my hand before he had a chance to respond. "Hannah didn't tell me. I know she can't speak about the cases that you and Declan are working on since she can't violate the rules of professional conduct. But it's been all over the internet, so she didn't tell me anything I hadn't already read."

"Trying to save my sister's ass, are you?" he teased, winking.

I liked when he softened. When he flirted. When he was so incredibly charming that I could picture myself wrapping my arms around his neck and hugging him.

"Honestly, it's been fucking wild," he continued. "It'll probably be the biggest case I'll ever work on—maybe in my lifetime.

Two social media giants at war, and Hooked doesn't want to settle. They want the world to know what Faceframe did, so they're pushing for a trial. Declan and I have so much fucking work to do. That's about as much as I can tell you." He raked his fingers through his scruff. "What did I see the other day on Instagram? You won an award from your company?"

"*Ohhh.*" I clasped my hands together. "Yeah, that." It had been a last-minute decision to post the photo on Instagram, but Hannah had yelled at me for not doing so, so I'd caved. "I won President's Club for the third year in a row. That award was for the highest book of business in my region, highest revenue increase within the entire company, and highest new sales in the western half of the US. In other words, I kinda blew every sales objective out of the water."

"Hell fucking yes." He picked up his drink and tapped it against mine. "Can't say I'm surprised. I knew you were a badass."

I shrugged after I took a sip. "I just love my job."

"And you're obviously really good at it."

"I guess I am."

His eyes moved around my face, like he was really seeing me for the first time. "People our age don't say that often. They work, grind, repeat. Hannah, you, and me, we're a minority when it comes to liking what we do."

"And being successful at it."

"Truth," he said. "There's a lot of competition out there. It's easy to fall into the cracks. Become invisible. Stay stagnant."

"Never." I held the glass between my palms, waiting for the vodka to stop burning before I took another drink. "That's not me. I'm not looking for attention, but I'm also not one who's going to lie on my back and wait to see what comes." When I realized what I'd said, I laughed. "I didn't mean it that way."

"But you did, and that's why we're here, Oaklyn. You didn't

lie on your back. You took matters into your own hands and told me what you wanted." He rubbed his lips together. "There's something so fucking sexy about that." He went silent as he continued to gaze at me, and while I tried to think of a response, he said, "Now, the question is, do I touch you before the starters get delivered or after?"

"I think the appetizers are going to be here pretty soon, no? That doesn't give you much time."

"Oaklyn, Oaklyn ..." He reached for my hand that was now gripping the edge of the table, pulling it toward him and flattening my palm on the wood. "You doubt my abilities, and I don't know why." He spread out my fingers and straightened them, and I couldn't help but feel the stirring of tingles as he gently touched each finger, outlining them slowly, eventually going across the back of my hand. "I don't need minutes to get you off with these fingers. I need seconds."

He was simply running his fingertips around the inside of my hand. Yet it felt like so much more.

Air was getting hitched in my throat. Goose bumps were spreading across my skin.

But aside from making me melty, he was showing me how small this table was. Even with my arms being much shorter than his, I could easily reach his side. And when it came time, he was going to have no problem making his way underneath to hit that spot between my legs.

"You still don't believe me, do you?"

When I went to look away, just to ground myself again and try to slip out of the sticky cloud he was keeping me in, he pressed against the center of my palm and ran his thumb to my wrist.

Whenever I got massages, they would do the same motion, repeating that move to relax the muscles in my hand.

Camden caused just the opposite.

There was no relaxation.

There was only fire.

But I wasn't going to give in. That was what he wanted, and I just wasn't that kind of girl.

"We'll see tonight, won't we?"

He laughed. A deep, almost-nefarious chuckle that vibrated through my whole body. "I want to know about your experience before me. What did it look like? How much of your body has been touched and conquered?"

I pulled my hand back and tucked it safely in my lap. "Why does that matter?"

"Because I want to know how much instruction you need. Like when your lips surround the tip of my dick, will you know how to suck it? Will you know how to swivel your tongue and how to pump your fist and what to do with my sac?"

My hand didn't stay in my lap for long. It almost immediately reached for my vodka, and I took several sips.

Before I could even respond, he continued, "Has your pussy been licked, Oaklyn?"

I shook my head as I swallowed, overwhelmed with the firing squad coming at me. "No."

"Those men you've dated, fuck, they were some selfish bastards." He spun his glass on the table, his fingers circling the rim, reminding me of the touch he'd used on my hand and how he'd made me feel. "Did you suck any of their dicks?"

I nodded. "But not all of them—and I've only dated a few." I thought back to the overnighters, the occasions when I'd been intimate with my exes. Memories that weren't as memorable as they should have been. "If I'm being honest, I don't know if I did a good job. I just did it, if that makes sense."

"Did any of them touch your pussy? Or finger you?"

I understood why he was asking these questions; his reasoning made perfect sense. He just spoke so freely about sex and was so open about the topic, but it made me want to completely shut down. I was hoping that would change once I actually had it. But discussing it with an expert, like Camden, made me feel even more of a novice.

"Just a little bit," I replied. "About as much as you saw me do to myself."

"And your ass?"

The exhale was loud and almost startling when it came out of me. "No." And because it felt important, I added, "That will be a first for me too."

"All mine, you mean."

The way his eyes were penetrating me wasn't something I could process.

Same with his response.

How is something on my body all his?

Unless ...

"All—"

"The tuna tartare," the food runner said, cutting me off, as he placed the dish between us. "It comes with sliced mango, avocado, capers, and a heavy garnish of ginger on top. It's served with fried wontons. And here is our famous shrimp cocktail. Six jumbo shrimp with our homemade sauce that's a mix between a cocktail sauce and a remoulade. Be careful; it does have a bite to it." He paused. "Is there anything I can get you?"

"No, thank you," Camden replied.

"Then, enjoy," the food runner said before he left the table.

"Looks like we're having seafood tonight," Camden said after several seconds. "I'm assuming the queen of sushi approves of that?"

I laughed.

Another detail.

"Yes, I definitely approve." I still couldn't help but wonder

111

what he'd meant about my butt being all his. "There's something I don't get."

He took a wonton off the plate and spooned some tuna on top of it. "All right."

"What did you mean by yours? You know ... when it comes to certain parts of my body."

He watched me while he chewed, and when he swallowed and wiped his mouth, a smile came over his lips.

It wasn't anything like the one he'd given to our server.

Or the one that had been on his face when I first came to the table and he greeted me.

It wasn't even like the ones that usually followed his laughter.

This was different.

This was consuming in a way I hadn't felt before.

"That's something I can't explain to you, Oaklyn. It's something I'm going to have to show you. And the moment you feel it, when your ass and pussy mold around my dick, like they were fucking made just for me, you'll know exactly what I mean."

TEN

Camden

Oaklyn was painfully gorgeous as she sat across from me at the table, looking like an animal who was on the verge of being hunted. I could tell she wasn't the type of woman who thrived off attention. When it came to discussing her personal life, her skin flushed, her breathing increased. She tried to change topics the first chance she got. And she was just as happy staying in the background, observing, taking it all in, listening—the exact thing she had been doing for most of tonight, aside from when she was sharing her accolades.

She'd been feeling me out since the moment she'd sat across from me.

Learning more about me.

Realizing that, even though I was a man who took no time to get to know the women I slept with, I wasn't going to rush things with her.

Despite the fact that she was going to be without me at the

end of all this, I wanted each lesson to matter. I wanted her to know that all of this had been planned for a reason—from the restaurant I'd chosen to the table I'd picked to the main course of tonight's dinner.

Not because I cared.

Fuck, I didn't know how to care.

But because she deserved it.

Unlike the men she'd dated in the past, there were others in this world who would scan their memory bank, choosing a place they thought she would enjoy. Who would know the menu would be in line with her likes. Who would look up the pictures of the restaurant's interior—since it was a minor detail that could be forgotten—to ensure the tables at the booths were short enough that they could reach to the other side to finger-fuck her pussy.

This wasn't just going to be a lesson.

This was going to be a night she'd never forget.

For me, it had already taught me so much about her past and the men she'd shared a little of her body with.

I was going to be the lucky motherfucker who got to show her what real pleasure felt like, who would appreciate her body in ways she'd never experienced. The guys before me—whoever those fucking idiots were—hadn't realized what they had. Or maybe they'd been intimidated by her attractiveness and success. Or maybe they had just been fucking losers who didn't give a shit about anything or anyone.

Whatever the case was, I was going to rock her entire world during each of these lessons.

I was going to set the bar the highest, and every dude who followed me would have to measure up.

And, *fuck me*, I couldn't wait to start.

I'd initially planned to do it right after we finished the appetizers, but the waitress returned and asked if we wanted main courses. I'd seen Oaklyn eyeing up the sushi delivered to the surrounding tables, so I ordered us some rolls to share.

Now that those rolls had been devoured and we turned down dessert and a second round of drinks was in front of us and I paid the bill, it was time.

No one was going to bother us; I'd told the waitress we were just going to enjoy our cocktails and we'd be on our way. Unless someone came by to give us more water, it would just be Oaklyn and me at this booth.

I took a long sip of the vodka, holding it against my tongue as I stared at her.

God, she was beautiful, wearing a long, loose dress that flowed all the way to her ankles, giving me perfect access when I needed it. The top cupped underneath her tits, showing just the right amount of cleavage. Her hair hung past her shoulders, curled in a way that reminded me of the morning after. She looked satiated from tonight's meal, her gloss long gone from her lips, her eyes slightly hooded from the first vodka she'd drunk. She knew what was coming and was trying to prepare herself, which made her almost antsy in her seat, shifting positions, moving her hands from her lap to the table and back.

I knew she wouldn't ask when.

She wouldn't make a single move.

It was all on me—the way I wanted it to be.

But keeping her in suspense, making her question when she would feel my fingers, was something I really liked.

More than I'd anticipated.

"What do you think, Oaklyn? Is it time to stop yourself from screaming?"

Her cheeks turned one of my favorite colors, and she gazed off toward the dining room, like my stare was too much for her. "That's why we're here, right?"

Yes.

But I couldn't lie; she'd been excellent company tonight.

And even though I was dying to touch her, I wasn't in a rush to get this over with.

I wanted her to learn.

But I also wanted her to enjoy this as much as I would.

"Should I come over to your side of the booth?" she asked.

While picking this restaurant, I'd planned every stage of the lesson, down to the placement of our bodies, and one of the reasons I'd chosen this booth was due to its small size. There were only about eighteen inches of table between us, allowing me to easily reach her.

To watch her.

To touch her any way I wanted.

Having her next to me would be the obvious.

I wanted the unobvious.

"I want you right where you are," I instructed. "So I can see you. So I can look into your eyes the whole time."

She reconnected our stares. "You're going to make this as challenging as possible, aren't you?"

"One, that's my style." I grinned. "And two, you picked the lesson—don't forget that." I dropped my hand under the table and rubbed across her upper thigh, giving her the tiniest sample of my touch. "Here's what I want you to do. Lift your right foot and put it on my lap." Her lips parted, and I cut her off with, "Don't ask questions. Don't say a word. Just listen to me and do each step."

She gripped the edge of the table, her eyes wide and alert as she followed my command, her heel landing on my thigh. With her leg high and stretched to my side of the booth, the bottom of her dress fanned across the open space, acting like a window blind, preventing anyone nearby from seeing in.

"See what I did there?"

She nodded silently.

Attentive and obedient.

Damn it, I liked that.

The moment I cupped the top of her foot, her breathing changed again. With her chest uncovered, I saw the way it rose and fell, speeding up as I massaged my way to her ankle, slowing as I lowered to her toes.

Her skin was so soft and smooth.

Delicate.

"I haven't even touched your cunt, and you're already so fucking turned on."

Her brows lifted. "How would you know that?"

"I can see it on you." I could all but smell it in the fucking air. "I can feel it on your skin."

"Impossible."

"*Mmm*," I moaned softly as her heel pressed against my hard-on—whether it was on purpose or not, I loved it. "Stop doubting me, Oaklyn. You'll know very soon how good I'm going to be to your pussy."

Her toes moved, and as I swiped across them, they wiggled and scrunched.

The only part about this situation that I didn't like was that her screams were going to be muted. Those were something I wanted to hear. They were one of the best parts about being with a woman, listening to the way I made her feel. But here, with Oaklyn, I'd have to rely solely on her quieted words, her expression, the signs she gave off, like the way her teeth were nipping her bottom lip.

"You told me you don't use toys." My fingers were now underneath her dress, crawling to her knee, her skin getting warmer the higher I got. "So, you're used to the way your own touch feels. But it doesn't sound like anyone you've ever been with has gotten you off by fingering you."

"You're right."

"We're going to change that. Right now." I moved in a little higher, the distance between us not even causing me to strain. I couldn't have been more pleased with this table and how unnoticeable my actions were from anyone looking at us. "Oaklyn, that's not the only thing that's going down tonight. There's something you're going to learn too."

She sucked in some air.

"Remember the purpose of this proposition." I gave her a second, allowing that to settle in. "You want me to teach you how to be the best lover, and a part of that is control."

It was obvious she wanted to feel good. She wanted to come. She wanted to know what it felt like when a real man touched her pussy. But the root of all this couldn't be ignored, or then we'd only be doing this for pleasure.

I couldn't allow that.

These lessons were designed to not only teach her, but to also scare her off, have her change her mind. And for this one, I knew just how I was going to do that.

"When you only have ten seconds to come, you need to use those seconds to your advantage. When your partner tells you to hold off, there's a reason, and you need to listen." I slid up a little higher, rubbing around the outside of her thigh, circling, moving extra slow as I reached the inside of her leg. "Every scenario is going to be different, but control is the common denominator, and that's what we're going to focus on. Show me you can take direction, and I promise I'll reward you." I inched up a little more, and what I found surprised the hell out of me. "No panties?"

She shook her head. "I thought they'd just get in the way."

That meant the silky skin beneath my fingers was the edge of her pussy. I'd already known she was fully shaved, that at the top of her lips was the most perfect clit, that about five inches down was the opening to her pussy. I'd seen it. I'd been close enough to touch it. To smell it. I'd just had no idea that it was going to be this soft.

This hot.

This wet, even all the way over here.

"You're craving me, aren't you, Oaklyn?" I didn't give her any time to respond. "Your mind is a fucking war zone with thoughts about how badly you want this. How you need this. How your cunt is desperate for this."

"I already want to moan."

Fuck yes.

"Let me hear it," I ordered.

She glanced to her side, into the open dining room, like she was checking to see if anyone was around.

"See that man in the red shirt, sitting at the table with who I assume is his wife?" I paused for her to find him. "Give him a reason to look over here." When her eyes connected with mine, I continued, "Make his fucking dick hard."

Her expression told me she was full of hesitation.

I needed to change that.

So, I flicked my thumb over her clit.

It was that simple movement, that rush of skin on skin, that earned me the sound I wanted to hear.

That, "*Ahhh*," that my ears were after.

I caught eyes with the red-shirted man and fucking smiled at him. "Damn, you did good."

There was greed in her gaze, a look that backed up the noise she'd made.

One that exploded with hunger.

One that showed me the fiery flames in her eyes.

"Now, I want you to do it again." The second the last word left my mouth, I flicked.

"*Ohhh.*" Hair fell into her eyes, and she didn't bother to tuck it back. "*Shiiit.*"

When the red-shirted dude looked this way a second time, there was a smirk on his face.

He fucking knew.

And I was positive he was getting a hard-on because of it.

"Like goddamn music," I told her. "Do you want more?"

She didn't think I could make her come in seconds.

She didn't think I was the expert I'd claimed to be.

I was just going to have to prove that to her.

"Yes," she sighed.

"Where do you want me?" I gently stroked her clit. "Here?" I opened her lips with a finger, brushing my way down until I reached her pussy, the wetness so much heavier and thicker in this spot. "Or here?"

"I ..." It seemed like she couldn't catch her breath. "I don't know."

"Because you're worried it's going to hurt?"

I dipped my fingertip into her pussy, and she moaned, "Oh God, Camden, *yesss.*"

My cock fucking pounded inside my jeans as I thought about what it was going to feel like when my tip was doing this. When it was experiencing this tightness. When she was soaking the condom with her wetness.

"Answer the question, Oaklyn."

"I don't think you'd hurt me—at least not doing this. Other things, you might not be able to help."

"You're right." I wouldn't slam her pussy with my finger. I wouldn't give her three fingers at once either. She wasn't ready for that. But anything I gave her tonight certainly wasn't going to hurt her. "Then, why don't you know where you want me?"

She reached for her vodka, guzzling several mouthfuls. She licked her lips and finally said, "Because I can't think straight.

Even this—which is basically nothing—feels completely overwhelming. I can't imagine what it's going to feel like when you give me more."

Now, that was the right answer.

My finger hadn't moved, the tip of it staying within her walls, sitting still while my thumb hovered above her clit. "Maybe I should make you come first. Get that out of the way. And then you can experience what control is really like."

"You mean ... you're going to get me off more than once tonight?"

I laughed.

The question was so innocent, yet she was so serious when asking.

"Yes, Oaklyn. You're going to come multiple times at this restaurant."

She shook her head again. "No. I can't."

"You can, and you will." I pressed the pad of my thumb against her clit. "I'll show you."

I focused only on the top, giving it the amount of pressure I assumed she needed, and swished it back and forth horizontally before I rotated my finger around.

I was met with an instant buck of her hips.

And more wetness.

Fuck, there was so much more of that.

"You like the way that feels," I growled softly.

"It's so different here"—she glanced to her right as a waiter walked by, smiling at him—"and with you doing it. There's nothing familiar about the way this feels." She inhaled. "It's a million times more intense." She paused. "I can't breathe."

"Wait until you feel this ..." I went deeper into her pussy, slowly sliding past my knuckle, where the tightness narrowed even more, and continued until it was fully buried.

"Camden." The sound came out as a moan, drawn out,

followed by her clasping my wrist. She held me there, squeezing, like she was trying to stop me from going anywhere.

"No one's ever been in this far, have they?"

Her eyes answered me, but she still whispered, "No. I've only let them in about an inch, nothing more."

I tilted my palm forward, arching my finger toward her stomach, and very gradually circled that spot. "And here?"

Her head hit the cushion behind her, and her eyes closed. "Where are you?" Her throat moved as she swallowed. "What is that?"

"Your G-spot."

"And I thought it was a myth."

I laughed. "Far from it."

"I'm going to die right here in this booth." Her eyes flicked open. "I'm not going to survive this. This is"—her head moved from side to side—"the most physically overwhelming experience of my life."

And I was barely fucking touching her.

Oaklyn had either been sadly deprived in the past or something about my touch set her off more than any other.

I didn't want to think too much about either, so I gave her what she wanted instead.

And that was more friction, more pressure, more pumping of my finger.

"Do you think that table can smell how turned on you are?" I nodded toward the one that was directly behind the red-shirted guy, where two dudes sat, both around our age and more than aware of what could go down in this booth. "Do you think they can smell the sweetness of your cunt?"

"Camden—"

"Answer me."

"Yes!" Her reply earned us looks from each of them, and I

rewarded her with an increase in speed. "Oh fuck"—she swallowed—"I think they can smell how you're making me feel."

Her lips stayed parted, and her back arched as she released my wrist. Her hands moved to the edge of the table, her fingers turning white as she held on. Her lips were wet from licking them, her eyes almost feral.

There was nothing more gorgeous than the sight in front of me.

Nothing that had ever made my dick harder, aside from the scene that had played out at my condo with her. Nothing that had felt as good as the way her pussy was clenching my finger, the way her clit was hardening under my thumb.

"Come," I demanded. I increased my speed again and growled, "Come for me, Oaklyn."

Her mouth opened like she was going to scream. She inhaled as much air as she could hold, and the second her lungs were full, she shuddered. "*Ahhh.*"

Each rock of her hips bumped my thumb, but I didn't stop.

I went harder, faster.

I watched the waves move across her face, the satisfaction filling her gaze.

I listened to the sound of her breathing, panting, until she made one final sigh of, "Camden," and her head fell back. "What the fuck was that?"

"The beginning." I was sure she was probably sensitive, so I stalled, her wetness turning thick on my finger. "And there's going to be a lot more."

Her head straightened. "I thought you were kidding."

"When it comes to your pussy, Oaklyn, I will never kid."

I carefully traced my thumb down her clit, each bit of movement showing in her expression.

"Tingly?" I asked.

"In ways I can't even describe."

I smiled. "I understand." I pulled my pointer finger back and added the tip of my middle finger. If she was ever going to fit my cock, I needed to gradually loosen her, get her used to a size that was larger than what she used when she rubbed one out. "This is going to feel a little different, but it's not going to hurt." I rotated both fingertips in her wetness, spreading it over my skin, pulsing her hole. And each time I did that, I swiped her clit with fast, hard strokes.

"Oh shit," she whispered.

"This orgasm is going to come quickly. Show me you can stop it."

"I don't know if I have that kind of power."

I smiled. "You do, and you will."

"Camden ..." Her teeth ground her lip as I began to probe her a bit more. "This is ... I don't know what this is."

"It's about to get better."

I wedged both fingers into her opening, holding one in front of the other, and gently wiggled them in, turning my wrist the whole time so she could feel the way they hit her from all sides.

"My God," she gasped.

"I knew you would like that."

She'd released the table, but her hands resumed their position there, her head lifting off the cushion behind it. That was when I drove the rest of the way in, delicately drawing those two fingers forward and back—all the while, I was pushing against her clit, holding the top, almost grinding my thumb against it.

"I want to scream." Her voice was so seductive.

"I know."

"I don't know how I'm going to stop myself."

"Control, Oaklyn. That's how."

The same way I was stopping myself from pulling her into my lap and plunging my cock into her. Because right now, at this very second, I wanted nothing more.

"Don't come," I warned when I saw her getting close, the red-shirted man now looking at her. "Stop yourself, but don't stop yourself from letting him know how good you feel." I nodded toward the first table, but kept my eyes on her. "He's watching. Why don't you give him a show?"

I waited to see her regain her control, but her clit was hardening.

"Look at me."

Her eyes were on him and slowly shifted to me, but I didn't think she was actually seeing me. She was off somewhere else, completely lost.

"Fucking look at me, Oaklyn."

She blinked several times.

"Do not come—do you hear me?"

Her chest rose, and she held the air in her lungs.

I didn't let her off easy. In fact, I made it even more challenging by increasing my speed, aiming my fingertips toward her G-spot again, adding double the pressure to her clit.

Her head pushed into the top of the booth behind her, moving up and down every time I slid into her. "I can't."

"Yes, you can," I roared, making sure only she could hear me. "Do whatever you need to do—put your mind somewhere else, talk yourself down, stare at that red-shirted motherfucker. I don't care, just don't come."

"Camden—"

"Would you like some more water?"

The waiter had come out of nowhere but was now standing at the edge of our table, holding a pitcher, gazing between the both of us.

I'd hoped this was going to happen.

To not only scare her, but to also teach her the ramifications of what voyeurism really entailed.

She'd wanted this.

She was definitely getting it to the extreme.

"Yes," I replied to him, "we'd both like more water."

Our previous waitress had cleared our table, except for both sets of drinks—the vodka and water.

And as he reached for Oaklyn's glass, staring at her, I didn't stop the pace I was using before he arrived, slipping inside her like she didn't have an audience.

Like I wasn't on the verge of making her come.

Like the scent of her previous orgasm wasn't floating in the fucking air.

"How was dinner?" he asked her. "Did it all meet your satisfaction?"

I grinned at Oaklyn as I replied, "Everything has been delicious." I tapped her clit. "Especially dessert."

"What did you have?" he asked.

"I'm having it right now," I told him.

With my free hand, I pointed. He probably assumed I was aiming at the vodka, but I was really targeting Oaklyn.

He chuckled. "Have a drink for me, man. The second this shift ends, I'm pouring myself one of those."

A grin pulled at my lips. "Good for you." I licked across them. "What did you think of dinner, baby?"

Oaklyn had stayed completely silent.

That was about to change.

Her eyes widened at the name I'd called her.

Or maybe it was from the way I was flicking her clit.

Or how she was doing everything in her power not to come.

"Great." She cleared her throat. "It was"—she brought in more air—"perfect."

Oh fuck, she had done good.

He picked up my water glass and filled it to the top. "Can I get you anything else?"

I kept my focus on Oaklyn when I responded, "I think we're good. We're just finishing up, as you can see."

And I hoped he could.

"Sounds great," he replied and left the table.

"I'm going to kill you," she exhaled. "I ... don't ... I don't even know."

That was how I wanted her. Lost for words. A bumbling fucking mess. With eyes that were rabid as she stared at me.

"You did everything I'd asked of you."

"I deserve a damn—"

"To come," I said, cutting her off. "Do it. Now."

Within a stroke, she was shuddering, her breathing much louder this time, the spasms inside her body shaking each of her muscles.

And mine.

"Camden ... *fuuuck*."

I drove into her pussy, twisting, turning, massaging her clit at the same time. "That's it. Let me feel it."

She rewarded me with an expression I wanted to lick off her face.

It was beautiful, making my dick ache to be inside her.

But it was also the type of enjoyment that came when you really knew someone's body.

When you knew you had mastered their pleasure.

And that was what I'd done with Oaklyn.

"You're fucking squeezing me," I hissed. "Goddamn it."

As she wriggled in the booth, I slowed my speed to a dull grind until I came to a halt.

I knew I could probably give her another orgasm, but at this point, I was sure her pussy was sore, and I didn't want to overdo it. Scaring her was one thing; causing her pain was something entirely different.

I pulled my fingers out and put them straight into my mouth, sucking the wetness off. She was delicious—in the way she looked, in the way she tasted, in the way she smelled.

Is there a more perfect woman out there than Oaklyn Rose?

Fuck.

And what the fuck am I thinking?

"You conquered lesson two," I said, occupying my mind so I didn't concentrate on the way I was feeling. "I didn't think you'd pull it off, not after the water incident, but you proved my ass wrong. How do you feel?"

Her foot dropped from my lap, and she settled herself in the booth, taking several breaths. "Like electricity is shooting through my body and I can't stop it."

I continued to gaze at her. "Do you want to?"

"No, but"—she surrounded her vodka with both hands—"this is the second time I've left you with this." I felt the sudden touch of her foot against my erection. She ran her toes against it for only a second, and then she was gone. "Remember, my offer always stands."

If she stayed here any longer, I would have her in the restroom. On her fucking knees. With her mouth open and her throat ready to take in my shaft.

It wasn't time for that yet.

Hell, I wasn't sure it would ever be time for that.

Because that would change everything.

It would make it about my pleasure, and that was a level we didn't need to reach.

I nodded toward her glass. "Drink up."

Her stare shifted to the vodka, and she took a long sip, setting the glass back down. "I have to drive. I think ... I'm good."

I nodded once more, this time toward the entrance of the restaurant. "It's time to go, Oaklyn."

"Are you heading out too?"

I brought my drink up to my lips. "I'm going to finish this first."

"Got it." She grabbed her purse, pausing for a few seconds, and then she stood. "Until lesson three, I guess."

There were so many things I could say.

So many orders I could give her.

And knowing how submissive she was, she'd follow through with each one.

It was safest to say, "I'll be in touch."

She smiled, a look of pure satisfaction on her face. "I can't wait." And then she disappeared from the dining room.

I drained the rest of the booze, my fists tight, my hard-on relentless.

I released my fingers to fish for my phone in my pocket.

I needed a fucking release.

I needed my best friend's ear.

I pulled up Macon's last text and started typing.

ME

Where are you?

MACON

At our favorite bar, my man.

ME

I'll be there in twenty. Order me a drink, motherfucker.

I shoved my phone back in my pocket and grabbed Oaklyn's drink, putting my lips on the glass, in the same place hers had been because her gloss had left a mark, and I let the rest of her vodka pour down my throat.

When I finished, I set the glass down and rubbed my fingers under my nose.

The ones that had been inside Oaklyn's cunt.

And I took a long, deep inhale.

ELEVEN

Oaklyn

The first thing I did after walking out of the restaurant and getting into my car was take out my phone and search for my best friend's name in the Contacts. Even though the drive back to my apartment would only take around twenty minutes, I didn't want to do it alone. Not even with music blaring in the background and the windows down. Neither of those would get me out of my head.

A place that, after tonight, was extremely jumbled and messy.

A place that, after tonight, was filled with images of Camden's hand and the intensity of his gaze and the smile that had tugged across his lips.

Feelings were shooting through me like fireworks.

I needed an escape.

A pause button.

And since I couldn't discuss the situation with Hannah, she

was the perfect person to call. She would get my brain fixated on something other than her brother.

She answered after the second ring with, "What are you doing right this second, bestie?"

I could hear the wine buzz in her voice, her tone telling me she was working on her second glass.

I laughed. "I called you. Shouldn't that be my question?"

"If you tell me you're busy, we're going to be in a huge fight."

"I'm not." I started the car and shifted into drive. "I'm actually driving, so I'm as free as can be."

"Good. Then, get your buns to Molly's."

I checked the time on the dash before I turned onto the road. "That's where you are?"

"And it's where you need to be."

Molly's was walking distance from my apartment and the spot where I usually met Hannah when we went out for drinks. I could park my car at home, and I wouldn't even have to order a rideshare.

Time with my favorite girl and a couple more drinks and immediately passing out when I got home sounded like the best plan for the rest of tonight.

"I'll be there in twenty-ish," I told her, but something struck me the moment I replied, and I questioned, "What are you doing there anyway? You never go there without me."

"Check your phone, babe. I've called and texted. I was giving myself another glass of wine before I marched my ass across the street to see why you weren't answering."

I'd seen multiple notifications on my screen before I searched for Hannah in my call log, but I'd just ignored them. And because my phone had been in my purse the whole time I was in the restaurant, I hadn't heard her call or text.

"Sorry," I replied. "I was at a work thing. But I'm on my way, and I'll see you soon."

"Hurry."

And I did. The traffic was surprisingly light enough that I got to my apartment in less time than I'd estimated, giving me a few extra minutes to rush upstairs and change my clothes. The dress, although extra flowy so no one could tell, was wet on the inside from the two times he'd gotten me off. I was sure it had dried, but instead of waiting, I put on a pair of panties and jeans and an off-the-shoulder top, and I took a little longer than I wanted to check my hair and makeup before I headed across the street.

I didn't know why I'd assumed Hannah was alone—she certainly wasn't a solo drinker. I just hadn't expected the entire family to be with her, but all three cousins—Dominick, Jenner, and Ford—along with their girlfriends and Declan were there, occupying three entire tables in the back of the bar.

The moment Hannah spotted me, she stood from her seat and shouted, "Oaklyn," with her arms out. "What took you so long, woman?" She hugged me tightly. "I was worried you'd changed your mind."

As I squeezed her shoulders, I took a quick peek at my watch. "I'm only seven minutes late."

"But you're never late."

I laughed. "I ran upstairs and changed. I was fancied up for work and was craving my Converse." I pulled away and went around the table, hugging all the family, noticing the only person who was missing before I took one of the open seats next to Hannah.

Camden had left after me—I was certain of that since I'd seen his sports car in the parking lot on my way out of the restaurant.

I wondered if he was coming here or going home.

Or heading somewhere to meet up with one of his fuck buddies—or whatever he called the girls he slept with and didn't care about.

That was something I didn't want to dwell on.

Something that made everything inside me start to hurt.

As I looked at Hannah, I wanted so badly to ask her if he was coming.

But I couldn't.

I needed to act as though I hadn't noticed his absence because, in this moment, I couldn't put my mind in a pre-Camden space to know whether that was a question I would have asked before.

He owned far too much of my mind now.

"What's the occasion for tonight's get-together?" I inquired instead as my best friend handed me a full glass of wine. "Did you guys land a big account? Win a trial? Or just a *why the hell not* kinda evening?"

"The latter," Declan said, reaching across Hannah to clink his glass against mine. "I don't think anyone at this table, including you, Oaklyn, needs a reason to drink."

I smiled at her boyfriend, the grumpiness to Hannah's sunshine. "You're not wrong about that."

"Still, we've all been trying to get together," Hannah said, "and it's almost impossible. Someone's always traveling or sick or can't get a babysitter"—she pointed at Ford and winked—"so tonight is the night we're all here. Even the Spades were able to join us."

"Macon's here?" I asked, instantly recalling the conversation Hannah, Camden, and I'd had about him at the bar when she mentioned—repeatedly—that she wanted to set me up with him.

"In the flesh," I heard from behind me.

Shit.

That was Macon's voice.

I could never forget that deep, gritty tone that dripped with lust.

I turned just as he was taking the seat beside me.

He held out his hand. "Oaklyn, it's nice to see you again."

"And you," I replied, clasping our fingers together, mine feeling so tiny against his.

"So, the two of you remember each other. Perfect," Hannah chimed in. "That saves me an introduction."

When I glanced at her, her smile was so large that it was cartoonish. Now, I knew why she'd wanted me to come here so badly—she was obsessed with getting Macon and me together.

"Macon and his brothers just got back from Hawaii, where they finalized the land for their newest hotel." Hannah nodded toward the two others who had just joined the table.

Cooper, the middle child, had almost a surfer look with golden-brown hair and dark blue eyes, and Brady, the oldest, looked like he had come straight from a Milan runway with jet-black hair and these piercing icy-blue eyes.

"Oh, yeah?" I said, turning my head to meet Macon's emerald gaze. "That had to be an amazing and exhilarating trip. I'm impressed you made it here tonight. Usually, I'm dead for a week after I travel."

"Mind over matter," he replied. "Besides, there was a rumor that you were coming tonight, and I wanted to see if it was true." His stare dropped to my chest and began to lower.

That was when I looked at Hannah.

This was all becoming too much.

And I pointed at myself and said to her, "A rumor that I was coming? Isn't it funny how rumors get started?"

"If I had to carry you over here, you were coming," Hannah said.

"That's one hell of a best friend, always having your back," Macon added, gaining my attention.

The guilt suddenly hit.

The thought of what had gone down tonight at the restaurant.

The feelings that I had of Camden that racked my chest as I sat here and looked at his best friend, Macon, who stirred nothing in me but a stale wind.

I lifted my wineglass and guzzled down several gulps.

"Some things that Oaklyn is far too humble to tell you are," Hannah said, leaning closer to me so she could get a better view of Macon as I swallowed, "she's one of the top marketing brand managers for her company, she just won President's Club, she's on a fast track of buying her own condo in WeHo, and even though she'd never admit it, she's the most incredible cook."

I loved her more than life itself.

In any other circumstance, I would appreciate what she was doing.

But not now, not with him.

Even if Camden was okay with it—and I assumed he was based on the conversation at the bar—I wasn't.

Nothing about this felt right.

"And I like to eat." Macon eyed me as the words left his mouth. "As for the rest, I'm extremely impressed, especially considering you're what, twenty-four?"

"Twenty-five," I told him.

"What type of marketing?"

"Digital mostly," I replied, "but I'll get whatever medium my client needs or what I think will best suit them. Unlike my competitors, it's about what's best for the client, not me."

"Always putting everyone else first," Hannah said. "It's no surprise she does so well; she's a pleaser at heart. The girl who will bend over backward and run the extra mile to make everyone happy."

"I don't know about that—"

"You're the angel of our duo—I tell you that all the time."

My stare slowly left her and moved to Macon.

"You're the angel ... is that right?" He paused. "Just how angelic are you?"

I didn't know how to react.

Or what to say.

So, I picked up my wine and shrugged.

I was sure if any other woman were sitting in this seat, she would have an answer, and it would sound something like, *Take me home, and I'll show you.* There was no question that Macon had that kind of charm.

It just didn't work on me.

I was too Camden-obsessed.

"We're talking the highest level," Hannah replied for me.

I casually and inconspicuously kicked her under the table, and she squeezed my hip in response. But it wasn't a normal pinch. It was the kind where she was urging me to get my flirt on.

"*Mmm,*" Macon moaned, the sound so low that it vibrated through me, "I like that." He ran his palm over one side of his beard and then the other, staring me down the entire time, like he was trying to decide what part of me he was going to devour first. "Maybe I need to ask you on a date and see for myself."

Oh God.

Macon glanced around the room, his stare eventually returning to me when he voiced, "What do you say, Oaklyn? Should we grab a drink sometime?"

His voice was suddenly so loud that it made my ears ring.

So was his question.

"I—"

My voice cut off when I felt a change in the air, like the pressure in the room was increasing, causing a sensation to grow over my body.

One that hadn't come from Hannah or Macon gazing at me.

They didn't have that kind of strength.

Only one person could affect me this way.

I looked up, and that was when I saw Camden, frozen several feet away from our section of tables, glaring at the three of us, like we were doing something wrong. That look only stayed on his face for a few seconds. It didn't soften or lighten. It transformed into an expression I couldn't understand.

But the feeling inside me was just as intense.

Since I knew Hannah and Macon were looking at me, I nodded toward Camden and said, "Look, Camden's here."

"Finally," Hannah said as Camden joined our table. "I thought you were never going to come."

He looked at me as he said, "I had something I needed to do first."

Something?

Or someone?

I didn't know what that meant or how I was supposed to read this situation.

I just knew that I didn't like this feeling.

Macon stood and man-hugged Camden, and once they released, Camden leaned across the table and kissed my cheek, whispering, "Looks like you're enjoying yourself," before he moved on to his sister.

For someone who had this uncanny ability to read me, he'd sure done a shitty job.

The moment Camden took a seat, Macon faced me again and said, "So, what do you think, Oaklyn? Is it a date?"

Without giving me a chance to respond, Hannah said, "I

told you I was going to set them up," to her brother. "And see? I totally worked my magic."

"You sure did," Camden replied to her.

All eyes were now on me.

I didn't know what to say.

What to do.

But I needed to voice something.

Even if it wasn't what I wanted, I didn't know any other way out of this, so I turned to Macon, and after a few seconds, I smiled, even grazing my lip with my teeth. "I'd love to go on a date."

TWELVE

Camden

I was seeing fucking red.

I wasn't technically allowed to be pissed. Oaklyn could talk to whomever she wanted. She could flirt her ass off with any of the Spade brothers. I'd even given Macon permission to take her out. Hell, she could pick up a random dude somewhere in this bar and go home with him.

I couldn't stop her.

I had no right to.

But that didn't mean I was happy about it. That seeing them together at a table, sitting so close, where he couldn't take his goddamn eyes off her, gazing at her like he was seconds away from taking her virginity, was making my heart pound and my fists clench.

I didn't like the way she was looking at him either.

I didn't even like that she was looking at him.

Fuck.

I lifted my hand to my face, rubbing my fingers under my nose, taking in her lingering scent.

An hour ago, she'd been mine. That perfect body spread out in front of me, urging me to touch whatever part I wanted, but I'd focused solely on that incredible spot between her legs.

I'd brushed my fingers over her softness.

I'd watched her face as the orgasms rippled through her.

I'd felt her pussy clench my fingers and the cum she left on my skin.

The cum I was smelling now.

And what, less than sixty minutes later, she was cozying up to my best friend, someone who was going to take her virginity and run?

Just like me.

Who certainly wasn't going to be soft or tender if he fucked her.

Because of course, he was going to fuck her, goddamn it, since she'd just agreed to go out on a date with him.

Something I couldn't wrap my head around.

Something I couldn't fucking stomach.

Something I couldn't watch a second longer or I was going to make a scene—and that was the last thing I wanted.

Hannah would then know.

Everyone would know.

And I couldn't let that happen.

I was just turning away from the new couple when I heard, "Where the fuck have you been?" from Dominick.

As he approached, I stood to greet him and went in for a man hug, relieved that I had something else to focus on.

"I met up with a girl, nothing serious, just got it in real quick," I lied.

The truth was, I'd gone into the restroom at the restaurant

and rubbed one out before I left to come here. It was my only option—my hard-on wasn't going to go away otherwise.

But, shit, I hadn't expected to see Oaklyn when I arrived at the bar.

When I'd texted Macon from the table, I'd assumed it was just him until I got into my car and read all the texts from my sister, telling me the whole family was there and waiting for me.

"Sounds like you," he replied, taking a drink from a tumbler that I assumed was full of scotch.

I needed a fucking drink.

Fast.

"And just like you before you got hitched."

He clasped my shoulder. "Not hitched yet, my man, but soon." He smiled. "Maybe one day, you'll know that feeling."

"Unlikely," I huffed.

"We'll see about that." He chuckled. "I'm headed to the bar, and it looks like you need a drink."

"I thought you'd never ask. Double vodka on the rocks."

"No mixer?"

I shook my head. "Tell them they can mix in more vodka."

"I'm on it." He squeezed my shoulder even tighter before he released me and walked away.

Unoccupied, my ears picked up on the conversation between Macon and Oaklyn. They were talking about his job, just some small-talk bullshit that I knew Macon hated, biding his time until he could get her naked and satisfying her need to know the man behind the one-night stand.

I knew his style.

Just like I knew he wasn't listening to a fucking word she was saying. He didn't care. He had no interest in learning about her. He just wanted to sleep with her.

If I turned in their direction, I would say something.

I'd call him out.

I would point my finger to the ground in front of me and tell Oaklyn to get her ass over here.

So, I went over to the other table where some of the guys were talking, and I wedged my way in between Jenner and Declan.

Jenner tossed his arm around my shoulders. "Glad you're here, buddy. Wasn't sure you were going to join us tonight. Macon said you might be too busy to come."

I stole a glance at my best friend, who had known I was out with a girl—I just hadn't told him it was Oaklyn. He was charming the shit out of her, smiling in that rich, enticing way, making her feel like she was the hottest girl in the room, that no one mattered in this world but her.

That shit needed to stop.

Now.

I faced Jenner and said, "The date ended early."

"No reason to drag it out all night after you get what you want, am I right?"

I nodded. "Exactly."

Except this motherfucker was as married as Dominick, and so was Ford, and, shit, Declan was really no different. Aside from the Spade brothers, I was surrounded by dudes who had been out of the game for a while.

I needed a subject change.

With my eyes getting a break, my brain needed one too.

"How was Hawaii?" I asked him. "Macon tells me you guys found land and you're set to build."

Jenner released me as he replied, "Wait until you see it. It's fucking majestic. I've been to every one of the Spade Hotels, and it's no secret that Utah is my favorite, but this property is going to be something else."

"When are we going?"

He laughed. "Say the word, my friend, and we'll take the jet."

Damn, that sounded like a good time.

Something I wanted.

Needed.

But taking off for a weeklong vacation in paradise would only make me question what was happening back at home, just like I couldn't stop wondering what was happening behind my back right now.

When I looked over my shoulder, my teeth ground together.

My fingers tightened.

"We'll need to plan something like that soon," I responded, glancing at Jenner again.

Dominick joined the group and handed me my vodka. "I had them make you a triple."

"Even better," I told him, and I immediately brought the drink up to my lips, swallowing several gulps.

As it burned the back of my throat, I glanced at the couple one more time.

The couple.

I couldn't believe I was actually fucking calling them that.

Not that they'd ever reach that status.

But still, they looked that way at the table.

And as though Macon could sense my stare, his eyes shifted over in my direction, and a smile grew across his lips. His eyelids then narrowed, and he nodded at me.

He fucking nodded, like he was accepting the piece of meat that I'd served to him.

That motherfucker.

I couldn't be mad.

Not at him or her.

This was my fault.

My doing.

I was the one who had told her that I didn't think she could handle this. That she was going to get emotions involved in the process of this proposition, and when we finished every lesson, she'd lose it.

A virgin as sensitive as Oaklyn surely needed some tenderness after a guy touched her body, and I'd warned her that wasn't the kind of guy I was.

But two lessons had passed, and she'd held it together each time.

She seemed fine.

She wasn't getting attached.

Yet here I was, staring at the two of them, practically snarling when he was only talking to her.

But it was his intentions that drove me mad.

It was his thoughts that I could see as clear as day.

It was the fact that she was mine.

Mine?

Goddamn it, Camden, what the hell is wrong with you?

Oaklyn Rose wasn't mine.

I didn't do that kind of ownership when it came to women.

I didn't do multiple nights in a row.

I did one-night stands.

I did women who knew exactly what I was after. I took care of them, and they took care of me, and it was a mutual agreement.

If I made her mine, that meant commitment.

A relationship.

A level I hadn't reached since high school, which my sister had recently pointed out.

What the fuck do I know about any of that?

Why am I even thinking about it?

Macon was gazing at Oaklyn again, their faces semi-close.

145

Their speech quiet enough that I couldn't hear it from over here.

The more I looked on, the worse I felt.

The harder my hands shook.

The tighter my chest became.

Tearing her away from him would do nothing but stir up drama that I wasn't going to deal with tonight—or anytime soon. I didn't need that kind of questioning from my sister. I didn't need that kind of shit from my cousins, considering they all knew I wasn't the type of guy to want more.

And I didn't need to make Macon feel like I was ripping her away over some surge of fucking jealousy.

What I needed was to get the hell out of here.

I brought the glass up to my lips and shot back the rest of the liquor, and the moment I pulled it away from my mouth and set the empty on the table, Declan clasped my elbow and said, "I'm going to steal Camden for a second," and he led me away from the group.

When it was just the two of us, I pulled my arm back. "I was just going to leave and head home."

"Not until I talk to you first."

He stood in front of me, eye-level, his stare almost haunting.

I couldn't imagine what he needed to speak to me about.

Work.

Hooked.

Another one of our cases.

Couldn't any of that fucking wait until we were in the office?

"Take it from someone who knows ... when you think you're being inconspicuous and not a single motherfucker is tuned in to what you're doing, there's always someone in the crowd who's watching. Who misses nothing. Tonight, because I haven't had enough of these quite yet"—he held up his tumbler —"that person happens to be me."

I searched his eyes. "I don't know what you're talking about."

"Come on, man. There's no reason to hide in front of me." He paused. "I saw your face the second you walked into the bar. The way you froze when you noticed your best friend chatting it up with Oaklyn. You ran right over there like a puppy whose owner was paying attention to another doodle. You're not fooling me."

"Bullshit."

He laughed. "Oh, it's bullshit that the entire time you were standing with Ford, Jenner, and me, you ignored almost everything everyone was saying because you couldn't stop staring at Oaklyn?"

Ignored them?

I had been talking to Jenner.

And then I wasn't because I was so focused on Macon and Oaklyn.

Had I missed what they were all saying?

This wasn't like me at all.

Shit.

I exhaled, my lungs so goddamn restricted that the air that moved through was as hot as lava.

"I thought so." He fisted my shoulder. "I'm not going to tell Hannah. I'll let you do that on your own when you think the time is right, and then she can tell you all the ways she's going to neuter you."

I shook my head. "Not going to happen."

"No? You think you can fight it?" He smiled. "Let's see how well that goes. Again, from personal experience, it only lasts for so long, and by the time you finally cave, you're so fucking wrapped up in her that you don't remember a moment before her."

I remembered the moments all right.

But none of them compared to Oaklyn.

I drove my fingers into the sides of my hair and pulled the strands. "I don't know." When my gaze fell, I saw the drink in his hand and grabbed it, shooting back the remainder of the booze, even sucking it off the ice. I wiped my mouth and looked at Declan. "I don't know what the fuck is happening to me."

"I do." He extended his arm, leaning back to really take in my face. "You're falling hard for her."

"No."

"What, you think you're so different from all of us, kid?" He nodded toward Dominick. "Different from what he went through with Kendall, his client's sister, and how hard he fought against being with her? And different from Jenner and Jo and how he didn't want to tap that because of her age and because she was his top client's daughter? Jesus, those boys like to mix with their clients." He chuckled. "And then there's Ford and his goddamn nanny, who he swore he was never going to date. Now, they're inseparable."

"And you," I gritted out through my teeth.

"And me, who was never going to settle down, never going to get tied up. I swore my life on it. Look at me now." He pointed at his chest. "I'm straight up in love with that woman. I don't care how much shit she gives me or how much hell she puts me through; she can do no wrong. I'll treat her like a queen until the day she dies."

"Jesus, Declan." I sighed, avoiding Oaklyn's table when I looked around the room. "I'm not saying I'm different from any of you guys. I'm just saying I'm not ready for all that."

"You're just not willing to admit you're ready. But you're fucking ready." He cupped my shoulder a bit harder before he released me. "That's all right. She's not going anywhere. At least not this second, but I can't promise she's not going home with your boy tonight."

A growl threatened to erupt in my chest as his words processed through me.

"You're going to let that happen?" he goaded.

"I can't stop it."

"Like hell you can't." He pushed on my back until I was facing my sister, who was talking to Ford. "Hypothetically speaking, if they weren't best friends and cousins and she wasn't mine—which is a stretch at this point, I know—and I saw the two of them talking the way they are right at this moment, my hands would be balled into fists, and that motherfucker would be leaving this bar with blood dripping from every crevice, two black eyes, and no teeth."

"Macon is my best friend."

"Does Macon know how you feel about Oaklyn?"

"We've talked about her some." I looked over my shoulder at Declan since he was positioned behind me. "But I haven't told him. Shit, I haven't even told you. You're just full of assumptions."

"Let's not play that game again. But if I'm able to see it all over you, don't you think Macon can too? And maybe he's doing this on purpose. And maybe the reason he practically shouted the question across the whole fucking bar was to make sure you heard him ask her out." He let those words simmer. "You know, to make you realize how you really feel about her. Because I'll tell you one thing; the best way to challenge someone's feelings is by taking away the one thing they want." He leaned in closer, his face not far from the back of my ear. "And from where I'm standing, that looks exactly like what Macon is doing."

Was Declan right?

That was something I hadn't even considered—there was no reason for me to consider it.

Those feelings didn't exist.

Do they?

This back-and-forth—I couldn't take it.

I was just under the assumption that Macon wanted her, that he, for some reason, wanted to be her first.

Which made no sense.

Not when he knew we were in the middle of our lessons.

Not when he knew Oaklyn wanted me to be her first.

This was getting more confusing by the second.

"While you think about that," Declan continued, "I want to give you a piece of advice. If you keep looking at Oaklyn like that, your sister is going to catch on, and she's going to call your ass out. Not tonight—she's had far too much wine for that to happen. But you know that woman has eagle eyes, and she sees everything. If you want to save yourself from that scenario and tell her in your own time, then I suggest you look away and watch yourself."

"You act like I've been fucking staring at her since I walked into the bar."

He moved around to the front of me. "Listen, kid, you can deny it all you want, but we both know there's no one in this world who's better at reading people than me. Don't make me spell this all out. Just listen to what I'm saying and take it for what it's worth." He shifted again, this time to my side so we were both looking at Oaklyn. "You should have seen her face when you came in. She didn't know what the fuck to do."

I slowly glanced at him. "Yeah?"

He nodded. "That's when I knew the feelings were mutual."

I hissed out air as my head moved from side to side. "I don't know, man."

"Trust me."

His chin rose again, aimed in the direction of the table, and I followed to where he was signaling.

Oaklyn was rising from her seat and heading for the restrooms.

"If you're going to make your move, do it now," he said.

"My move?"

"Yeah, my friend, I mean, claiming what's yours and not your best friend's."

I held the back of my head with both hands, fingers stretched wide. "Shit."

"And let me quickly give you another piece of advice. The restroom? Bad idea. There's way too much family in this bar. The girlfriends will find out, and they'll tell Hannah. Don't go in your car either—you've had far too much to drink. Go outside. There's an alley between the bar and the building next door. It's the perfect spot."

"How do you know about the alley—" I raised my hand. "On second thought, I don't want that answer."

He laughed. "Listen, I'm not saying I haven't been in an alley with your sister. I'm just saying I haven't been in *this* alley with her."

"My fucking ears are melting, Declan."

"Go." He pounded my shoulder with his fist. "Take what's yours and don't give her back to him."

THIRTEEN

Oaklyn

I stood at the sink, letting the water wash over my hands even though the soap was long gone. I just needed a moment to myself. To think. To recap the last thirty-ish minutes since I'd arrived at the bar.

Each of those minutes spent under the heavy gaze of Macon Spade.

He had certainly been laying it on thick. Asking all the right questions. Acting as though he were interested in everything in my life. Heck, maybe he was; I didn't know.

I just didn't have the heart to tell him he was wasting his time.

Especially when Hannah had been hovering around us, working her magic to make sure Macon saw all the best qualities in me, doing everything in her power so the two of us would click.

She was looking out for my best interests, and aside from being Mr. Sexual, Macon seemed like a really nice guy.

I was just relieved he hadn't yet asked for my number, making me question if he was really going to take me on a date. Without those digits, I didn't know how a meetup could go down. But if he happened to slide into my DMs or get my number from my best friend, I would come up with every excuse in the world not to hang out.

If the last two lessons had shown me anything, it was that Camden Dalton was the man I wanted to be with.

Oh God, I just loved everything about him. The way he dressed, the way he carried himself, the way he was so career-driven. When he looked at me, I felt it in every part of my body. When I got him to smile, his happiness and pleasure spread all the way through me. And then there were his looks—something that didn't usually matter to me, but Camden was the handsomest man I'd ever seen.

I didn't care that he was grumpy at times or that his communication wasn't always the best or that he'd earned himself a reputation for being the biggest bachelor.

He was perfect for me.

But there were two serious problems. The first was that Hannah would never allow us to be together, and the second was that Camden didn't feel the same way about me.

Even worse, he really wanted nothing to do with me.

Once lesson five ended and Camden moved on from me, I would have to find a way to endure the pain. To act as though I wasn't feeling this excruciating level of hurt every time I was in his presence.

Somehow, someway, I'd survive.

I always did.

He wouldn't be the first boy who broke my heart, and each time, I picked myself back up and moved on.

This time would be much harder. Much more devastating.

Unlike any of the ones before him.

Because Camden hadn't just been in my life for a couple of weeks and these feelings hadn't just been born; they'd lived inside me for quite some time. And I was going to give him something I'd never given to anyone else.

He'd told me I couldn't do that without falling for him.

He was right.

It seemed impossible to wrap my head around a future where I'd mourn what we had—even though we had almost nothing—but it was inevitable.

And I'll have to find a way to pick myself up again.

That was what I repeated in my head as I stared at my reflection in the mirror, my skin turning pruny from the water, and I focused on my eyes first.

Eyes that had gazed into Camden's earlier tonight as his hand reached across the table to finger me.

And then I moved to my cheeks.

A set that flushed every time I thought of him.

And shifted to my lips.

A mouth that was dying to be kissed by him.

And finally, my teeth.

Ones that bit into my lip just to stop myself from telling him how I really felt.

Those words would get me nowhere.

All they would do was prove to him that I couldn't handle the proposition, and I wouldn't give him that satisfaction.

But, damn, this was hard.

I turned off the water and glanced away from my reflection, wiping my hands on a paper towel. I made sure my skin was dry before I tossed the towel in the trash and headed for the door. My fingers circled the handle and pulled it toward me, my feet stumbling to a stop the moment I stepped out.

It was the sight before me that had completely knocked me off-balance.

One I hadn't been prepared for.

Why was this tall, muscular, devilishly gorgeous man standing outside the women's restroom?

"Hi," I whispered to Camden, his eyes already fixed on mine. "Are you okay?" I tried to think of why he would be here. "Are you waiting for someone?"

"You."

My heart began to pound. "Yeah?" I swallowed. "And why's that?"

"I'm going to take you somewhere."

I didn't know what to do with my arms, but they felt so incredibly heavy as they hung at my sides, so I wrapped them around my stomach. "Right now?"

He nodded.

"Okay," I replied.

"Do you trust me?"

"Always." I took a deep breath, unsure if that kind of honesty was the right thing to give him.

His hand lifted, and he gently grazed it across my chin. "Oaklyn ..." he said softly in a tone Camden never used. "Fuck me, you're perfect."

A word I'd just used in my head to describe him.

And when he'd said it, I could feel his emotion.

It was sitting in my chest, squeezing me so tightly.

He found my hand tucked across my hip and linked our fingers. "Come with me."

There was a door not far from the restroom. I hadn't noticed it when I came in, but he took me through it. We walked behind the bar, past the dumpster, where a few of the employees were smoking, and we entered a side alley that was wedged between this building and the one beside it. The alley was completely shut off from the street, mostly dark, just specks of light that filtered in from the streetlamps. We were about halfway down from where we'd entered when Camden stopped, positioning my back against the brick of the building, standing closely in front of me.

What are we doing here?

And what does he want from me?

"I didn't want to have this conversation inside the bar or outside the restroom. My sister might be drunk at the moment, but if she sees us together or if one of the girlfriends do, Hannah will start questioning, and I don't want that. At least not yet."

"I get it."

But do I?

I had no idea what he meant by the *yet* part.

"Oaklyn," he began, and I could feel him searching my eyes even though I couldn't see that level of detail in the alley, "I need you to be honest with me about something."

"I've never lied to you."

"That's not what I mean or what I'm inferring." He took a breath, his exhale hitting my face even though he was so much taller. "What I need to know is, are you interested in Macon?"

Macon?

That's what this is about?

His best friend?

Who Camden has been all for setting me up with?

"I find him interesting, and he's a nice guy," I said, "but, no, I'm not interested in him in that way—or any way for that matter."

He released my fingers, and they went to my neck, tilting my face up to him. "You're saying you don't want to go out with him?"

I thought I'd answered that question, but he obviously needed more reassurance. "No, Camden, I don't want to go out with him. The reason I've been talking to him is to appease your sister, who's relentlessly tried to keep us connected all night."

And to make you jealous.

Something I would never admit.

"I needed to be sure before I did this." His hand moved up my face, stopping at my cheek, his fingers spreading, his thumb stretching to my lips, where he traced the top one, rounding the corner before moving to the bottom one.

"Do what?" I whispered.

There was plenty of wine flowing through me by this point. Not to mention, I was almost completely in the dark, unable to attempt to read his eyes or know the next move he was going to make. I could mostly only rely on touch, and his was sending off so many signals.

Signals that something was about to happen.

And that something was going to change everything.

As he got closer, his cologne was more prominent, as was the liquor on his breath. His hand gripped me harder, his thumb leaving my mouth, his other fingers diving into my hair, holding my strands in his palm.

"This."

One word.

And the timing of it only allowed me to take a short breath before his lips were on mine.

Camden had kissed me the night we agreed to the proposition.

That'd felt more like a test. A way to determine if we had any chemistry or if I could even come close to satisfying him.

This was different.

This was a need.

A want.

With the way his lips surrounded me, how his tongue circled mine, he wasn't just taking. He was breathing me in.

Inhaling me. Claiming me, like this was far more than a lesson.

And my body immediately responded.

My back arched off the brick as my arms shot up, hugging his neck, pulling our bodies together, and I felt the hardness of his erection and the muscles in his chest and the strength in his hands as he held me.

Within a few seconds, his fingers slid up to the top of my head, and then his arms extended out straight, his palms pressing against the wall above me.

I was in a cage.

Full of Camden.

And there was nowhere else I'd rather be.

But I was overflowing with questions, and the moment he pulled away, I wanted to ask them.

I let the silence simmer. I let him graze my cheek with his rough whiskers, his nose sliding across to my ear and down my jaw.

"Why?" I asked softly. "Why did you need this?"

He continued to tickle my face, the tip of his nose dragging over my chin and up to the other ear, where his mouth hovered. "Because I can't stop thinking about your lips." He kissed my lobe, sucking it. Releasing it to add, "Because I can't stop thinking about you."

"But you just had me, Camden. Your finger was inside me tonight."

"Not that." He inhaled and exhaled again. "More, Oaklyn. I want fucking more."

My eyes closed even though I didn't need any additional darkness.

Seeing me with Macon had triggered this reaction. My attempt at making him jealous had paid off.

Emotions had finally entered the picture.

That thought couldn't have made me happier.

But that didn't mean I was going to let him off so easily. If he wanted me and he wanted more, he was going to have to work for it.

"You warned me," I said. "You were the one who set the boundaries. Who said feelings had no part in this proposition."

He reached for my hands, locking our fingers, and held them against the wall, far above my head. "I know what I made you promise."

"And now, you're reneging on that promise because you've realized I'm the woman you want. Or maybe it's that you just don't want me to date your best friend."

His face moved in front of me. "You're looking for answers. I don't have those right now."

"Then, what am I doing out here?"

His lips hastily slammed against mine, his body on top of me, pushing me even harder into the wall. There was urgency in the way he kissed me, in the way he glued us together, how he unlocked one of my hands to run it over my neck and past the side of my breast, straight down my side. When he reached my ass, he rounded my cheek, squeezing before he gripped the back of my thigh and lifted, angling my leg so it was now around him.

With my hand free, I was able to touch him, feel his heart pound as he made out with me. I lowered to his abs, the muscles tightening as I traveled to his belt, stalling, building the courage to continue my journey toward his hard-on.

Oh God.

My palm cupped the massive bulge, my fingers running down the length, feeling him moan into my mouth as I rubbed it, tasting his vulnerability. His sounds got louder as I circled my thumb across his tip and lightly tickled the bottom of his shaft.

He pulled away, and even though I couldn't see the hunger in his eyes, I felt it.

"I'm taking you up on your offer." His lips moved my face to the side, my ear now touching the coarse brick while his mouth pressed against the center of my cheek.

Breathing me in.

Biting me.

"You want my lips," I said.

"I want them sucking the tip of my dick."

"Now?"

"Yes."

"Here?"

"Fuck yes."

"Is this a lesson?"

He paused. "Only if you need one. Why don't you show me how good you are first? And if you require direction, I'll give it to you."

This was the last thing I had expected.

Any of this was actually.

But I wanted to give him the same amount of pleasure that he'd given to me tonight.

I wanted to make him scream.

I wanted to taste his orgasm, like he'd licked mine every time I came in front of him.

"I'll do anything you want me to."

His mouth moved to my ear again, and his lips pressed against the shell.

Two breaths.

Both short and extremely hot.

And then, "Get on your knees."

FOURTEEN

Camden

I'd ordered Oaklyn to her knees.

I didn't want to think about what I'd just admitted to her. I didn't want to process her endless questions and come up with answers.

What we were.

Where this was going.

What this was going to look like.

I didn't know.

All I knew was that when I'd dragged her into this alley, I'd had to kiss her.

I had to take what was mine.

And I wasn't going to leave here without claiming her mouth with my cock.

But the only way she was going to be able to follow through with that was if I released her hand, which I was holding against the brick wall, using a grip that prevented it from moving. Her other hand was fisting my hard-on through my jeans, stroking my length up and down, cupping my sac, preparing for the mouthful she was about to get.

I didn't want her to doubt anything I'd said.

I didn't want her to wonder.

So, I left her ear, where I'd been hovering, and I slowly moved to her mouth and ravished those fucking lips. I wasn't gentle. I didn't take my time, like I had when we first entered this alley. My tongue slipped through the opening, and I inhaled her taste.

Her sweetness.

Her submission.

Fuck me, Oaklyn was everything.

What I needed, what I wanted, she gave it to me.

And when I couldn't wait another second, I released her fingers and lips, and I returned my palms to the wall. "Now, take what you've been asking for."

"With pleasure." Her hand left my cock. "God, finally."

Since she was positioned against the brick, all she did was slide down, reaching up to get at me. She started with my belt buckle, followed by my button and zipper. When she tried to lower my boxer briefs, I slipped my cock through the hole—something I wasn't sure she knew about, but that kind of training was for a day when there was more light.

Her hand was so delicate as it circled my shaft, her breathing speeding up as she lowered to my sac. "My God, Camden, you're huge. This is never going to fit inside me."

"It will. I fucking promise you that."

I would do anything to be able to gaze down and see her face as she eyed my length and width, to view her expression as she contemplated what it was going to feel like when I took her virginity.

But this alley of darkness prevented that.

I could only see tiny specks of her face, a glimmer from the whites of her eyes.

I had to rely solely on feel.

"Now, suck," I told her, holding the back of her head, leading her to my cock.

Every bit of movement came as a surprise. There was no way to prepare for it.

That was why I hissed the second she wrapped both hands around my base, aiming my erection toward her mouth.

"*Mmm*," she moaned.

I felt her breath.

Her lips.

And then that moan continued as she took in my tip, the inside of her mouth vibrating over me. With it came an instant heat. Suction. Wetness. Like I was inside her cunt, but I could feel the thickness of her tongue as she used it to rotate around my head.

"*Fuuuck.*" I pounded my fist against the brick. "Just like that, but go deeper."

I wanted to give her the freedom to make decisions. I wanted her to choose where she wanted to go and how she wanted to do this.

But there was pure alpha in my blood.

I couldn't give up the control.

And Oaklyn couldn't help but listen and take my demands because she did exactly what I'd told her, swallowing a few more inches, bobbing over that new amount of space.

It felt incredible.

The feel of her skin.

The warmth of her mouth.

The pressure she was using.

Fuck, I could come right now.

"Yes," I urged her on. "Fucking yes."

I could feel the slickness of her hair as it got caught between her hands and lips, so I bunched her locks and held it behind her head. "Now, use your hands. Get them wet so they slide easier. And what you can't cover with your mouth, rub with your palms."

She raised her hands to my tip, where I assumed she was collecting some of her spit, and pumped my shaft. She was soft but needy with her strokes, and every time she lowered and rose, I rocked my hips forward, driving my dick through her grip. While her hands did the hard labor, her tongue stayed on my crown. Sometimes flicking back and forth. Sometimes circling. Sometimes staying flat.

But with each push, I moaned.

Louder.

And fucking louder.

"Do you taste that?"

I knew a bead's worth had leaked out and was waiting for her. Since her mouth hadn't left me, it had to be on her tongue. The saltiness dissolving, owning.

Claiming, just the way I wanted it to.

"*Yesss*," she replied as she took a breath.

"That's my pre-cum. You're going to get a whole lot more of that in a couple of minutes."

"I want more." Her hands dropped to my base. "Give me more, Camden."

She shot to the center of my cock, her throat opening to take in even more of me. The fullness caused her to breathe harder, sounds of pleasure coming from each of her exhales.

She was doing just what I wanted.

She was trying to suck the orgasm out of me.

"Now, twist." I held her knuckles to show her what I was

talking about. "Just like I did to your pussy tonight. You want to add friction to every side."

She instantly followed my order, giving me the perfect balance.

My head fell back; my mouth opened. "Yes. Like that. Fuck."

I'd only given her a few tips, and, damn it, she was already giving the meanest head.

"Faster, Oaklyn." I fisted her hair even tighter, keeping her on a short rein. "Suck it like you want me to fill your mouth with my cum."

There was a change in her movements. She was attempting to take me in deeper. The suction stronger as her cheeks hollowed, concaving so the inside rubbed against me too.

My feet widened, getting a better stance, my hand moving higher on the wall.

"Hell yeah," I roared. "I want you to try to deep-throat me."

I was positive her eyes were wide and fearful as she gazed up at me.

I just couldn't see them.

"Have you done that before?"

She breathed, "No," over my tip.

"Then, I want you to soak your mouth with as much spit as you can hold. Don't swallow any—you need all the lubrication you can get."

As my order processed through her mind, I could feel the wetness building. Each time she took in my dick, her spit was thicker.

"Perfect. Now, relax your throat." I gripped my base, taking the place of her hands, using my other palm to tilt her head back. The new position would be easier on her, allowing her to take more of me in. "Don't worry; I'm going to go slow."

Like I'd promised, I didn't drive straight in. I went gradually. I used the little patience I had. And I listened to her sounds, determining her comfort level, and that was how I dipped into her throat.

Man, it felt so fucking good.

I was three-quarters of the way in, and she was as tight as a goddamn lock.

With a tongue that was soaked.

And a mouth that was just the temperature I liked.

She was giving me everything I'd asked for. Not because she had to. Not because I'd demanded it. But because she got as much pleasure out of it as I did—the same way I'd felt tonight at the restaurant.

When a woman wanted to give pleasure for her own benefit, well, shit, there was no bigger turn-on than that.

"Oh fuck," I growled, pulling back and sinking my way in. "You have no idea how incredible this feels."

But what felt even better was when she was moving with me. When her hands were around the bottom of my dick, her lips longingly focused on my crown.

I released my base and lifted her face, returning her to the original position, ordering, "Make me come." My hands flattened against the brick, my eyes closed, and my throat fucking hissed through every inhale and exhale. As she bobbed, I began to fuck her face, giving her that surge, power. "Suck it, Oaklyn. Get that fucking cum out of me."

It wasn't going to take long. Not by the way she was stroking my bottom half and licking around the top. Her mouth was still so full of spit. The heat inside there had been upped several notches, giving me that warm, slick feel.

I pushed my weight into the wall as the tingles started in my sac.

Erupting.

Igniting.

"That's fucking it," I encouraged. "Yes!"

She must have sensed how close I was getting—maybe from the way I bucked into her mouth or the pants that were releasing from mine—because she was going faster, giving me more suction.

And within a few more pumps, I growled, "I'm going to fucking come."

My moan came out like a gritty scream, a sound she hadn't been able to give me earlier.

But she'd earned this from me.

"Fuck!" I drew in air. "*Yesss!*"

The first shot came out hard and pooled on her tongue.

She didn't stop.

She didn't even slow.

She kept up the movements, draining out another stream from me, the thickness aimed at the back of her throat this time. And still, she continued going, pulling out my orgasm, emptying me.

"Oaklyn! Goddamn it!"

When her hands left, I circled my fingers around my shaft and rolled my grip forward, making sure she'd gotten everything, adding the final drops to her tongue. I then released my dick to reach for her, pulling her up from the ground and positioning her against the wall before I tucked myself into my boxer briefs. I raised my zipper and secured my button, and once my hands were free, I found hers and held them above her head, aligning our mouths.

"Fuck me, you're good at that."

"Thanks to you and your direction."

Even her voice was satisfying.

"Nah. You knew what you were doing before I began barking orders. I just opened things up a little."

She laughed so lightly. "Now what?"

"I kiss you."

"Even though I just swallowed—"

I didn't give her a chance to say another word before my lips were pressed against hers and I was sucking her tongue into my mouth.

FIFTEEN

Oaklyn

"I miss this apartment," Hannah said from my couch, gazing around the living room, where we'd shared endless memories over the last couple of years. "I miss you."

"Miss me?" I lifted the bottle of wine off the coffee table, pouring some into two glasses, one of which I handed to her. "Why, silly? I'm here. I see you constantly. We text all day, every day. There's no reason to miss me." I clinked my glass against hers before I took my first sip.

"I don't know. It's just that living with Declan, as much as I love it—and I really *looove* it—it means I see you less, and that's the part that I hate."

"It just means that we need more girls' nights, so work your magic and make that happen. Deal?"

She smiled and nodded.

I grabbed the plate of fancy deviled eggs I'd made when I got home from work and held it in front of us. "I haven't made these before, but the food blogger I follow described them as

169

sinful, and every recipe I've made of hers has been spectacular."

"I'm ready for some sinfulness." She lifted one of the halved eggs and took a bite. "*Ohhh*, she's right. They're incredible."

"*Mmm*," I groaned. "She was." I looked at the Tupperware that Hannah had set on the table when she first came in. "What did you make?"

"Your favorite."

My brows rose, and I was hoping she was going to say yes when I asked, "Nutella brownies?"

"Only for my bestie."

I shimmied my shoulders. "Heart you—hard."

She laughed, tucking her legs underneath her, and she pushed into the corner of the couch. "I couldn't sleep last night, so boom, we have gooey, chocolaty yumminess."

I popped the rest of the egg into my mouth and wrapped my arm around the top of the cushions, bringing our bodies closer. "What's going on, babe? Why aren't you sleeping? Is it a work thing? A Declan thing?" I paused. "Oh God, I hope it's not a Declan thing."

"No, it's definitely not Declan. Things couldn't be more perfect there." She took another egg off the plate and nibbled at the bacon I'd sprinkled across the center. "You'd think he'd be able to, you know, bang me straight to sleep, and most of the time, he can, but the past couple of weeks, shit, things have been so rough at work."

"Talk to me." I twirled a chunk of her hair around my finger. "Tell me what's going on."

She took a deep breath. "I'm so grateful for the position I'm in and the reputation I'm starting to earn in the legal industry. It's everything I've always wanted and more—"

I put my hand on her arm. "You're justifying yourself. You

don't have to do that. It's me. I know you appreciate everything you have. You don't take it for granted, even for a second."

She nodded, her eyes briefly closing. "I'm just stressed." No longer giving me her profile, she slowly turned toward me. "I've got a full caseload. I'm going up against some of the worst bastards in the business—not as ruthless as Declan, but they're still brutal. I really have my work cut out for me, and it's been weighing on me, like thousands of pounds collapsing onto my chest."

Her lips tugged into a grin, showing no teeth—a look that I knew well, and it told me she was about to be her most vulnerable.

"You have all these goals going into law school, these plans and aspirations for what life is going to look like when you start your associate's role. And then you take the bar, and everything is moving so fast that you don't have a second to sit back and process. And then you get thrown right into a position, and you're in the thick of it with clients and cases. But when you actually stop to breathe and it all hits you, it's the most over-whelming moment." She gripped her wine with both hands after pouring more into her glass. "That's where I am now. Overwhelmed and semi-drowning and extremely sleep-deprived."

I'd known Hannah for so long. I knew each of the phases of life she'd referred to. When she and Camden were just kids and all they talked about were the lawyers they wanted to become. Followed by her undergrad years and then law school and the long, arduous hours she put into prepping for the bar.

Hannah hadn't stopped once.

She worked harder than anyone I knew.

It had only been a matter of time before all the stress finally caught up to her.

I reached for the brownies and opened the lid, taking one

for myself and handing her the other I'd grabbed. "Take it from someone who knows you better than you know yourself. Maintaining the stamina and speed you've been going at for quite some time isn't easy, but this is just another hurdle, and you happen to thrive off challenges. I don't care if it's Declan or Camden or some other cutthroat, furious monster you face in the courtroom; you're going to crush them. I have zero doubts about that. So, take a second if you need to. Take some deep breaths. Book a day at the spa—heck, I'll join you." I slid my fingers across her shoulder and squeezed. "What I know, with absolute certainty, is that you've got this. You'll figure out a pace that works for you, and sleep will be the result. But remember, you can still rule the world if you're yawning all the time. It's allowed."

She chowed down half the brownie, talking from behind her hand as she said, "Looks like, in the meantime, I'm just going to have to keep up my middle-of-the-night baking and spoil everyone at the office with the different brownie combinations I come up with." She licked the Nutella off her fingers.

"Don't forget me from that list. I want in on the flavor tastings."

She laughed. "Deal. I love you." She took a drink of her wine. "Enough about all that. I want to move on to happier things, like you and Macon."

My eyes widened as I finished my brownie. "Excuse me?"

"Don't *excuse me*, girl." She smiled in such a knowing way. "You both disappeared from the bar at the same time. I might have been drunk as hell, but I noticed, and I know something went down that night. So, spill it."

I slid back a few inches, filling my lungs.

How am I going to get out of this?

I wanted more than anything to tell her what was really happening with Camden. That I had such incredibly strong feelings for her twin brother. That he was the only man I wanted to give my virginity to.

But I feared her reaction would put the biggest strain on our friendship, and I couldn't handle that.

But not telling her, keeping this secret, felt horrible, especially considering I usually told her everything.

"I swear, nothing happened, Han. It was literally a coincidence that we both left at the same time. I went to the restroom. When I came out, one of my clients called, and that tied me up for a bit." I swallowed, thinking of how Camden's hands had really done all the tying and then his dick, followed by a full-blown make-out session before we both came back inside. "It's the same as what I told you at the bar. My story hasn't changed."

She eyed me as she ate the rest of her brownie. "But you've changed."

I pointed at my chest. "Me?"

She nodded.

"How?" I pressed.

"How do I put this ..."

As she thought about the right word to use, a part of me started to freak out.

What if she knows something about Camden and me and is about to drop that little nugget? What if she is going to ask something that I won't be able to deny?

Camden had warned me that Hannah would be able to see right through me, that if I ever mentioned his name with a dreamy-like, telling smile, she would immediately know something was up.

Did I do that earlier?

Did I even mention his name?

Oh God, suddenly, everything was a blur.

"You're acting almost lighter, if that makes any sense—like

you just got laid—and I want to say happier, but I can't really say that because you're the happiest person I know. Nothing brings down my positive petunia."

I laughed so hard that I snorted. "We both know I didn't get laid."

Even though her head turned, her eyes stayed on me. "But maybe something else happened."

"Something else? Like what?"

Her grin was still stretched across her lips. "Why don't you tell me?"

I could deny the obvious—or what she thought was obvious.

Or I could roll with it and see where it took me.

"You're right; something happened."

"Oh my God, I knew it." She set her wine on the table and fully turned toward me, inching closer until our knees touched. "Tell me everything. Was Macon all swoony? Was he—"

"Hold on. It wasn't Macon." I brought the glass up to my lips and swallowed several times. "It's ... someone else."

"Who?"

I hated this.

The feelings it stirred.

The need to lie.

This wasn't who I was.

Hannah deserved better.

She deserved the truth.

"Someone I've known for a long time," I started. "But it's honestly not even worth talking about. It's just some minor hookup stuff." More lies, but I didn't want to get into the proposition. I didn't want to talk about the lessons. They were too special to me to discuss. "We're just having fun. I don't know if it's going to turn into anything serious." As I stared at her, I could tell she was on the verge of inquiring who he was, so I added, "Before you ask, you don't know him."

She put her hand up in the air, like I was preaching a sermon. "I fully support this, especially the fun part, but you're really okay with the physical aspect of all this? You're a relationship kind of girl, and—I say this with all the love in my heart—you're not the kind of woman to just give your body to a man. I mean, you've waited this long. I hope he's special? And deserving?"

"Don't worry; I'm not there yet." At least that part was semi-truthful, considering we were only approaching lesson three. "Lots of stuff to do before we get *there*, there, you know?"

"I get it." As she continued to analyze me, I could feel her gaze all the way in my chest. "I can tell how happy you are. You haven't stopped smiling." She patted my knee. "Is this amazing guy the reason things didn't move forward with Macon?"

This was turning into quite a web.

But it seemed like she believed me.

"Macon Spade, the playboy," I said, sighing. "The truth is, he didn't even ask for my number." I chugged down more wine. "He made no effort to get in touch with me, but, yes, that's the reason."

She stole a corner off one of the brownies. "Do you want him to?"

"No."

She laughed. "That was a quick answer."

"He's not right for me, Han. He's a super-nice guy, handsome, and he has all the qualities I'd be looking for in a man, but no."

"And this mystery man is the right guy?"

Is Camden perfect for me?

He didn't like to commit.

He didn't do relationships.

He was the ultimate bachelor.

But I couldn't stop the way I felt about him. The sparks

that set off every time I was in his presence. The way my heart throbbed when he said certain things to me. The way I found his grumpiness so sexy, his hands so ravishing, his scent so enticing.

If only he felt the same way about me ...

"Yes," I replied. "He's the right guy. I just don't know that we're going to end up together. Things seem to work the way they are, and I have to be okay with that. I can't force someone to want more."

Her brows rose. "How long has this been going on?"

"Not long." I grabbed her hand to reassure her. "Not even long enough to sort out everything that's happening." I finished my wine and set the empty glass on the table. "I was going to tell you when things between us made a little more sense." She didn't seem convinced, so I continued, "You know I tell you everything. This just came on fast and out of nowhere."

She nodded, rubbing her thumb over my wrist, like she was taking my pulse. "You know what I think?"

Oh man, I wasn't sure I wanted to know.

"What's that?" I asked.

"I think he's going to come around and realize you're perfect for him. That you're everything he's ever wanted and he won't let you go." Her eyes narrowed. "And there's a chance he's already come to this conclusion. He's just not ready to admit it. Guys are different from us. It sometimes takes them a bit longer, like Declan. You remember how long he took to come around."

The nervousness in my body caused me to laugh. "Why do you think he's going to change his mind?"

"If he has any brains at all, he will. He'll see how amazing you are and how stupid he would be to let you go."

"Maybe." I shrugged. "But none of the others I dated had that kind of epiphany."

"*Hmm.*" Her stare intensified. "Something tells me this one is different. Just a feeling I have in my gut—and I'm always right about these things." She was about to say some more when her phone vibrated on top of the coffee table, and she reached for it. "It's Camden."

"What?" My gasp was far too loud. "It's not Camden!"

"I was talking about who's texting me."

"Oh." I laughed, trying to play off my strong reaction, and I looked away from her and pulled out my phone from the top of my sports bra. "What's he up to tonight?"

"He's with Macon and Declan. I'm sure they're getting into all kinds of trouble. They usually do when they're together."

"Interesting." When she glanced up from her cell and looked at me, I questioned my response and added, "Sounds about right."

She grinned, stalling for a few seconds before she typed him a reply.

I took that moment to also send Camden a text.

ME

> Your sister guessed there was a guy in my life. Who knows how, but she did. I think I've steered her away by telling her it's someone she doesn't know, but she hasn't made it easy. She really is a little PI; you weren't kidding.

"Mystery man?" Hannah asked when I slipped my phone away.

I hadn't realized she'd been looking at me.

Damn.

"Oh, it's—"

"You know what?" she said, cutting me off. "I already know that answer. I can tell by the way you're smiling."

SIXTEEN

Camden

"Here's the tequila you ordered," the waiter said as he set three shots on our table. "Can I get you anything else—"

"Another round," I replied before he even finished speaking. "And keep them coming."

I grabbed one of the small glasses he'd just placed down and drained every drop from it. There was so much vodka already flowing through my veins and such a buzz tingling through my body that I didn't feel the burn as the tequila passed through my throat. In fact, I barely even tasted the harsh liquor.

I went to reach for another shot when Declan cut me off and said, "I know you're not taking mine, asshole." He surrounded the other two small glasses and gave one to Macon.

Macon nodded at me and joked, "Greedy motherfucker."

"Listen, I need it more than the both of you," I replied.

"And why is that?" Macon countered.

Instead of responding, I reached inside my pocket to pull out my phone that was vibrating. I was sure it was just my sister responding to the text I'd sent a few minutes ago, telling her she'd better be prepared for a rough night because I was sending Declan home shit-faced.

But it wasn't Hannah.

OAKLYN

Your sister guessed there was a guy in my life. Who knows how, but she did. I think I've steered her away by telling her it's someone she doesn't know, but she hasn't made it easy. She really is a little PI; you weren't kidding.

A guy in her life. That was an interesting way for Oaklyn to word it.

Fuck, she probably didn't know what to say since after the night at the bar and the goddamn blow job, I wouldn't talk about what was happening between us or what I wanted.

I didn't know.

Shit, I still didn't know.

I just knew I wasn't going to let her anywhere near Macon.

ME

How did my sister guess there's a guy in your life?

OAKLYN

My smile.

ME

Oaklyn, I fucking warned you.

OAKLYN

> I can't help it, Camden. You make me smile—that's all. I didn't realize it was plastered all over my face until she called me out tonight. Trust me, I did everything I could to throw her off.

ME

> What were you thinking about?

OAKLYN

> The other night.

"I think we just got our answer," Declan said.

My eyes slowly lifted from my phone. "Your answer to what?"

"Why you need all the goddamn drinks," Macon replied and nodded toward my cell. "I'm assuming that's your girlfriend?"

"My girlfriend?" I laughed. "I know you're not talking to me." I glanced at Declan, and he was gazing at me too, grinning like a fucking fool.

"Oh, I'm fucking talking to you all right," Macon replied. "I could tell by your face when you were looking at your phone that it was a message from her."

I set my phone on the table, turning it over so they couldn't see the screen, and busied my hands with my tumbler of vodka. "First off, she's not my girlfriend. Second of all, I'm not talking to you about Oaklyn after the stunt you pulled the other night at the bar."

Macon leaned his arms on the small table, the buttons at his wrists banging against the wooden top, the sound repeating as he linked his fingers together. "I think we need to address that so-called stunt."

"For what reason?" I barked back.

"Because it worked."

I looked at Declan just as he said, "See, I fucking told you so."

"Jesus Christ." I ran my hand across the top of my hair, forgetting that it was gelled. But that didn't stop me. I even did it again.

"When we first spoke about Oaklyn, it was obvious she meant something to you," Macon voiced.

I took a sip, and once I swallowed, I casually asked, "And why would you think that?"

"Because it was a talk, Camden, and you wouldn't fucking talk about her. I couldn't get anything out of you, and that's not like you. But what I did hear and gather was that your head was all over the place and you didn't know how to process your feelings, so I came up with a little plan."

"I don't want to hear it," I hissed.

The last thing I needed was my friends helping me out when it came to women.

Oaklyn and I were moving at just the right speed. I didn't need these two motherfuckers scheming behind my back like I was incapable of making a decision.

I was a grown-ass man.

"But you're going to hear it," Declan demanded.

And to ensure I was listening, Macon even clutched my shoulder before he said, "My plan was to see if you got jealous when I gave your girl a little attention. Once I saw you walk into the bar, I laid it on thick, and I made sure you heard me ask her out. You should have seen your fucking face."

"I thought you were going to reach across the table and strangle your best friend," Declan said to me, chuckling.

I glanced between the two, finally admitting, "I wanted to."

"Like I said, it worked," Macon declared. "You just needed a kick in the ass to realize what and whom you wanted, and I was happy to do the hard labor." He squeezed before releasing me. "Not that flirting with Oaklyn was hard on me. That girl isn't just easy on the eyes; she's—"

"Watch it, you fuck."

My best friend laughed at me. "Just testing you again—and you passed."

My head shook back and forth, and I sighed. "What you were saying before, why do you think your little plan worked?"

Macon adjusted his position, leaning back in the seat and crossing his arms. "Oaklyn left to use the restroom, and you suddenly disappeared too. Around twenty minutes later, the two of you returned, seconds apart, but she came from one side of the bar, and you came from the other, trying to be sly, which any sober person would have figured out."

"I know you want to keep it a secret for now, so you're lucky the only two sober ones were me and Macon," Declan added. "A few less glasses of wine, and your sister would have been all over that."

Macon eyed me down. "Are you going to tell me that was a coincidence?" He grinned. "I hope you do. That'll be a fun fight for me to win."

I emptied the rest of the booze in my glass, scanning the bar for our waiter, who was supposed to be returning with more tequila.

"And I'm also going to give you some shit about wanting to strangle me. I get that my idea worked and all, but you'd better not think I would ever pull that shit for any other reason. You know I would never fuck with a friend's girl—whether you're in a relationship or not. I do some wild stuff, but that's a territory I won't enter."

I remembered the rage that had boiled through me.

The red I'd seen, clouding my vision.

"He was a goddamn mess about it," Declan told him, like I wasn't sitting at the table. "He missed every clue, brother. I had to tell him your real intention." He paused. "And I think that only reaffirms that our boy has some strong feelings for Oaklyn."

I couldn't believe what I was hearing. "You know I'm right here, don't you? Fuck."

I needed a break from these bastards, so I lifted my phone and turned the screen toward me.

"Look at this motherfucker, getting on his phone like we're not in the middle of a conversation," Macon said about me. "Avoiding telling us what happened between him and Oaklyn at the bar that night, refusing to comment about how angry he was with me."

"He's running like he's being chased by the police," Declan said.

"I believe, in your world, you call that guilty as charged," Macon continued.

The two of them laughed while I rolled my eyes and typed.

ME

What about the other night?

OAKLYN

The way you got all growly when you thought I wanted your best friend. How you pulled me outside, into the darkest alley, and went all alpha on me.

How you kissed me.

How you took what you wanted from me.

How you ordered me onto my knees.

My dick was already getting hard.
Fuck me.

ME

Do you know what I can't stop thinking about?

OAKLYN

I'm pretty positive I can guess ... my mouth.

"So, what are you going to do about Oaklyn?" Declan asked, gaining my attention. "Are you going to tell your sister you want to date her best friend? Are you just going to keep it a secret and hope Hannah doesn't find out?"

"I haven't even had that talk with Oaklyn," I admitted, relieved when the waiter showed up with our shots.

"Three more tequilas," he said as he placed them in front of us. "Anything else—"

"Another round of shots. And you might as well bring me two more of these." I held up my almost-empty vodka.

Macon and Declan nodded, signaling they wanted refills as well.

The second the waiter was gone, Macon said, "Hold on. You haven't talked to Oaklyn about any of this? And she has no idea how you feel?"

How I feel?

Something I hadn't even admitted to these guys, but they clearly had that answer without me saying a goddamn word.

I blew some air through my lips. "It's complicated."

"Because you like her and you're not ready to tell her? That's what you consider complicated?"

I no longer gave a fuck about the gel in my hair and grabbed the front that I'd spiked, tugging each of the strands. "Listen ..." *What the hell am I going to say? What is my reasoning? Why does all of this feel so hard?* "I don't know what the fuck I'm doing. I've never really wanted to be in a relationship before. And now, I'm here, and it's Hannah's best friend, and Hannah will have my ass when she finds out."

"And to top it all off, you're about to take Oaklyn's virginity." Macon's brows rose. "Unless you already have?"

"I haven't," I replied, "and that's all I'm going to say about that."

"A virgin, shit." Declan chuckled. "What, you're not going to tell us what you did to her in that alley?"

"Fuck no."

Declan reached across the table and gripped my arm. "It's all right, buddy. I get it. I wouldn't say a word either—and not just because you're Hannah's brother and those details wouldn't be appropriate." He continued staring at me. "You care about her."

I filled my lungs. "Yeah, I do."

"And you want more with her," Macon stated.

I nodded. "I think so."

"You fucking think so?" Macon pushed.

I released my hair and held the glass, taking down everything but the ice. "I know I don't want her to be with you"—I nodded toward Macon—"or him." I made the same gesture at some random dude in the bar. "I don't want anyone touching her ... but me. That's what I know. And I also know I enjoy being around her. Talking to her. Listening to her." As I halted, I saw her face in my mind. "She's beautiful and sweet and kind and brilliant. Man, is she brilliant."

"Wait, wait. You're telling me you listen to her?" Declan challenged. "I wouldn't have pegged you as a man who listens."

I shook my head. "I don't, but with her, I do."

"She makes you a better man," Declan said.

I thought about what he'd said. I really let those words sink in. "She does, and I haven't even really let her in yet. I can't imagine how I'm going to feel if we get together."

"You mean, *when* you get together," Macon corrected.

"But Hannah—"

"Don't make this about Hannah," Declan said, interrupting me. "You do what you need to do with Oaklyn first. Figure out where you want things to go with her. Talk to her, tell her how you're feeling. And when it's time, you sit your sister down and lay it all out on the table."

"I agree with him," Macon added. "He gave you good advice."

"And you don't think I'm going to make it worse by not immediately coming clean with Hannah?"

Declan rolled up his right sleeve. "I was in your situation not that long ago, except I had to go to my best friend and tell him I was dating his much younger cousin. A best friend who also happened to be my boss." He hissed out some air. "But I didn't stop at Dominick. I also spoke to Ford and Jenner." He finished the rolling and moved on to his left sleeve. "At the time, not only did I think my job was at jeopardy, but I also feared how they would respect me as a friend. That shit was tough. I got through it, and you will too."

"I'd take telling those three guys over Hannah any day of the week," I confessed.

"She can't be that much of a hard-ass," Macon said.

Declan laughed.

And I emptied the ice into my mouth, crunching down the pieces before I said, "It's not that she's a hard-ass; it's that she's my twin. Her respect means everything to me. I don't want to disappoint her. I don't want to upset her. And you know what would hurt even worse?" I couldn't believe I was saying this. That I was even thinking it. "If she doesn't think I'm good enough for Oaklyn. That would fucking destroy me."

"She puts her on the highest pedestal," Declan said.

I nodded. "She deserves that placement. She's such a good

fucking girl. So much better than me." The back of my throat burned as I said, "I don't deserve her."

"Because you've been a dog with women?" Macon asked. "Come on. Every dude at this table has slept his way around this town. We've all done things we're not proud of. But that doesn't make us bad people. It just means we think with our dicks."

"What he said," Declan mumbled. "Besides, I'm no better than you, so if Hannah wants to be with me, then there's no reason why she wouldn't want you to be with Oaklyn."

"Maybe," I whispered. "Or maybe she'll fucking gut me for taking Oaklyn's virginity and despise me for going behind her back and going against the promise I made that I would stay away from all of her friends."

"Have some faith, my friend," Macon said.

As the waiter returned to our table, I held my phone and typed a reply to Oaklyn's message, knowing my response was going to surprise her.

ME

Well, you're right; your mouth has certainly been on my mind. Like I told you that night, you really know how to give head, and I'd be lying if I said I didn't want it right now.

But there's another thing that I haven't been able to stop thinking about. That's the way you looked at me when you came out of the restroom and saw me standing there. The expression on your face.

OAKLYN

Really? I was just so shocked to see you. I wasn't expecting you to be there. At all.

ME

Shocked, yes. Unexpected, of course. But I saw more than that, Oaklyn. More than excitement. More than just pleasure.

OAKLYN

Like if there was anyone in the world I wanted to be standing there, it was you?

ME

Yes.

OAKLYN

And that's just how I felt.

That's why I can't get this smile to leave.

ME

I don't want it to. It looks too beautiful on your face.

OAKLYN

Now, I'm blushing.

ME

Don't get too red. I don't want my sister asking any more questions.

OAKLYN

Well, she already knows I'm crushing on someone. When she asks who I've been texting—and I'm sure she's going to—I'll just tell her it's him. Mystery Man.

ME

That's my name, huh?

OAKLYN

For now.

I could easily lead that into a different discussion. A conversation we needed to eventually have.

But that wasn't going to take place over text.

ME

This Friday, are you free?

OAKLYN

I can be.

ME

I'm going to pick you up at your apartment at 6 p.m.

It's time for lesson three …

OAKLYN

I can't wait.

SEVENTEEN

Oaklyn

"Hi," I said as I slid into the passenger seat of Camden's Porsche, impressed with the fancy interior and red leather and how it smelled so clean and new.

"I'm sorry I didn't come up to get you. I looked for parking all along your block and another two blocks in each direction. There wasn't a single spot open."

With the front seat of his sports car so compact, Camden looked even taller than his six-three height and even broader than his extra-muscular build.

He also looked positively delicious with his beard just trimmed and edged, wearing a black button-down and jeans. The collar of his shirt was open just enough that it showed a hint of his dark chest hair, his signature leather bracelets around the wrist of the hand that gripped the steering wheel.

I breathed in the scent of his woodsy cologne as I replied, "Don't worry. It's much easier for me to come down and meet you. One of the downfalls of high-rise living, as you know." I smiled as I shut the door and reached for the seat belt.

He pulled into traffic, weaving his way across two lanes. "I think my high-rise-living days are going to be short-lived."

"Oh, yeah?"

He shifted into another gear, and the hum of the engine vibrated through me. All that did was set the embers in my stomach on fire, ones that had begun to spark the second he called to let me know he was parked outside my building.

"I'm going to start house-shopping."

I turned toward him, an excuse to stare at his profile. "Now, that's fun. Are you going to sell your condo? You haven't had it that long."

And I knew just how long that had been since I'd attended his housewarming party. A night I so desperately wanted to tell him that I didn't want to wait the full year and complete the proposition sooner. I just hadn't had the nerve.

"I'm going to keep it as an investment property and rent it out."

"Okay, Mr. Business." I laughed. "No, that's a really great idea."

"Well, I can't take all the credit." He turned at the light. "When I was at the bar the other night with Declan and Macon, the night you were with Hannah and we were texting"—he quickly glanced at me, a grin climbing over the most enticing lips—"I was telling them about my plans, and they suggested it."

"I think it's amazing."

"You do?"

I nodded and knew he couldn't really see me, so I added, "Yes, I do."

"You know, my cousins are going to inherit The Dalton Group whenever my aunt and uncle retire and pass it down.

That'll consume those guys to the point where they won't need another venture. But me, I want a side hustle, so I can retire long before them. I'm hoping this is just the start of many investment properties."

"That's admirable, Camden, and extremely inspiring."

When he stopped at the light, he gazed at me. "Thank you."

"What else do you guys talk about during guys' night?" I giggled, feeling the heat move into my face. "I imagine the conversations take on quite a life of their own once some heavy drinking is involved."

"And you wouldn't be wrong."

"Hannah said Declan came home in pretty rough shape."

He swiped his thumb over his bottom lip. "I wasn't any better. I was actually probably worse off than him."

When his hand left his mouth, I expected it to return to the steering wheel.

But it didn't.

It slowly reached for me, grazing the bottom of my chin. "Nothing is off-limits when I'm with the guys. We discuss anything and everything." His palm moved to my cheek, his fingers diving into my hair. "Except the heavier and physical details involving you."

I was taken aback by the softness in the way he was touching me and the words he'd just spoken.

He was just so gentle, which was so unlike Camden.

Almost loving.

And if the car behind us hadn't honked, alerting him of the green light, I wondered if he would have kissed me.

But as soon as the sound hit our ears, his hand was gone, and his car was moving again.

"I need to know ..." I started, hesitant, unsure if he would even reply. "Why am I the exception?"

The question made him smile.

A sight I wanted to stare at forever.

But a second after I finished speaking, something hit me, and I asked, "Or is it that you don't talk about me because you don't want Declan to know in case he says something to Hannah—"

"Declan knows. So does Macon."

I allowed that information to process through me before I said, "Oh."

He downshifted as he approached the red light. "I assure you, Declan won't say a word to Hannah, and Macon is a vault."

"If you told them, I assume you trust them."

He slowly looked at me. "That's the thing, Oaklyn. I didn't tell them."

"Then, how did they know?"

"Apparently, they saw it on my face."

They saw *it* on his face.

Which meant they saw an expression similar to the one I'd been wearing when Hannah came to my apartment the other night and called me out about Mystery Man.

Is that what I do to him?

How I make him feel?

Oh God.

"So, they saw your smile and immediately knew it was because of me?" My cheeks had already reddened and felt hot. Now, they felt like I was holding a blowtorch against them.

He checked the light and shifted, his stare staying on the road as he began to drive. "For Declan, yes. He saw me walk into the bar the evening Macon was hitting on you, and I guess by the way I looked, he put two and two together."

When he paused, the tingles in my stomach rose to my

chest, my heart pounding as I really thought about what he was saying.

"Macon is a different story. He knew long before Declan, but, yeah, he pretty much put it together too."

"Camden"—I took a deep breath, knowing the risk involved with asking this question, knowing I could get an answer I didn't want to hear—"I don't understand. What did they put together?"

He stayed silent until he approached the next light, the car coming to a halt at the same time his eyes locked with mine. "Oaklyn ..." His voice drifted off as he looked at me, his gaze changing with each second. Deepening but softening at the same time. "I didn't want to have this conversation in the car. I wasn't even sure I wanted to have it tonight."

I swallowed, my throat feeling so tight.

I was still so unsure if he was going to say the words I was dying to hear or if this was going to go in a very different direction.

"Why does it matter where you say it?" I asked. "What's more important is that I hear it, right?"

He nodded, his hand leaving the gearshift again, this time landing on my leg. "I don't know when it happened. Maybe when we were twelve. Maybe it was after the first lesson. I'm not sure. But something changed." His fingers circled around my knee, gripping it, and I could feel the warmth of his skin through my jeans. "This is more to me than just lesson after lesson."

If I'd thought my heart was pounding fast before, it was nothing compared to this. I was sure it even came through my voice when I whispered, "I know."

"You feel it too?"

I tried to take in more air. "Yes."

"Then, it won't come as a surprise when I say"—his hand

moved higher to the center of my thigh, around the side of it, where he wedged his fingers between the seat and me—"I can't stop thinking about you. That even though I'm not sure how to do this and what exactly *more* looks like since it's something I have no experience with, it's what I want." He went silent, his head shaking back and forth, and with each swipe, I watched him turn just a little more vulnerable. "Because at the end of all this, when we complete lesson five, there's absolutely no way that I can even fathom letting you go."

The pounding in my chest turned to an explosion, and for a second, I debated on whether I should make him grovel. If I should remind him of the warning he'd given me about not getting emotionally involved. If I should not reciprocate his confession and let him sweat it out, wondering when and if I was ever going to come around.

But that wasn't me.

I wasn't going to look at the man who I'd been crushing on since I was a girl and tell him a lie. I wasn't going to make him wait to hear my truth.

I was going to take exactly what I wanted—what I'd always wanted.

So, when my lips parted, instead of responding, I moved the seat belt behind my back and threw my arms around him and pulled our bodies as close as I could get them. "Camden," I said softly.

His face was in my neck, the roughness of his beard scraping my skin—a sensation that was so welcome. "I have so many feelings for you."

My eyes closed, and I squeezed my lids together. "I've had feelings for you since I was twelve."

He chuckled, a sound full of surprise and cuteness. "Really?"

"Really."

I released him, knowing the light was going to turn at any second, and as we both glanced through the windshield, we saw that it already had.

He pulled his hand back but brought mine with it and set my palm on the gearshift, cupping my hand while he shifted. "I want to tell you something," he voiced, his gaze still on the road. "I had every intention of using these lessons as a way to get you to change your mind. It's not that I didn't want to be the guy. I just wanted to make sure you knew what kind of guy I was. I thought these steps would give you a better picture. But, shit, Oaklyn, we're on lesson three, and you haven't wavered even a little on your decision. Not even after I asked you to get on your knees."

"Nothing you can say will scare me."

He rubbed his thumb across mine. "Unless it involves anal."

I used my free hand to gently punch his arm. "You and anal. Seriously, I can't even."

He lifted my hand and kissed it before returning both to the gearshift. "I still want to follow through with the lessons. Enjoy things just the way I planned and take our time since there's no reason to rush it." He quickly glanced at me. "And I want to do the same with us. Go slow. See where things take us. Figure this all out together, given that this is all new to me and the physical part is new to you and we have the Hannah thing to deal with." He paused. "Are you all right with that?"

That was everything I wanted. For us to feel each other out and learn how to make this work.

Besides, we couldn't go public until we talked to Hannah, and I knew that was going to be a massive hurdle, one I wasn't looking forward to.

But now that we'd had this conversation, I was curious how it was going to affect the upcoming lessons, especially tonight's.

If I would feel a change in Camden's touch, in his reactions, in the way it all played out. If lesson four would really be something he'd never experienced before—an answer we'd semifought about through text and I'd told him the man I fell in love with would give me one of his firsts instead—or if it would be something he made me choose.

"Yes," I said. "I like that idea."

"Good."

I couldn't get the smile to leave my face. It felt like it was permanently etched there, that Camden Dalton wasn't just a person, but an entire mood.

"You know I won President's Club through my company, and today, I got one of the gifts, which is airfare and a stipend toward a hotel. I texted Hannah and asked her if she wanted to come on the trip with me, and we're going in two weeks." I shoved my hand between my knees as the weight of the secret suddenly hit me. "I'd better be careful with how much wine I drink while we're gone because our little PI is going to try to get everything out of me and I can't cave."

"Where are you going?" He peeked at me before he turned at another light.

"Sedona. We're staying at a Spade Hotel, and we're going to spend our mornings hiking and our afternoons at the spa. I can't wait."

"Sounds like the perfect trip for you two."

I took a long, deep breath. "I'm just suddenly feeling a little guilty."

He pulled into a lot, the building brick and unmarked, unless there was a sign that I had missed out front. He parked the car and turned off the engine before facing me. "Don't, Oaklyn. She's going to find out when the time is right. Now, this is all about us, and there's no reason to feel guilty about anything."

"Okay."

He squeezed my fingers. "I'm serious. We're going to tell her, and it'll all be fine."

Air rushed through my lungs and out my lips. "Are you sure about that?"

"Yes, I'm sure." He lifted my hand off the gearshift and placed it on his lap. "Let's focus on something a little happier, shall we?"

I glanced toward the building again. "Where are we?"

When I looked back at him, a smile was warming his handsome face. "I can't wait to show you."

EIGHTEEN

Camden

I met Oaklyn on the passenger side of the car, my hand immediately going to her lower back as I walked her toward the entrance of the building. I could feel her gaze on me every few steps, trying to read my face, trying to goad me into telling her where we were.

The building was extremely inconspicuous on purpose, but if you were an LA local, like me—and her—it was a place everyone knew about.

I was surprised she didn't.

Or that she hadn't guessed where I was taking her since she'd picked this lesson. I would have thought our first stop would be obvious. But my girl was on the naive side, and she probably assumed I would surprise her with a sex toy instead.

That wasn't the case.

I wanted her involved in every step of the lesson. I wanted her to decide which toy I would use on her body.

Or, if I was lucky enough, I would get to use multiple.

I placed my arm around her shoulders, pulling her close to me, pressing my lips against the top of her head.

Breathing her in.

Fuck, this felt good.

A feeling that shocked the hell out of me, the same way the next couple of minutes were going to do to her.

But, damn it, I really liked this. Holding her near me, inhaling her tangerine and blueberry scent. Looking down and seeing those gorgeous blue eyes gazing up at me.

Trusting me.

I wanted more.

I ground my teeth across my lip and whispered, "Are you ready for this?"

She laughed, the sound born out of pure nervousness.

I was learning all of her noises.

What they meant.

And this one was so obvious.

"No. Yes." She smiled even bigger. "I honestly have no idea," she finally admitted.

"You're going to enjoy it. I promise."

We reached the front door, and since the glass was tinted, she wasn't able to see inside. I gripped the handle and pulled it toward us, looking down at the top of her face as we walked in.

We weren't more than a few paces past the door when she glanced up at me. "A sex shop, huh?"

"A sex *toy* shop."

Her eyes widened. "Do I look like a deer in headlights?"

Her pureness was something I fucking loved about her.

"Don't worry. You'll learn quickly. I'll be your tour guide."

A quick scan of the layout told me there were multiple sections that held no interest to me. We didn't need costumes or stripper heels. We had no use for movies or edible lube and paint.

There was only one area of the store that I really wanted to focus on.

So, I linked our hands, and I led her toward the back, where the toys took up an entire massive wall. "Let me give you the rundown." I walked her to the end of the wall—the perfect place to start since the toys in this spot would throw her straight into the deep end. "It's all broken down by category, and here" —I pulled one of the plastic packages off a hook, holding it in front of her—"is all about the ass."

"Ass?"

"These are butt plugs, Oaklyn."

"*Ohhh.*" She sucked in some air. "We're literally talking about the booty."

With my thumb, I outlined the top of the rubber plug and held my lips toward the back of her ear, saying softly, "The pointed tip makes it go in easier." I ran my thumb toward the middle. "Do you see these rims, how they bump out every inch or so before they narrow, almost like the shape of a Christmas tree?"

"Yes."

I pressed my mouth against the shell of her ear. "Think about the way that would feel. How you'd have to stretch every time to get over each of the rims." I nibbled her earlobe, releasing it to say, "If I was sliding this in slowly, you'd hold your breath during each hump, anticipating how it was going to feel as it sank deeper inside you. If it would pull. Burn. Fucking tingle." I exhaled against her, knowing my breath was reaching as low as her neck, where goose bumps were starting to rise. "But if I was going fast, you'd be opening and closing every second, like going over speed bumps in the road. And while I was doing that to you, I'd rub your clit." I moved my lips to her neck, needing to taste the warmth there. "Or maybe I'd lick it. Press my tongue against it. Flick it back and forth and get you off with my mouth." I licked up to her ear. "Would you like that?"

"Yes, please."

"You want me to fuck your ass with this plug and eat your cunt at the same time?"

"*Yesss* to the eating part." She touched the plug, covering the whole length, eventually looking up at me. "Are you really going to get this?"

"No."

I put it back and reached a little higher up, taking a different one off the hook. This one was metal rather than the rubber that we'd looked at first, and the description showed that it vibrated. It was the same size as the previous one, the smallest one they had here, and it didn't have the grooves; it was smooth and flat.

"This is what I'm going to get you." I set the new one on her palm. "The metal will feel entirely different from the rubber, and so will the flatness. And when I turn on the vibration, you're going to feel such a mix of sensations." I wrapped my arm around her waist, gradually tracing her side before making my way to her butt, squeezing the cheek closest to me.

"Camden ..." Her voice changed. It quieted, turning almost sultry.

"Imagine what this will feel like when it's filling you. Pulsing inside you." I moved to the center, my finger carefully traveling up and down the line. "When you're puckering from how good it feels." Since she hadn't looked at me, I cupped her chin and directed her gaze until it hit mine. "I want to hear how loud you scream when you come with this in your ass." I took her lip into my mouth, grazing my teeth across it, ultimately letting it go. "But not tonight. I'm going to save that for another time." I paused. "Relieved?"

She searched my eyes. "I don't know what I am right now." She swallowed. "I think I'm a lot of things."

"Wet."

"Yes. A lot of that."

I heard the sound of someone approaching, and I pulled my hand away from her cheeks and turned toward the noise, seeing a sales associate make her way closer.

"Sorry, I was helping another customer when you came in." She glanced from me to Oaklyn, tucking a chunk of purple hair behind her ear. "Is there anything I can help you find?"

I handed her the metal plug. "We're going to take that, if you want to set it up front for us. I'll be up there in a little while to pay. We're just going to keep shopping."

"Perfect. Let me know if you need anything."

Once she was gone, I turned Oaklyn toward the wall again, standing behind her with my hands on her navel. "Just in case you didn't know, the butt plugs come in all sizes." I pointed toward the bottom, near the floor. "Those are the largest ones, and then they decrease in length and width." I raised my hand to where I'd grabbed the metal one. "As you can see, big to small, and we got you the smallest."

"Hold on. You're telling me some people use *that?* Camden, it's the size of my forearm." She turned around to face me, and I knew she was referring to the plugs by the floor. "I mean, no judgment, but ouch."

I smiled. "Different strokes for different folks."

I held her cheeks, rubbing my thumbs across her lips before I kissed her.

I just needed a taste.

I needed her heat against my tongue, and I took it quickly, deeply, until I separated us. "Come on." I held her waist and brought her a little farther down the wall. "Now, we're moving on to dildos. How much do you know about them?"

She shrugged. "I've seen them, of course, but I've never used one."

"Do you know about all their bells and whistles?"

"They literally whistle?"

I laughed.

Fuck me, she was adorable.

"I mean, I suppose some might." I held my hand up, drawing a circle in the air over the entire section. "This is probably the most creative toy they make since it's so diverse and it comes in all shapes and sizes. They can twist. Rotate. Vibrate. Some even play with your clit at the same time." I took one of the rabbits off the wall and showed her the ears. "This part presses against your clit. They circulate and vibrate while the dildo is inside you. And the dildo"—I held her hand and rubbed it against the coiled silicone—"it turns, and the bead-like texture hits your walls while it's moving."

"My God."

"Too much?"

"I know I keep saying this, but I just don't know." When her stare reached mine, she added, "However, you seem to know everything about this."

I aimed my mouth over hers. "I might not know how to date women, but I know how to please them, sex toys included."

She wrapped her arms around my neck. "I guess I picked right, then."

"You picked me—is that what you're calling it? Wasn't it more like a proposition?"

"Snagged. Scored. And now refuse to let go of."

"*Mmm*." I held the bottom of her ass, gripping it tightly. "I like the sound of that."

She kissed me before she said, "I'm happy you do."

I put the rabbit back and pulled a glass one off the wall. It was far too large for her, but I wanted her to feel the hardness of it. "They also make dildos out of everything—glass, rubber, silicone, plastic. And each material will feel different."

She pushed her thumb against the long glass shaft. "This looks like it feels relentless."

"Too harsh?"

"Maybe." She shrugged. "I think I almost want something kinder."

I leaned into her face, breathing her in. "But you picked me, and I'm not even fucking close to kind."

She smiled and laughed. "You're just a little grumpy—that's all—and I love every second of it."

I put the dildo back and grabbed a small bullet. "This might be more in line with what you need." I held the package in front of us. "The size is perfect, just a little bigger than my thumb. It's made of silicone, so it'll slide right in."

She tried to feel the material through the plastic covering. "It has the texture of hard bubbles."

"Yeah, just along the top. It'll make things a little more interesting when it's inside you."

A half-smile tugged at her lips. "Interesting, to say the least."

If she kept looking at me like that, I was going to take her straight back to my car and eat her in the goddamn front seat.

Fuck.

I cleared my throat. "The bottom of the bullet is ribbed, so that'll add a different dimension as well." I nuzzled my nose against her cheek. "I'll make sure you feel every bit of it." Once I pulled my face away, I showed her the wire loop at the end. "This is what I'll hold to make sure it doesn't get lost."

"You mean, inside me?"

"Yes."

She was quiet for a moment. "Like a leash."

I chuckled. "Something like that."

"And this part over here"—I tapped the top of the packaging, where there was another bullet shaped device, but this one was made of plastic—"is the remote. I can be up to ten feet away and change the speed."

"Why would you want to be ten feet away?"

"Why?" Her innocence was making my dick so fucking hard. "What if I tied you to my bed and went into the other room so you couldn't see what I was doing, and I wanted to surprise you with a change in speed? What if I put you in a bath and made you leave the bullet in your pussy, and I went into the bedroom to relax? Just two examples. I'm sure I could come up with more."

Her teeth found her lip and bit down. "I like those."

"You'll get them—both and more. I promise."

She continued to stare at it. "I'm a fan of the size." The half-smile turned to a full grin. "That"—she pointed at my dick —"is intimidating as fuck, but this"—she nodded toward the bullet—"is something I can probably handle."

"You're going to handle me too," I growled against her mouth. "Every fucking inch of me, and it's going to make you come so hard that you're going to scream."

She whispered, "When?"

Our talk tonight had changed things. Even though I'd told her that I wanted to carry through with the lessons, I had gotten the sense that she didn't believe me.

That we were going to skip right to lesson five now that I'd told her I wanted more.

I held her cheek. "After three and four, I'm going to take your virginity."

"So, we're still really going to have five lessons?"

I lowered my hand to the center of her back. "There are no more lessons, Oaklyn. I'm no longer trying to scare you away. I'm also not trying to get you prepped for another dude. You're mine. Every fucking piece of you is all mine." I kissed her softly. "What I'm doing is taking small steps to get there, so we don't rush things. I want you to experience every type of physical pleasure before we have sex."

She flattened her hands against my chest. "I love the sound of that."

"Good. Now, we have more shopping to do." I tucked the bullet under my arm to free up my hand. "I think this is the smallest and calmest dildo they have, but are there any others you want to look at?" I wrapped my arm over her shoulders. "Any others you'll let me try on you?"

She focused on the wall, checking out all the different options, the lengths, the widths, the upgrades. "I think I'm sold on the bullet."

"Then, let's move on." I guided her toward the last section of the wall. "These are vibrators. They don't go inside you; they just press against your clit."

"Gosh, they have every single angle covered, don't they?"

"Baby, there are a lot of spots on your body that can make you come." I took a thin six-inch hot-pink wand off the wall and gave it to her. "The mushroom head sits at the top of your clit, and this one has six different speeds. And"—I read the description—"it can even beat to the rhythm of a song if you connect it to a playlist."

She laughed.

"They have heads that are much larger"—I nodded toward the top of the section—"and wands that are girthier and longer that have endless speeds. I don't think you need something that large or complex." I held the back of her neck, claiming her. "You have a tiny little pussy. This one will work perfectly."

She gazed up at me with flushed cheeks. "And it's pink, such a girlie choice."

"That too."

"Looks like we have our toys. Now what?"

I growled as I leaned forward and ravished her lips. This time, I went slower. I didn't hurry. I didn't pull away for several seconds either. When I finally did, I held her stare. "We go home and play."

NINETEEN

Oaklyn

"You know, it was between this and sushi," Camden said as I took my last bite of filet. "Did I pick a solid choice?"

It was a chunk of meat that he'd grilled to perfection with caramelized onions. Although he'd tried hard to take over cooking the veggies and potatos when we got back to his condo after visiting the sex toy shop, I'd insisted on helping out. So, while he manned the grill, I stayed at the stovetop and sautéed a medley of sundried tomatoes and bok choy, roasted corn and snow peas—vegetables I'd surprisingly found in his fridge. And instead of baking the potatoes or boiling them, I'd thinly sliced them, coating the outside in heavy seasoning, browning and crisping them before I added cheese.

"Not just a solid choice. An amazing choice. I really love meat and fish; you can never go wrong with either." I set my fork down to lift my wine. "This dinner has been perfect." I glanced around the table that had already been set when we arrived, the lights that had been dimmed, the way the sunset was coming in through the tall windows that showed such a vast, beautiful view. "I wasn't expecting this, honestly."

"You thought I was going to pick you up at six, take you to a sex toy store, and not feed you?" He leaned back in his seat, having finished his meal as well, holding his drink close to his chest.

His recap sounded almost cold.

But that wasn't how I'd felt while I was putting on a little makeup and getting dressed for tonight. When he'd called from downstairs, saying he couldn't find a parking spot.

I just hadn't been sure what would happen after the lesson, if there would even be an after, and I'd assumed that, once it was over, we'd grab something to eat, or I'd make something once I got home.

I certainly hadn't expected this.

This was date-like.

Thoughtful.

And extremely romantic.

"I thought you were going to put things in my mouth. I just didn't think those things were going to be food." The moment I finished speaking, my cheeks instantly reddened.

I wondered if there would be a time when I could chat about the physical stuff between Camden and me and I wouldn't blush. When a discussion like that would be so normal that it would be as if we were talking about the steak we'd just eaten. And since the beginning of this proposition, I'd wondered once lesson five came and went, would I ever be touched by him again?

The car ride today had given me that answer.

But, still, it was so much to process, to take in, to think about what exactly this was going to look like, given that we had to be extremely careful and make sure Hannah didn't find out.

Even so, he'd made me the happiest woman in the world.

"Oaklyn"—he paused to exhale and shake his head—"I might be heartless, but I have manners. Of course I was going to feed you something other than a sex toy."

He didn't understand.

He'd taken my statement the wrong way.

"All I meant was that this has been strictly about the lessons. You made that clear ... remember?" My voice lightened. "I didn't anticipate anything else, including food."

"And now, it's not about the lessons." He wiped down one side of his beard and then the other, his stare so intense that I felt it everywhere.

All it did was make me smile harder. I couldn't hide the way he made me feel. "Which I love more than anything. Granted, you did feed me before lesson two, but the restaurant had been somewhat strategic since the table was perfect for what you wanted to do; the choice of cuisine just happened to be a bonus. Sometimes, meals can hint at more, and this setting certainly gives me that vibe."

"Tell me why."

I took a large drink of my wine, continuing to hold it while I said, "Out of all the places you could have chosen that evening, you took me for sushi, which is one of my ultimate favorites. Something you knew I would really enjoy." I let those words hit. "And tonight, you debated on what I would like, wavered, and switched things up, hoping I would devour the steak like sushi. Do you know how thoughtful that is? When you could have just stopped for some Mexican fast food before taking me home."

"I don't plan on taking you home tonight."

"Is that so?" I took a breath, his gaze making that almost difficult. "I had no idea you were this sweet."

"You're making me sound soft, Oaklyn, when everything in me, including my dick, is so fucking hard right now." He held his drink as he leaned into the table, surrounding the glass with both hands.

Oh God.

That look.

It was positively sinful.

"Sweet isn't soft—"

My voice cut off as he pushed his chair back and came over to my side of the table, where he knelt in front of me. He slid the base of my chair until I was directly facing him, spreading my legs, placing them on either side of him.

"You can call me whatever you want, but when you feel what I'm going to do to you tonight, you're going to realize there's nothing soft or sweet about it."

I was quivering.

Pooling.

Barely breathing.

I circled my legs around his lower back, bringing him in even closer, and once I had him locked in, his hand went to that spot between my legs.

Pressing.

Holding.

"That fucking heat," he growled. "I want to sink my dick into it."

I wanted that too.

It was time.

I didn't care that we hadn't completed all the lessons and we were supposed to be taking things slow—however he had worded it in the car. I wanted this.

I wanted him.

But before I could tell him that, he said, "Not tonight. Get that idea right out of your head. We have two more lessons before that happens."

"Camden—"

"No." His hands went to my face, aiming my stare at his. "I'm not going to fuck this up. I care about you too much." He paused, gazing into both of my eyes. "Oaklyn, all I've ever done my whole life is rush shit. Take what I wanted from women and then left. It never meant anything. There were never any feelings involved. I don't want that with you." He held me tighter. "I want to do it right. I want to take my time. I want to give you something I've never given to anyone else."

"Camden ..."

"That's why lesson four is so important."

The lesson that I'd asked him to come up with on his own, the one thing he'd never experienced with another woman.

There were so many different directions in which he could spin that lesson, and my brain was already reeling with possibilities.

But I didn't want to get ahead of myself.

I wanted to focus on the now.

This moment.

I wrapped my arms around him.

"Tell me you understand," he asked.

I nodded. "I absolutely do."

And I appreciated it more than he would know. In fact, my eyes were threatening to well with tears before he kissed me.

Slowly.

A speed that only emphasized everything he'd just said.

And when he pulled away, he kept our faces close. "That doesn't mean I'm not fucking dying to touch you. Hell, I can't even wait another second."

He was suddenly lifting me off the chair and into his arms, my legs wrapping around his waist, my hands gripping the back of his neck, and he carried me into his bedroom.

Like I was weightless.

Like I was his possession and he was going to do everything to please me.

When I landed on his bed, I realized this was a room I'd never been in before.

But like the others, this one was just as romantic.

A fireplace had been built into one of the walls and was roaring with flames. The curtains had been drawn, and through them, the sun was casting its warm glow across the whole space. The decor was black and charcoal, wood and stone—all rich in texture.

A room that was as sexy as the way he was looking at me.

He backed up a few paces and nodded toward the spot next to me. "Open it."

I didn't even realize what he was talking about until I looked at my side and saw the rectangular-shaped box that was secured with a black ribbon and bow.

I glanced between him and the present. "You got me something?"

"I got *us* something."

I pulled the ribbon, sliding it off, and lifted the top of the box, moving the tissue paper aside to pull out the slinky, silky sexiness.

"Camden," I breathed as I held the lingerie in the air, "this is gorgeous."

The nightie was a dark emerald green, outlined in black lace, with spaghetti straps. Cups that would fit my breasts and a shape that would hang over my body just loose enough that I could move freely, but tight enough that it would show my body, especially since it would land far above my knees.

"I want you wearing that when I come back." He reached for the bag of sex toys that he must have placed in here before dinner. "I'm going to go wash these."

As he walked into his en suite with the bag in his hand, I

quickly stripped off my clothes, starting with my shirt and jeans and then my bra and panties. I took the nightie from where I'd placed it on top of the box and slipped it over my head, the soft material tickling my skin as it lowered down my arms and chest, my stomach and thighs.

There was a mirror on the wall next to Camden's bed. A placement that I found a little strange. I was sure it was there for a reason other than checking out his outfits in the morning. I walked over to it, and as I took in my reflection, I adjusted my breasts and straightened the bottom hem of the dress.

Emerald was a color I never wore. I leaned more toward blue since it matched my eyes.

I was surprised at how much I liked it. That he'd been able to choose my size and a style that would fit my body type without asking his sister for those specifics.

"Fuck me," I heard from behind me, the sound like a growl.

Just as I looked over my shoulder, he was there. Inches away. He reached for me, wrapping his arms around my stomach, and his face went into my neck, breathing me in.

His hard-on bulged against me while he was shirtless, wearing just his jeans.

My body lit up, tingly and aching to be touched.

"You look incredible," he exhaled into my skin. "Like a fucking dream."

I reached up, holding his neck, my eyes briefly closing as his lips traveled to my ear. "Why green?"

I couldn't stop my curiosity even though I more than approved of his decision.

"I wanted to see what my favorite color would look like on you."

I smiled. "And?"

He took my free hand and held it against his erection. "Does that answer your question?"

I laughed. "According to you, you've been hard since we finished eating."

"Then, let me tell you." As he glanced up from my neck, his body still bent down, he kept his mouth close to my cheek while we both gazed at my reflection in the mirror. "Oaklyn, you're the most beautiful woman I've ever seen. Your mind. Your face. Your body. Just look at yourself. Look at what I get to touch." He slowly ran his hands down my sides and over my hips. "And kiss." He rounded my butt and went to my thighs and gradually rose to my chest. "And love." His hand flattened on my stomach, his lips aligned with my ear. "You're fucking perfect. Every inch of you. And every single one of those inches is mine." His hand lowered, this time to that spot, the one he'd avoided since I'd been standing here, and he pressed his palm against it.

The sensation caused me to moan, "Camden." I inhaled sharply, my back arching into him. "*Yesss.*"

"Is that all it takes?" He pushed harder. "A little pressure, and you're going to come for me?"

"I could."

"But you won't. Not yet. We have so much playing to do." He was guiding my chin down so my face was pointed at the mirror again—something I hadn't even realized I'd stopped looking at. "I want you to watch yourself."

His hand moved behind him, and when it returned, he was holding the hot-pink wand. The size wasn't as intimidating as some of the others at the shop. The color was inviting. And because his hands were so big, it looked tiny in his grip.

"This is going to feel so fucking good," he whispered in my ear. "I'm going to put it on your clit." It was just a few seconds of warning before the rubber was on me, sliding in between my lips, gliding up and down. "I can feel how wet you are."

My breaths were coming out heavier, my eyes closing.

"Watch yourself, Oaklyn," he repeated. "I want your eyes on your cunt. I don't want them to leave—do you hear me? I want you to see everything I do to you."

My eyelids flicked open, and I moaned, "This feels ... I don't even think I have words."

"Wait until I turn it on."

That statement served as another warning. I didn't even have time to fill my lungs when the vibration shot through me. My fingers gripped his hair, holding on for dear life as the intensity took over my body.

"Oh my God," I cried. "What"—I gasped—"is this?"

"The fastest orgasm of your entire life." He gave my earlobe a bite and licked it to soothe the sting. "I want you to see how beautiful you look when you come."

Because of the placement of the vibrator, my nightie was as high as my belly button, revealing the way my legs were spread and the V between them, the way he had positioned the wand against me.

I didn't know what was happening.

My body was barely holding itself up, and without the help of his arm that was wrapped around the center of me and the rock-hard muscles behind me, I wouldn't have been standing.

There was just too much going on inside my body.

The bursts were starting, building.

Churning.

"Fuck!" I yelled. "*Ahhh!*" My hand clung to the locks of his hair, my hips lifting forward and sliding back, moving on their own, the waves turning into this fierce, relentless cycle. "Camden!"

As I sucked in air, a flame ignited in my pussy, and it boomed harder, faster, more flickers adding to the growing fire.

I couldn't stop what was happening.

I wasn't even sure I could see my reflection any longer.

I was in this hot cloud of steam with this immense strength wrapped around me.

And I was instantly lost.

"I've got you," he said in my neck. "I'm not going to let you go." He kissed. He breathed. He might have even bitten. "Now, fucking come."

I was already there.

But that demand sent me diving over the edge, grasping for him, for air, for anything that I could hold on to that would keep me in this place, this feeling, this moment that was unlike anything I'd ever felt.

"*Ohhh!*" I heaved. "Yes!"

Shudders pounded through my body, pulsing from the inside, causing my stomach to ripple in movement. Camden held me even tighter as I bucked against him. And like the waves that had rocked through me earlier, these came in heavy crests, each one slapping me, firing through me.

"Fucking beautiful," he hissed.

I couldn't breathe.

I couldn't stop.

I couldn't even slow.

This feeling was just crashing through me, and when I finally made my way past the peak, I felt the energy drain through my toes. The sensitivity crept its way in until the pleasure quieted to a whisper.

Camden knew and turned the vibrator off, and it was suddenly gone from my sight.

"Now, I need to taste you." He held up my dress, showing my pussy while he traced the outside with his fingers. He was so soft, careful, just brief grazes of skin against skin. And when he had what he wanted, he lifted his hand to his mouth. "Fuck yes. I can't wait to eat your pussy."

I couldn't wrap my head around that.

Things felt far too delicate down there after what he just did.

I needed a second.

I needed ... him.

I pulled my body off his, where I'd still been giving him most of my weight, and I turned around to find his button.

Zipper.

Once they were undone and his pants were lowered, I slipped into the hole of his boxer briefs—a place I'd learned about in the alley—and I wrapped my fingers around his hard-on. While holding his stare and his cock, I let him know this was, "Mine."

"You keep touching me like that, Oaklyn, and you're going to make me come."

I felt a hard bite on my lip, my teeth not wanting to let it go, but I did to reply, "That's what I want."

"*Mmm.*"

I fisted the bottom of his dick and pumped to the tip, rubbing my palm over the top before I lowered down his long, thick shaft. "I can't wait to have this."

"Baby ..." His mouth was in my neck. "Tell me."

"I've never wanted anything so badly in my life." As my hand bobbed, his was between my legs. "I want to know what it feels like. How you're going to make me come. How you're going to stop yourself from splitting me in half."

He growled, "That will be difficult, especially with how good you're going to feel." He kissed the back of my ear. "I have a feeling your pussy is going to mold right around me, milk the cum out of me."

I didn't know where it had come from, but he was rubbing the bullet over my clit. The hard bubbles that I had seen earlier through the packaging along with the material of the bullet made such an interesting combination.

One that was almost overwhelming.

"That's it, Oaklyn. Stroke my fucking cock."

But now, he was doing more than just touching me. He was circling the entrance of my pussy, spreading my wetness.

"You're so turned on; this is going to slip right in."

My hand didn't stop. It moved faster. "Can I handle the size of it?"

I knew it was small, but it was still larger than his finger, and that was the most I'd experienced so far, and even during those scenarios, I hadn't had a whole finger, just a half.

His arm lifted from my navel and went around my neck, pulling my upper body against his chest. "I'm going to make it fit." He slowly dipped in just the round tip. "You're so fucking tight."

My hand stalled, waiting, anticipating, as I breathed through the expected pain.

But there wasn't any.

Not even when he went in a bit deeper.

Or when he turned the bullet, making sure I felt the texture as it rubbed against the inside of me.

"Oh God," I exhaled. "That feels incredible."

"I knew it wouldn't hurt, but if it did, I would have felt you tense up, and I would have immediately stopped."

He gripped my neck with more strength so he could take on the rest of my weight. And I gave it to him with ease, particularly when the bullet was all the way in.

"I'm holding the leash, and I can feel you pulsing around the silicone."

As I did just that, I regained the speed in my hand, giving him just as much pleasure. "I want more."

"Greedy," he moaned. "I didn't know that about you, Oaklyn."

"I just want you."

"You have me in your hand."

I did, quite literally, but I hoped he meant that in every way.

"I want you to get used to the way it feels before I turn on the vibration." My head rested under his chin, and he was staring at me. Hungrily. "In the meantime, I'm going to do this." His thumb was on my clit, and he began to strum it like an instrument.

My hair ground against his chest as I pushed into him. "Camden," I sighed. There was so much going on, so many different feelings. "Damn it, that feels good."

I made sure he didn't just hear me, that he felt me, too, in the way I held him, how hard and deeply I caressed him.

"You'd better slow down," he warned.

But I didn't want to.

I wanted to watch him lose himself.

"No," I fought back. "Your orgasm is also mine."

He bent his head, his eyes never leaving me when he dived into my neck. "Is that right?"

"Yes."

"Then, you're getting this." The second he finished speaking, the vibration turned on.

Even though it was slow, it came on strong.

Enough so that I screamed, "Camden!"

"Fuck yeah, I love that sound. Let me hear it again."

I didn't have to try. It was there, burning my throat to get out, and as my lips parted, I shouted, "Yes!" And when I drew in more air, I added, "Oh fuck!"

"I want you to come at the same time as me." He lifted his face from my neck and pressed his lips against my cheek. "And I'm going to come right on your fucking ass." Satisfaction was spreading across his face. "That's it, Oaklyn. Don't fucking stop."

I was no longer aware of how I was even touching him, what I was doing. All I could focus on was the bullet, the flick of his thumb.

The tingles.

The build.

The spasms moving through me.

And they were coming on with a ruthless intensity.

"Oh shit," I moaned.

He held my face, aiming it toward the mirror, keeping his hand on my cheek as he began to thrust his dick through my grip. "I cannot fucking wait to be inside of you. To have this be your pussy. To make you scream this loud with my cock."

"I want you."

"Show me." He increased the vibration, his hand moving quicker as well. "Show me how you're going to come when I fuck you." My eyes started to close, and he tightened his grasp. "The rules haven't changed. You're going to watch yourself shudder and scream."

And I did.

Because it came on so instantly.

"Camden!"

A shout followed his name, one that came with a raging rush that blasted through my body. And in that moment, even though I was completely adrift in trembles, I became fully aware of what I needed to do for him, and I glided my hand up and down his length. He turned even harder, his momentum stopping for just a second, and that was when I knew.

When I heard the deepness of his moans.

When I felt the warmth on my butt, a stream followed by another.

"Oaklyn," he groaned. "*Fuuuck.*"

I was done.

A shuddering disaster that couldn't make sense of every

feeling ravaging my body, but I held on to him—his dick, his neck—and I let the motions work through me, screaming, "*Ahhh*," as I neared the highest point, quieting as I started the descent.

Camden was just as loud.

He jolted just as much as me.

And he gripped me with just as much power.

Until there was nothing but stillness and breathing.

He sighed into my neck, loosening his grip to kiss down my shoulder and up to my face. "You're covered in me."

"I can feel it."

His sounds told me he liked that, that it was another way for him to claim me.

Own me.

Dominate me.

"I need to get you in the shower, and then we're going to have some dessert."

"Dessert?"

He smiled as he turned me toward him. "They're not my sister's brownies, but they're pretty solid." He hovered above my lips. "And, yes, I know those are your favorite. I saw your post from the other night."

TWENTY

Camden

When my eyes opened, Oaklyn was sleeping on my chest. Her arm was around my stomach. Pieces of her dark hair were tickling the bottom of my chin. Her body only moved to breathe, a slight lift as she inhaled, the heat from her exhale warming my flesh.

So, this was what it felt like to watch the morning rise on a woman's skin.

To feel her wrapped around you all night.

To not maneuver your way out of bed a few seconds after you were done, never to return.

This was what *more* looked like.

Felt like.

A place of contentment so out of the norm, but a place I didn't want to leave.

In fact, as the glow from the sunlight trickled in through the curtains—a reminder that we needed to get up—I only held her tighter.

Monday had come fast, considering we hadn't left my condo since we'd returned here Friday evening after the sex toy store. Saturday morning, Oaklyn had made us breakfast, which eventually led to lunch. Then, dinner was delivered, and another night was spent in my bed.

With her in my arms.

Sunday had looked almost identical to Saturday.

And now, the two of us had to part, go to work, leave each other's presence for the first time in days.

From this place we kept calling *more.*

A place that still didn't involve sex because we'd decided to wait until Hannah knew the truth about our relationship.

And for the first time in my life, not being intimate was my choice, and leaving this bed was the last thing I wanted.

Since we still had a few minutes before we had to get up, I carefully slid my way out of her grip, replacing my body with a pillow so she had something to rest on, and I went into the kitchen to make us coffee. Once I'd learned how she took hers, I'd had creamer delivered over the weekend, and I added some to her cup before I returned to the bedroom.

She was just starting to stir as I climbed into bed, kissing her forehead, whispering, "Good morning."

Her beautiful eyes opened, a smile instantly dragging across her lips. "*Mmm.* Morning."

"Here." I handed her the cup and leaned my back against the headboard, crossing my legs on top of the comforter.

"What time is it?"

"Almost seven."

She took her first sip and groaned. "What's your day look like?"

I traced across her bare hip, loving that I'd demanded she sleep naked and that she'd listened. "Horrific since I didn't work at all this weekend." My hand paused as I grinned.

225

"Hooked is going to monopolize my entire day, but I have two other cases to prep, so somehow, I'm going to have to be three people at once. Tell me about your day."

"Not nearly as stressful as yours. Lots of paperwork. I need to tweak some campaigns. I might be meeting with a client later this afternoon if they don't reschedule on me."

"Does that happen a lot?"

She pulled the blanket up past her chest and positioned herself a little higher on the pillows. "Often enough. This one is local, which makes it much easier. But a few times a quarter, I hit the road and travel to my accounts that aren't in California."

"How far do you go?"

"My farthest is New York. I'll actually be going there a few weeks after I get back from Arizona for just a couple of days." She rolled onto her side to face me, resting her cheek on her palm, balancing the coffee on a pillow. "Why? Will you miss me?"

I chuckled, lowering the blanket so I had an unobstructed view of her body. "I already do." God, her smile was fucking gorgeous. "You've spoiled me the past few days. I've gotten to kiss you whenever I wanted. Today's going to be rough without that perk."

And that was something else that had surprised me this weekend.

That I would crave her lips so often and would lean toward them, taking them at random moments when the pressure built up to the point that I couldn't stand it.

That I'd constantly touch some part of her body, my hands needing the heat from her skin, the softness, the feel of a curve.

"So, you are going to miss me. I love that. And I love that conversations like this do that to you." She nodded toward my shorts that I'd slipped on before grabbing us coffee.

I adjusted my hard-on. "It's not the conversation, Oaklyn.

It's you. Looking at you." My voice lowered as I added, "Touching you." I left her hip to run my fingers over my hair. "And as much as I want to spend all morning with my hands all over you, I've got to get in the shower. I need to be at the office before Declan so I can get a little work done before all hell breaks loose."

"You go do that, and I'll make us some eggs."

Still holding my coffee, I dived my face into her neck, taking in that fruit smell that didn't fade regardless of how many times she had showered at my place. I nuzzled that spot—one that was becoming a favorite—and scraped my beard against it, hearing her giggle in response.

I kissed her cheek before I pulled back. "See you soon."

I forced myself out of bed and into the bathroom, where I turned on the water to a steaming temperature and stepped beneath the spray the moment the glass shower walls began to fog. I hurried through the movements, washing my hair and body, and once I got out, I shaved underneath my chin and edged the sides of my beard, brushing my teeth before I put on my suit. The last things I did were spray on some cologne and tuck my wallet and phone into my pocket, finally making my way toward the kitchen.

I was just passing through the living room when I spotted Oaklyn. She was dressed in one of my button-downs, standing at the gas range with her back to me, a spatula in her hand. Her long hair fell down her back in waves, her hips swaying to a song playing through my built-in speakers.

Even though the shirt was so baggy on her, I could see the outline of her ass and those delicious, lean, toned legs.

A view so fucking perfect that I ached.

Although the physical steps were coming on slow—a choice that I'd made and I had every intention to uphold—everything else was happening fast.

The amount of time we were now spending together.

The way I felt about her.

The way I was looking toward our future.

There was just one thing that still held me back. Goddamn it, I needed to have that conversation with my sister sooner than later. I just wasn't ready to go there. I wanted to continue to feel things out for a little while longer. And then I'd take on the wrath that she was going to give me and the turbulence that could potentially follow.

"What are you doing over there?" Oaklyn asked, pulling me away from my thoughts as she looked at me from over her shoulder.

"Admiring."

"Me too. You, in that gray suit and black tie ..." She hissed out air through her lips. "You look beyond handsome."

I leaned against the wall as I continued to stare at her, my arms crossing, feeling the pull of my jacket and the metal of my cuff links. "Nothing compared to you."

"I'll fight you on that."

"Fight me, huh? That would be one hell of a wrestling match." My gaze narrowed as it dipped down her waist and ass and legs. "Jesus, don't tease me, Oaklyn. I have less than ten minutes before I need to leave, and comments like that will have me calling in."

"In that case, you win."

She winked and carried the pan over to the island, plating two fried eggs for each of us, followed by some toast that had just popped up from the toaster. She buttered both pieces and brought the plates to the table, where I joined her after I grabbed us more coffee.

"This is nice." She held her mug with both hands, watching me take my first bite. "The before-work thing, I mean. Now that Hannah is living with Declan, I only cook for myself. It was so strange for a while since we'd lived together for so long and I always made breakfast for two."

I dipped the toast into the runny yolk and groaned as I chewed.

I didn't know how she had made eggs taste this good, but, shit, they were fucking fire. "You can make me breakfast anytime you want."

"That would mean I'd have to stay the night."

I looked up from my plate. "And?"

Her grin grew. "You'd better get out of here. Fast."

I laughed and inhaled the rest of my food, downing my coffee as I brought the plate into the kitchen and set it in the sink along with the mug. When I returned, I turned Oaklyn's chair until she was facing me and knelt to pull her into my arms, holding her tiny body against mine.

"Stay as long as you want," I told her. "There's no reason for you to rush out of here."

She circled her arms around my back, her head on my chest, where she'd slept all night. "I didn't bring my laptop, so I really do need to go home."

"Don't you dare touch those dishes. My housekeeper will be here in a little while, and she'll clean up."

"But—"

"No buts. You cooked, and since I'm out of time, my house-keeper will clean." I gave her a final squeeze and stood. "I'll text you later."

———

"My assistant said you phoned about an hour ago," Easton voiced after I answered his call. "Did you get everything you needed?"

I lifted the Hooked file from the mess on my desk, trying to remember why I'd even called him. I'd been at the office for four hours, and it felt like a month. I was in the midst of juggling all three cases, and it was too much for my fucking brain.

I peeked inside the folder, reading the notes I'd written earlier, and it all clicked. "I did," I replied. "She sent over the documents I needed."

"How's it looking?"

I set the file down and pushed my back into the chair, my eyes closing, my hand rubbing across my forehead. "We're making headway. We've got our team working on the weekends to log all the data we'll need to show in court. This morning, I listened to the conversations you'd recorded that we're going to use for evidence. I'll tell you what; Declan and I can't wait to present those."

"When anyone fucks with me, the Boston comes out, and I hit record so fucking fast when that opportunity presented itself."

I laughed.

Jesus, I missed that city.

Bostonians had a rawness that LA locals just didn't have.

"It's a good thing you did," I told him. "That proof alone could win you the case. But that doesn't make our job any easier, not when you go up against a social media giant like Faceframe."

"That's why we hired the best. Now, go work your magic and let me know if you need anything else."

"Will do," I said and hung up.

I was just opening Hooked's file again when there was a knock at my door.

Goddamn it.

I couldn't go a fucking minute without being interrupted.

"Come in," I yelled, and I flipped through the top couple of sheets, reading some of the data I needed to memorize. "Yes?" I asked whoever was standing there without looking to see who it was.

"Hi."

That voice.

The softness of it.

I glanced up, and Oaklyn was smiling in my doorway.

"To what do I owe this pleasure?"

She laughed, her cheeks turning a color that looked fucking amazing on her. "I'm having lunch with your sister. She's still in a meeting, so I thought I'd come in and say hi." She glanced around the space. "I've never been in your office."

"Make yourself comfortable." I opened my arms, hoping she'd rush in and fall into them. To be extra cautious, I growled, "But lock the door first."

She didn't move. "I think we both know that's a bad idea." She gripped the frame of the door as though she needed to stop herself from entering. "But I think a good idea would be to have dinner at my place tonight."

"Yeah?"

She nodded, tucking a long piece of hair behind her ear, showing an earlobe that I was dying to bite. "I'm cooking."

"Say no more."

"Is that the only reason you're coming over? To eat more of my food?"

That dress and the way it fit her body—*fuck me*—it was just the sight I needed to get me through the rest of the day.

I kept my voice low when I replied, "I'm coming over because I can't stay the hell away from you." I linked my fingers together, my hard-on pressing against my suit pants, threatening to burst right through the seam. "You're all I've thought about all morning. And being with you tonight is going to be the best thing that's happened to me all day."

231

Her teeth were on her lip, grazing back and forth. "Then, I'll see you tonight." Her fingers released the frame, and she gave me a quick wave before she was gone.

The view of my empty doorway now was almost painful to look at.

But that spot was quickly filled just a second later by Declan. He glanced from me to the hallway, where I imagined Oaklyn was walking, before he looked at me again, making his way into my office, chuckling as he took a seat in front of my desk.

"Visiting you at work, I see."

I crossed my arms over my chest. "She's having lunch with my sister. But one day soon, she'll be coming here just for me."

Declan nodded. "Sounds like things are moving in the right direction, and that goddamn smile on your face confirms it."

"They're definitely moving." It didn't matter how hard I pushed on my chest; the feeling inside of it wouldn't go away. These sparks, shit, they were relentless. "There's just a giant elephant standing between us."

"You'll handle that when the time is right."

I sighed. "That's what I've been telling myself." I adjusted my tie, the feel of it almost choking me, before I rested my arms on my desk. "Things are good just how they are. But eventually, we're going to leave my condo or hers, and I just fucking know we'll run into one of my family members, and the secret will be out."

"Here's a tip, brother: don't let that happen. Tell her before she hears it from someone else. That'll fuel a beast in her that you don't want to fuck with."

TWENTY-ONE

Oaklyn

I opened the door to my apartment, where Camden stood on the other side, his arms stretched high on the doorframe, showing biceps that were bulging and a stare that wasn't just hungry, but also feral.

"Oaklyn," he grunted.

That stare didn't just lock with my eyes; it moved up and down my body.

"Hi." I inhaled deeply, his gaze becoming achingly overwhelming, and everything inside me was starting to tingle. "You're right on time."

My God, he looked incredible.

The backward baseball hat. The fitted white T-shirt. The gray sweatpants that hung low on his waist, showing the outline of his dick and a hint of his crown—a sight I hadn't at all been prepared for.

"I ran home to shower and change, so technically, I am a few minutes late. You don't mind, do you?"

Before I could respond, he was kissing me, gripping my butt, squeezing my cheeks. He was aligning our bodies so there wasn't even air between us, giving me a taste of his mouth— something I'd missed since this morning—and a dose of his woodsy, citrus, and amber scent, which I'd been teased with when I went to his office before lunch.

Once he finally pulled away, he eyed me up and down before he passed to walk inside.

"Do I mind?" I laughed from behind him, checking out this angle of his outfit. "I definitely don't mind you coming over in gray sweatpants. In fact, you could wear those every day, and I'd be the happiest girl alive."

He smiled at me from over his shoulder.

That simple expression set my whole body on fire.

"You prefer sweats over the suit I wore today?"

"*Hmm.*" I shut the door and followed him into my kitchen. "You honestly look good in everything. But those"—I nodded toward his waist when he faced me—"I very much approve of."

He winked. "I have them in every color, Oaklyn."

"Other colors don't matter. It has to be gray." I bit my lip before I emphasized, "Always wear gray."

He chuckled. "Noted."

When he reached for the bottle of red wine that I'd opened earlier and left on the counter, I said, "I picked up some vodka. Would you rather have that?"

I was just walking by him to grab the liquor, but I didn't make it more than a pace before he cinched my waist and pulled me over to him.

"Look at you, being all thoughtful."

"I know what you drink."

He nuzzled his face into my neck. "But do you know how I prefer you?"

I ran my fingers across his hard, chiseled back and up his defined shoulders. "Naked?"

"Fuck yes, but if we're talking about clothing, I want you in yoga pants. Now, I just have to see you in green ones."

"Why yoga pants?"

"Because it shows this"—his hand was behind me again, gripping the same spot he'd touched in the doorway—"and I'm fucking obsessed with it."

"But it's yours."

His face hovered above mine. "Hearing you say that will never get old." He kissed me again, his tongue slowly sliding into my mouth, his hands moving up my body, stopping when his palms reached my cheeks and his fingers extended over the side of my head. He kept us locked until he whispered against my lips, "What did you make? It's all I can smell."

I laughed at the way he growled the last word. "I kept things simple."

"Even your eggs aren't simple, Oaklyn. I don't believe dinner would be either."

I felt the droplets that had fallen down his neck and soaked his shirt from his wet, showered hair. "I really did. I just threw together a lasagna."

His grip tightened. "Lasagna? You fucking didn't?"

"With meat and extra ricotta."

His stare intensified, gazing between both of my eyes. "Just like my mom makes it."

Growing up, I'd spent enough dinners at the Daltons' house to know the meal that neither of their children ever missed. Mrs. Dalton was known for her lasagna—a dish that she had mastered so well that none of them ever bothered to order it in a restaurant because it wouldn't compare to hers. If I was going to attempt to duplicate her signature dinner—one that I knew Camden loved more than anything—I needed to make sure it was perfect.

What I didn't tell him was that I had made two batches, both completely different, to test which one came out better.

I was thoroughly impressed with the results.

"Not exactly like your mom's, but similar-ish."

This time, he just pecked me, leaving his lips lingering on mine while he said, "You know that's my favorite."

"And some homemade bread as well."

There was no warning; he just scooped me up, moving so fast that I didn't even have time to take a breath, and I was suddenly in his arms. My legs circled his waist, and my hands went around his shoulders. And while we stood in the middle of my kitchen, I expected him to set me on the counter.

But he didn't.

He didn't move at all.

He just held me, smiling.

"Looks like I picked the right thing to cook tonight," I said, laughing.

He shook his head, but it wasn't in agreement; it was more like he was in awe. "Oaklyn ..." He didn't say any more for several seconds. "There are moments, like when I watched you making breakfast in my kitchen this morning, and when you came into my office this afternoon, and now, when I just want to stare at you."

"Why?"

"Why?" he mirrored, but he wasn't challenging my question. It sounded like he was trying to come up with the right words. "I've always found you so incredibly beautiful. Ever since we were kids. And I'd be lying if I said I didn't notice all the times you bent over in front of me, or when you were in a bikini in our pool, or when I came to your apartment to visit my sister and you were walking around in workout clothes. But never during any of those times did I ever think I'd get to touch you. That I'd get to put my lips on you. That I'd get to be the first guy to be inside you."

My heart was exploding not only from his candor, but from his expression too. The way his eyes were softening while he looked at me. How he saw me in a way that no other man ever had.

"There was so much fucking temptation every time I was around you. There were instances when I had to actually walk into another room, so I didn't flirt my ass off with you or brush a piece of hair off your cheek—any excuse just to touch you and talk to you more. Because I knew that even though those were small acts, if I allowed myself to do them, they would lead to my hands wanting to be all over you." His focus shifted from my right eye to my left, scanning equally back and forth. "You've always been this perfect girl in my mind, Oaklyn. Never did I believe we would be here. That every one of my desires would be coming true. That you would be mine. So, yeah, there are times when I just want to stare at you and remind myself that it isn't a fucking dream. That I get to do this"—he pressed our lips together—"any goddamn time I want."

I thought my heart couldn't swell any larger.

But it happened.

My chest filled with so much emotion that I almost couldn't hide it from my eyes.

"I know exactly what you mean. I've felt the same way for just as long." I rubbed my nose against his cheek, inhaling his scent and feeling the roughness of his beard. "You have no idea how badly I want to talk to Hannah about you and just boast at the fact that I've finally gotten the man I've been dreaming about for all these years. How I want to put one of our selfies on Instagram. How I want us to go hiking at Runyon Canyon and go to my favorite restaurants and even a concert without the fear of running into one of the Daltons, who I swear are everywhere in this city so we'll inevitably bump into one of them."

"I promise you're going to get all of that very soon."

A worry came over me.

One that made me want to clarify and say, "Camden, I don't want you to think I'm rushing us. This pace is perfect. I'm not trying to force us into something you're not comfortable with. I just hate that we have to be a secret."

"Stop." He kissed me. "I want everything you want. You're not alone in this." He continued to gaze into my eyes, holding me like I was weightless. "How about right before you go to Arizona with Hannah? That'll give us a little more time, and we'll have a better idea of what things look like between us. You'll get to clear your conscience and then take off to the mountains with her."

I took a deep breath. "Ugh, I don't know if that's the best idea. I almost think we should tell her after we get back. What if she's so mad that she won't want to go? Or it could turn our trip into something awful."

"Then, we'll tell her when you get back."

"Okay." I filled my lungs again. "I like that plan."

Just having something set in motion gave me the smallest amount of relief. It was this in-between, this waiting, this unknown that was eating at me.

"Once we tell her," he said, "nothing is going to change between us. I want you to know that."

I squeezed my legs around him. "Even if she hates the idea of us?"

"My sister's opinion isn't going to force me to let you go, Oaklyn. Not a fucking thing in this world can do that. It's taken me a long time to get here. I'm not returning to my bachelor life, and I won't let a day go by where you're not mine."

I rubbed my nose across his and whispered, "Best answer ever."

"I don't want to set you down because then you'll be too far away from me and I'll start craving you again, but I'm dying to try this dinner you made, and I don't want it to get cold."

I couldn't stop smiling. "Let's eat."

He reluctantly set my feet on the floor after he kissed me, and I hurried over to the lasagna cooling on the stovetop, the layers settling. I cut two pieces and plated them. I added slices of the bread I'd made and brought them over to the table, where Camden was pouring us some wine.

"Wine now, vodka later," he said as I eyed his glass. "There will be a later, right? Or do I need to worry about my sister randomly showing up?"

"She calls first. Always. So, even if she came, we'd have enough time to hide you somewhere."

"Now, wouldn't that be interesting?"

I sighed, lifting my fork and placing my napkin on my lap. "Let's not even think about it."

"Good call." He glanced down at his dinner. "This looks fucking delicious." He even leaned his face close to the pasta to smell it. "*Mmm.*"

"Remember, it's different from Mom's. I added some veggies and more meat than she typically uses—"

"*Fuuuck.*" His head leaned back as he chewed, his eyes closing. "Oaklyn, you've done it."

I was so nervous that I hadn't even taken a bite yet. I just knew what it tasted like from the tiny sample I'd tried before he came. "Really?"

"*Mmhmm.*" His neck straightened, and he looked at me. "It's better than Mom's."

I shook my head. "No. It can't be—"

"It is. Trust me. I'm blown the fuck away right now." He

took a piece of the bread and dipped it into the sauce and moaned as he bit off the red-soaked corner. "Holy shit. This is amazing too."

I laughed as I sliced my fork through the cheese and noodles and brought some up to my mouth. "Wow," I said from behind my hand, "it is good."

"Where did you learn how to cook like this?"

I finished chewing and shrugged. "My mom taught me a lot. She can make anything taste yummy, but I think most of it came from all the years Hannah and I spent in this apartment. She was homebound with endless studying to do, so I had lots of time to experiment. And, as you know, your sister sugarcoats nothing, so when my creations sucked, she told me, and I got better."

He took another bite, groaning before he said, "You know I come from a family of eaters—not just my immediate family, I mean, but my cousins are all a bunch of foodies as well. I'm saying that because I can tell the difference between someone who cooks just to eat and someone who cooks with love."

I smiled before I took a sip of my wine. "Thank you. I really do love it."

He was quiet for a moment, staring.

His gaze hitting every spot again.

"I think it's time."

I sucked in some air, holding it in my lungs. "Time for ..."

He chuckled. "I told you that wasn't going to come until lesson five, and we're now on four."

"And here I thought, you were going to budge."

"I am. I'm giving you something I've never given to another woman."

My heart started to pound the same way it had earlier tonight when I was in his arms. "So, you don't want me to come up with a fantasy for this lesson?"

"No. This one is all on me." His thumb swiped his lip even though there was nothing on it. "Next Friday, after work, I'm going to pick you up. I need you to pack an overnight bag."

"To stay at your condo?"

"We won't be sleeping at my place. But that's the only detail I'm giving you."

TWENTY-TWO

Camden

"I'm dying to know where we're going," Oaklyn said from the passenger seat of my car minutes after I picked her up from her place.

She'd asked the same question every time I saw her this past week—when she popped over to my place for a quick dinner, during the lunch we had at her apartment when I was able to sneak away from work, even when we talked on the phone.

From the moment she'd gotten into my car, I'd kept her hand locked underneath mine, resting on the gearshift. But now, I lifted it toward my mouth, kissing the back of her knuckles.

Even her fingers smelled like tangerine and blueberry.

God, this fucking woman.

It was taking every ounce of strength I had not to skip right to lesson five and finally get the chance to be inside her. Once I reached that point, I could be with her whenever I wanted.

She certainly wouldn't mind if we fast-forwarded things.

Hell, she'd all but fucking begged for it during lesson three.

But, damn it, I couldn't.

I wanted things with Oaklyn to be different.

And I didn't just want to tell her that she'd changed me, that she had made me realize she was everything I wanted, that there was no way I could imagine my life without her.

Those were things I wanted to show her.

Completing lesson four and slowly moving to five was one of the ways I could do that.

Along with everything that I had planned for tonight.

Still keeping her hand near my mouth, I quickly glanced at her. "I think you're going to like it. No, fuck that. I know you're going to like it."

"I already do."

I turned at the light, moving our hands back to the gearshift. "You know, Hannah came into my office today and mentioned that she'd invited you out with the girls and you couldn't make it. It's funny; she always used to bring you up, and most of the time, I didn't pay attention. Now, I'm on full fucking alert."

She laughed. "I told her I was going out with Mystery Man."

I gave her another quick peek. "She's still letting you get away with calling him that? And hasn't demanded a name? I'm shocked."

"I think she knows I'm not ready to name him. That would make things more serious, and she thinks things are just super low-key between him and me. If I tell her we've progressed, the questions will come fast and hard." She squeezed the side of my hand with her thumb. "I hate lying."

"I know, baby." I sighed. "It's only for a little longer."

"Did she ask you what you're doing tonight?"

"Of course." I slowed at the light. "She wanted to know why I wasn't hanging out with Declan and our cousins."

Her brows rose. "What did you tell her?"

I chuckled. "Well, if I told you that, it would ruin tonight's surprise, so ask me that question in a little while."

"Deal." I felt her eyes on me while I started driving again. "The Hollywood Hills, huh?"

My area of town was where we'd now entered.

I had known she'd have questions once we got here, and I didn't blame her. We weren't surrounded by hotels, like some of the other areas in LA, and now that we were in the residential section, she had to be wondering why she needed an overnight bag.

I held off answering and just smiled, knowing she was still looking at me, and when I pulled up to the gated entrance and entered a code, I said, "We're here," and I finally glanced at her.

"Here?" She gazed through the windshield at the large house that was nestled on the side of the mountain. "I don't get it."

"You will." I got out of the car and grabbed our bags and met her at the passenger side, linking our hands. "Come on. We're going inside."

We walked up the driveway, and I opened the front door by entering another code. Leaving our bags on a bench in the foyer, I slowly took her deeper into the house.

"What do you think?" I asked as we passed the office that sat just off the foyer, followed by the dining room, and we stopped once we reached the massive kitchen. From here, the open floor plan extended into the large living room, a built-out deck, and an infinity pool, all overlooking the Hills.

"What do I think?" she repeated. "This house is positively stunning."

"Wait until you see the primary bedroom."

Her eyes were loaded with questions as I led her through the living room and into the primary wing, where I showed her the en suite, a shower that was also a steam room, and the his and hers walk-in closets. And, lastly, the bedroom had a sitting area, a fireplace, and access to the patio.

Fully furnished in a style that wasn't exactly mine, but that didn't matter. The home was over the top, outfitted in high-end upgrades, and a square footage that could never be outgrown, no matter how many of the bedrooms were filled.

We were standing in front of the floor-to-ceiling windows, taking in the view, when I slipped my arm around her, pulling her to my side, pressing my lips against her head. "Could you imagine waking up to this every morning?"

"That would be such a dream."

I breathed her in, my eyes closing as I inhaled her scent. "What if it didn't have to be a dream? What if it could be reality?"

That question earned me her eyes. "What do you mean?"

"The house is mine, Oaklyn. I just have to sign the last bit of paperwork, and I'll be able to take possession of it."

"You're kidding?"

I turned her toward me. "But before I give them that signature, I wanted you to see it. Feel it out. Give me your approval."

A smile grew across her face that was so incredibly beautiful. "My approval?" She was searching my eyes. "Why?"

I took a deep breath.

Fuck, I'd thought so much about this moment.

What I would say.

How I would feel.

The way she would react.

Those were the questions that had plagued me when I first toured this home and again last night when I came for the final walk-through.

Am I getting ahead of myself?

Am I moving way too fucking fast?

I hadn't even told my sister about our relationship, yet I was already thinking about the next steps, planning them, even moving forward with them.

A step that was bigger than I'd ever taken.

But one that felt right, especially now that I was standing in this room with Oaklyn, the woman I wanted to share it with.

"You asked me to give you something I've never given to another woman." My hands moved to her cheeks, aiming her face up to mine. "You wanted it to be a part of a lesson, and I gave you a fucked-up response and made it about sex, which was fitting at the time—at least, I thought so. But things have changed. Even though I continue to call them lessons, they're no longer about teaching, and what's happening between us isn't just physical. That's why this—what I'm about to say, how I'm feeling—it's not part of lesson four. It's so much bigger than that. It's so much more. And where we're going, shit"—my head shook back and forth as I stared at her—"I've never been surer about anything in my life."

"Camden ..." she whispered, her hands pressed against the backs of mine.

I grazed my nose against hers and pulled back to say, "I saw this house and immediately thought, *I want Oaklyn to be here. Living with me. Experiencing life within these walls, at my side, the two of us together.* And I could have just purchased it, signed the deal, and brought you over. I didn't want that. I wanted you to look around and see if you loved the space as much as I do. If you could see yourself being here." I moved my lips closer to hers. "With me."

Her eyes filled with emotion. "Camden ..."

"*More* is a word that's weighed on me. It could mean so many different things. But I knew when I came to this house, *more* meant sharing this spot with you. It meant taking that step. It meant saying the words that I've been feeling. Oaklyn" —I bit my lip because I was so fucking tempted to bite hers—"I love you. I think I've loved you since we were teenagers. And I want this. I want us. Even if it's not right now or next week or, hell, even in the next few months, I want us to be in this home together."

"I love you too," she cried. "Camden, I think I've always loved you. I've wanted us since as long as I can remember. To be able to say those words to you. To be able to kiss you." The first tear dripped from her eye. "The view isn't just a dream. Being with you—that's the dream."

"I'm yours."

"I still can't believe it." She blinked away another tear. "There's no better feeling."

I ran my thumbs under her eyelids, catching the drops before those fell. "This house is coming fully furnished. Everything in here will be mine. I did that on purpose. I didn't want to bring what's in my condo because that's mine or what's in your apartment since that's yours. I want us to design this home together, to pick out what we like. Until that happens, we have a place to sit, and a table to eat at, and a bed to sleep on, and art and decor to look at." I kissed her softly. "There's no rush. We have all the time in the world."

She circled my neck and hugged her body against mine. "I love you. I know you just said it, and I did, too, but now, it's my turn to take that lead. And getting to just say it ... I can't even describe what it's like."

"You don't have to." I held the back of her head. "I already know."

I squeezed her so tightly while my face was pressed into her neck, my eyes closing as my hands climbed down her body, moving to her ass. "This is our room tonight."

"We're staying here?"

"The paperwork is on my phone. The second I sign and the money is transferred, the house is mine."

She leaned back to look at me. "Really? That fast?"

"Yes."

She gazed around the bedroom and out the window before connecting our stares. "I really can't believe it. It's all so gorgeous. And I know there's lots more in this house that you haven't shown me, and I can't wait to see all of those rooms too."

My hands rose to her neck. "Do you have any second thoughts, any worries—"

"No. Wait, I take that back." She gradually filled her lungs, the happiness fading from her expression. "Hannah is definitely a worry. What if she hates us? What if she wants nothing to do with me and despises you for this? What if ..." Her voice drifted off, like the next thing she was about to say was just too hard.

"Oaklyn, your trip with her is coming up soon. We're telling her the second you guys get back. If things turn rocky, we'll go a little slower. We'll keep working on her. We'll show her why we're meant to be together. Eventually, she'll come around."

I was trying to be as positive as I could.

But I'd be lying if I said I wasn't worried.

And I knew I was doing this backward. Hannah should be told before I signed the closing documents. But, goddamn it, it just wasn't working out that way. If their trip hadn't been planned, then the conversation with my sister would have already happened.

I won't regret this, I kept telling myself.

Despite how fucked up the timing was and the order of the

way everything was going down, I wanted Oaklyn, I wanted this house, and I wanted it for us.

I just hoped Oaklyn wouldn't have any regrets.

I just hoped that however things ended up with my sister, Oaklyn wouldn't grow to resent me.

And I just wished more than anything that I knew how Hannah was going to react.

Fuck.

She slowly nodded. "Okay."

"Are you sure?"

She sucked in a breath, one that was so deep that I felt it. "The only thing I'm sure of is that I love you."

A smile grew across my lips. "That's all I needed to hear." I glanced at my watch. "Craig should be arriving just about—" My voice cut off when I heard the front door open. "Never mind. He's here."

"Who's Craig?"

"Dominick, Jenner, and Ford's private chef."

Her brows rose. "And he's cooking dinner for us? Here? Tonight?"

I gave her a kiss, growling, "I hope you're hungry."

"You're unbelievable."

I kissed her again and then found her hand, locking our fingers together before I brought her into the kitchen, where Craig was starting to set up.

"Welcome," I said to him and shook his hand. "Craig, this is Oaklyn, my girlfriend."

"Nice to meet you, Oaklyn." The moment he released her, he voiced, "Nice place you have here and one hell of a kitchen. I'm excited to cook in it."

"Thanks for coming," I said.

"I was able to get all your requests. Dinner should be ready in about an hour and a half. We'll start with some appetizers. I need about thirty minutes for those. Thirsty?"

"Yes," Oaklyn replied.

"I found some great wines that'll pair well with what I'm making tonight." He opened one of the bottles and filled two glasses he'd found in a cabinet. "Cheers."

"Cheers," I replied. I handed one of the glasses to Oaklyn and took the other for myself.

I brought her outside onto the patio. I turned on the fire that ran along the back of the pool, along with the fireplace that was in the sitting area, and I put on the pool lights before joining her on the couch. My arm slipped over her shoulders as we took in the sick view.

"Pretty magnificent, isn't it?"

"That's quite an understatement, Mystery Man." She smiled as she looked at me. "I'm still in shock that I'm going to live here with you someday."

"Whenever you're ready."

She exhaled, gripping the wine like it was going to fall. "Really?"

"Again, it doesn't have to happen right away, but, yes, really. That's what I'd like." I held her chin, tugging her bottom lip with my thumb. "You're going to be my wife one day. And then everything I've built—the condo, the others I plan to buy, the investments I intend to make over the next couple of years —it's all going to be ours."

Her eyes squinted, squeezing, and a whole new set of tears rolled past her lids.

I leaned into her face. "Yes. You heard me right. I said *my wife.*"

When her eyes opened, I saw everything I'd ever wanted— things I hadn't even realized until Oaklyn made that proposition.

When Macon and Declan forced me to admit what I'd been pushing away.

When my whole life changed.

When I came to the conclusion that I couldn't go another fucking day without her being mine.

"I'm obsessed with you," she declared. "I'm talking next-level kinda love."

I laughed. "You say that now, but I told my sister I was meeting up with a realtor tonight who was going to show me a few places and that I fully intended on banging her." I paused. "Still love me?"

She pounded my arm. "Yes ... *dick*."

"For the record, I'm not banging you tonight, so get that thought right out of your head. But we are completing lesson four—something I've thought long and hard about."

"Oh, yeah?" She took a drink of her wine. "And what's that going to look like?"

"Something that's going to make you fucking scream."

TWENTY-THREE

Oaklyn

"Fuck me," Camden hissed as I walked into the bedroom, wearing the lingerie set my man had surprised me with.

Who would have thought he would be into something so sensual? I hadn't, but I certainly loved it. This one was a different style of nightie than the first one he'd given me. Still the same color green, but it came with a matching pair of boy shorts, and the material was all lace and see-through.

"Get over here."

He was slightly sitting up on the bed with an arm behind his head and his legs crossed, wearing only a pair of boxer briefs.

Every ripple and muscle on his body was on full display.

But it wasn't just the incredibly sexy sight that had me aching, that had my heart thumping, that had wetness already pooling between my legs.

It was also the bed that he was actually lying on and the fact that it was going to be ours until we picked out a new one.

One detail in a treasure trove of information I'd learned just a few hours ago.

And the best gift anyone had ever given me.

But that wasn't all. There was even more that had unraveled tonight.

Camden had told me he loved me.

Words that only reconfirmed everything I felt for him.

Words that I'd been dying to hear him speak for over half my life.

Words that I cherished.

Not only because they had come from the man who had my heart, but also because I'd never heard them from another guy.

Camden Dalton had so many of my firsts.

I stopped near the fireplace, feeling the warmth from the roaring flames, and I held on to the wall, giving him a full-length view of my body. "You like?"

"Not like. I fucking love."

I smiled, turning so he could see the back.

"You know, when I picked that out, I envisioned the way your body would look in it, and, fuck"—he shook his head as I faced him again—"you're even sexier than I imagined."

I glanced down at the outfit, my hand returning to the wall. "It's beautiful."

"Oaklyn ..."

I gazed up at him. "Yes?"

"Come here. Now."

My smile grew as I made my way over to him. Once I was within reach, his hands were on me, my giggle getting even louder as he pulled me onto the bed, his body now hovering over mine. His hard-on pressed against me, the tip rubbing my clit, the friction causing me to moan before he cut off my sounds by ravishing my lips.

"Oaklyn," I heard again. This time in a much deeper tone that also came with his hands roaming the lace that barely covered me and a bite from his teeth as he gnawed my lip. "I'm going to try something completely different with you. This might be a little outside your comfort zone, so you're going to have to trust me."

I took in the deepest breath. "You brought the butt plug ..."

He laughed, now holding my face. "No. We're not doing that tonight."

"Then, what is it?"

He reached across me toward the nightstand, opening the top drawer, and when his hand returned, he was holding a blindfold and two pieces of rope.

"I'm going to tie you to the bed and blindfold you." He nuzzled my neck with his face. "What that means is, you're going to have to rely on your other senses. You can't touch me. You can't see what I'm doing. You'll only get to feel." He lifted his face, our lips inches apart. "And I'm going to test you by using more than just my hands and mouth, and the only choice you'll have is to take what I'm giving you." I went to comment, and he continued, "Don't worry; nothing is going to hurt. It's going to feel fucking incredible."

My exhale came out as a moan, my body already ready to experience everything he'd just described. "I don't doubt that." The tingles between my legs began to spread toward my chest. "I've never been tied up."

"I have a feeling most of the things I'm going to do tonight, you've never had before."

"*Ohhh.* Now, I'm really curious."

He kissed across my collarbone and up to my cheek. "Any concerns?"

"No."

"Good. You're going to fucking love this."

He moved his legs to either side of me, straddling my body as he took the first piece of rope and looped it around my wrist. Once it was knotted, he then tied it to one of the slats of the wooden headboard and did the exact same thing to my other wrist.

I was bound, my arms stretched wide, the rope allowing zero give.

I couldn't slip my hands out even if I wanted to.

His eyelids narrowed, his mouth rising in one corner as he took me in. "How do you feel?"

"Tight."

"Interesting answer. But you're not uncomfortable?"

I pulled at my hands. "No-ish."

The blindfold was in his hand. "How about when I do this?" He stretched it over my head, securing the front across my eyes, the band over the back of my hair, waiting for me to adjust on the pillow before he continued, "You're still all right?"

I took a moment to answer, to really feel out my body, for the darkness to lighten, which, of course, it didn't. "It's a strange feeling."

"How about when I do this?"

There was heat directly on my nipple. Like the sun was shining above it, causing it to pucker, my back to arch. The fieriness only lasted a few seconds, and then there was wetness and lapping, a slippery feeling as my nipple was flicked back and forth.

His tongue. It had to be.

Followed by a strong blow of air.

"Oh my God," I gasped, trying to rein myself back in because, suddenly, I felt completely out of control. "Camden!"

"Just what I thought. You're going to fucking love this."

He moved to the other side, but this time, the sun was gone, and the only warmth came from his mouth, where he gave me a burst of hard, relentless sucking.

I wanted to grab his hair and tug it.

I wanted to reach down and fist his cock.

But I was tied to this bed.

And the only thing I could do was scream.

So, that was what I gave him.

"*Ahhh!*" I drew in more air. "*Fuuuck!*"

The second my voice let up, he gave me his teeth. He didn't bite. This was nibbling, where he added a short flicker of pain before he soothed it with something soft.

Something that felt like the swishing of bird wings.

Goose bumps covered me.

My breathing turned labored.

My legs spread, even more so as he moved his way down my body.

But those tiny pulses didn't leave; he just spaced them out on different spots, first on my chest and then slowly dipping vertically down my navel.

"What is that?" I asked, not realizing I was pulling at my wrists, the rope gnawing at my skin. Still, I couldn't stop. It was as though I needed the pain to offset all this pleasure.

"It doesn't matter. What matters is that it feels good."

"Oh God, does it."

"How about this?"

There was a wave of movement. A sensation that almost felt like eyelashes kissing my skin, similar to what my mom would do when I was a kid, but the distance it swept was much longer. Wider. And the feeling was a combination of tickling and this erotic buzz.

"I'm dying," I groaned, my back lifting, my head driving into the pillow beneath it.

"You just want more?"

"*Yesss.*" Just as I filled my lungs again, I yelled, "*Ahhh!*" This time because something freezing was on my nipple. "What the hell is that?" My back fell against the mattress, and the coldness moved to my other breast. "Ice?" I swallowed. "Is that what it is?"

"Wait until I press it on your cunt."

My toes ground into the bed as he dragged the cube down my chest and stomach, stopping at the top of my boy shorts.

"They look so fucking perfect on you. I hate to take them off." He gripped the sides of the panties. "But they have to go."

And just like that, they were gone from my body, my bareness completely out in the open, and the first thing I felt was air. Like he was blowing as hard as he could across my pussy.

"Fuck, you're gorgeous."

My legs attempted to close, but he kept them open, maneuvering some part of his body on each of my inner thighs so I couldn't move them inward.

"Do you know how fucking hot it is that I can tie you up and you completely trust me?"

I felt so exposed.

Devoured.

Desired.

And even though I couldn't see him, my vision filled with white fireworks on a black background. I felt his stare scanning every part of me.

"And how badly I want to be inside you right now?"

"You can."

"Don't tempt me, Oaklyn. We're at four, not five."

"But—"

My voice cut off when his tongue touched down.

Landing.

Wiggling.

On that fucking spot.

A feeling I'd never had.

And with it came silence.

Because I couldn't process.

I couldn't think.

I couldn't even react.

I could only take.

My hips lifted, angling him there, trying to keep him from ever leaving.

What he gave me was a slow, gradual lick that started at my entrance and lifted to my clit.

I didn't need more.

That was enough.

And it was more consuming than I'd ever felt.

When I could finally comprehend what was happening, when I found my voice, when I was able to release the feeling through sound, I let out the longest, most honest exhale, along with, "Camden ..."

"*Mmm.*" He was dragging the wetness from the bottom of me to the top. He wasn't hurried. He wasn't using strong pressure. He was just loving me there. "I've waited so long to do this. To know what you taste like directly from your pussy rather than licking you off my finger or yours. To feel your goddamn heat on my tongue." His voice turned to a whisper. "Oaklyn, you couldn't possibly be more perfect."

Just when I was going to moan.

Just when I thought this couldn't feel any better.

Just when I was positive there was a build happening inside me.

Everything changed.

It turned ... frozen.

"Oh shit," I cried. "Ah!"

The ice was on my clit.

But that wasn't it. There was a fullness now too.

One that came from a finger that was carefully sliding into me.

I wasn't sure, but it felt like he was twisting his hand as he dived in, hitting me from every direction.

"You're so fucking tight," he hissed.

I hadn't known the location of his face until his words hit my stomach.

"I can't get enough of you, Oaklyn."

The ice was circling my belly button, melting and dripping.

Down, down, *dooown*.

And he licked each droplet.

"I can't." I tried to hold in air, my head shaking back and forth. "I just can't."

"You're lost, aren't you?"

My head nodded. "So far gone."

I heard a crunch, assuming it was the ice he was chomping, and suddenly, there was something cold against my clit. Like little shards were stuck to the flatness of his tongue, which he was pressing onto me.

He didn't move.

He didn't lick.

He just stayed like that, his finger going in deeper, aiming toward that spot I remembered so well.

The one toward the inside of my stomach.

The one only Camden had touched.

And once things started to warm down there, when the ice was fully gone, he replaced the frost with speed. Pressure. Those came from his tongue, pointed at the top of my clit, rubbing it.

Horizontally.

With an amount of friction that caused everything—even my voice—to scream.

"Oh shit!" I shouted.

Waves were rocking in my stomach, sparks flying across me.

Moving.

Rising.

"Camden!"

"Let me taste your cum." He licked harder. "Come for me, baby."

My orgasm rose to a peak. It happened so quickly that I hardly even felt the climb.

It was just there.

At the highest point.

Holding me hostage, causing every part of me to shake.

Tremble.

Shudder.

"Fuck!" I screamed. "Camden, yes! *Yesss!*"

He began to move so fast—his hand, his tongue—licking me through the crest and past each swell until I turned still.

"That was so fucking sexy," he growled, kissing up and down my pussy.

He was soft.

Tender.

Just when I thought he was going to take off the blindfold and release my wrists, there was a new feeling on my body.

It took a moment before I could figure out what it was.

I was far too sensitive to differentiate what, where, and how —my senses getting mixed and jumbled—but after a few seconds, I realized it was the eyelash kisses.

Which, after a few sweeps, I was certain it was a feather.

It went over my nipples, rotating around them, over and under my breasts, moving from one side of my chest to the other until he was brushing it between my legs.

The touch of the feather felt like a whisper.

Light.

Fragile.

All I could do was moan.

"And you thought I was done." His statement vibrated across me because his lips were on my clit. "Except I'm not. I need to watch you come again."

He was in my head.

I didn't know how.

But he knew.

"What are you doing to me?" I said so softly.

His finger was still inside me, having calmed after I came, but it was now moving again, covered in my wetness, sliding with ease.

"I'm giving you everything I've been dreaming about." He licked me. Hard. "Now, give me what I want."

I no longer felt the feather.

All I felt was Camden.

His hand between my legs, his tongue on my clit, his attention solely focused on dragging an orgasm out of my body.

It wouldn't take long.

It couldn't.

Not with the way he was caressing me.

Driving me.

Pushing me forward.

"That's it," he growled. "Fucking come."

My body was desperate to take back some of the control, so I ground into the rope, burning my wrists, and I pressed my thighs against his cheeks until his beard was roughing up my skin.

Even though this all teetered on the edge of pain, I was relishing from the blend.

Lifting.

Bucking.

Urging myself toward his mouth.

Within a few plunges of his finger and taps from his tongue, I was shuddering.

"*Ohhh* my," I drew out. "*Fuuuck!*"

Once the words were gone, there were sounds that burst from my lips, shouting in every tone as I quivered past each surge, slamming into me like I was a shoreline.

The flutters were in my stomach.

My chest.

They even shot down my legs.

And I stayed there, almost suspended, halfway between the tremors and stillness, while he licked away, keeping me in that space until I fell.

Until there was nothing left.

Until everything turned calm.

"So beautiful." He was kissing my pussy. "Oaklyn ..."

"*Mmm.*"

"I want you to come again."

I tried to laugh, but I just didn't have the energy. "I need to touch you first."

"What are you going to do to me?"

"What do you want?" I asked.

"That's not the way this works. If I'm going to release your hands, I need to know what you plan to do with them."

I could barely think.

My breath was still coming out in pants.

"I want to use them to hold the base of your dick while I suck it."

"You want to give me head? Fuck."

A grunt filled my ears, followed by movement on the bed, and there was a quick squeeze of my wrist before I was released. The identical thing happened to my other hand until I was suddenly free.

I immediately reached for the blindfold, and he stopped me.

"Open your mouth."

I did as I had been told.

"Goddamn," he roared as he traced his tip around my lips, eventually sliding it in between them.

I closed in, running my tongue over his crown.

"Oaklyn ..."

The blindfold was gone, and I blinked as I got used to the dimness in the room, taking in the sight of him as he surrounded my body with his dick in my face and the look of hunger in his gaze.

A stare that covered every part of me.

I gripped his base and sat up just enough that I wouldn't choke.

"Now, suck," he demanded.

TWENTY-FOUR

Camden

My hands left my keyboard, where I'd been typing a reply to Easton's last email, to pick up my phone from my desk. A smile growing over my face as I read Oaklyn's text.

OAKLYN

> I'm not going to lie. Working from the patio with my toes in the pool is kinda amazing.

ME

> Think of it as your soon-to-be new office.

OAKLYN

> Don't tease me, Camden. I could seriously get used to this.

Leaving her in bed this morning after spending the weekend at our new house had been fucking painful. When my alarm went off, all I wanted to do was wrap my arms around her and bury myself in her warmth.

Monday had come much faster than I wanted.

If I didn't have to be in court on Wednesday, I would have considered calling in. But I really needed to be in the office, prepping for the case, and even though we hadn't yet moved any of our personal things into the house, I'd encouraged Oaklyn to stay. Her text from earlier had told me she was going to take a rideshare to her apartment to grab her laptop and more clothes and planned to return.

I was happy as hell to hear that she was back at the house.

ME

I want you to get used to it, baby.

OAKLYN

I guess it's still a little hard to believe that someday, very soon, we're going to be living here. Together.

ME

Technically, we can now. It is officially our house.

OAKLYN

Nuts. Seriously. Just NUTS.

ME

What's nuts is that you're so far away from me right now. I've been thinking about you all morning.

OAKLYN

I know. I wish you could come home.

See what I did there? ;)

ME

Seeing you call it that ... sexy as fuck.

OAKLYN

<3

How's work?

"Hey," I heard my sister say from my doorway, "got a second?"

I slowly glanced up from my phone, making sure my expression stayed as aloof as possible. "Sure."

She closed the door and took a seat in front of my desk. "*Sooo* ..." As she crossed her legs, a sly grin crawled over her face. "How was the realtor?"

My sister was fucking relentless.

If I wasn't trying to hide my relationship with Oaklyn, maybe I wouldn't be so annoyed by her question. But the excuse-slash-lie that I'd given my sister a few days ago wasn't going to be a conversation starter.

I pointed at the pile of files on my desk. "I'm drowning in work, and I've got court in two days, which I'm sure you know —you know everything." My gaze narrowed. "*Sooo*," I mocked, "discussing a situation that's never going to turn into anything can't be the reason you came into my office."

"Someone's cranky this morning. What, she didn't put out?"

I wasn't going to ask who *she* was.

I assumed my sister was still on the realtor topic.

"Hannah ..."

Her smile widened. "At least tell me how the house-hunting went."

Oaklyn and Macon were the only people who knew I'd closed on the house, and I'd stayed in that perfect bubble all weekend long. Everyone else thought I was still touring properties; they had no idea I'd secretly been working on this closing for weeks. If they did and they knew I'd purchased a house, they'd want to come over and see it, and I just didn't want my time with Oaklyn to be interrupted.

But the truth needed to come out since I'd be moving in next week.

"The hunt is over. I bought a place."

Her eyes widened as she reached across my desk, squeezing my arm. "Oh my God, I'm so excited for you. Is it one of the listings you sent me?"

I shook my head. "This house never hit MLS. It was a pocket listing, so I couldn't send you the information."

"Tell me everything about it."

I laughed. "How about I just bring you there sometime this week and you can see it for yourself?"

"*Yesss*! Perfect." Her grip lightened, but she didn't pull away. "I'm so, so happy for you."

I returned her smile. "It has everything I was looking for in a house. Size. Views. A sick media room. Since it came turnkey, I'm going to leave all my things at my condo and rent that place fully furnished—I'll make more money that way—and my plan is, over the next year, to pick up a couple of more properties and rent those out too."

"I love this for you. You're kicking ass, my brother."

"Well, I just know that as much as I enjoy law, it can't be my only gig. I want more."

"You're going to get more. I'm sure of that." She released me and settled back in her seat. "You know, I was over at Ford's house the other night for dinner, and it's funny; he and Sydney were talking about moving too. I guess they want a bigger place. And then Craig was telling us that he'd just bought a house as well. It seems everyone is hot for real estate right now."

Craig knew all about my new house and the private dinner I'd thrown for Oaklyn.

Since he was my cousins' personal chef, I'd asked him not to say anything to Dominick, Jenner, or Ford about coming to my place and cooking for us.

I'd tried to cover my ass.

But I wondered if he'd kept my secret since my sister was notorious for getting people to open their vaults.

I was going to poke a little and see if anything came spilling out.

"I saw Craig recently," I admitted. "He didn't mention anything to me about moving."

"No? Huh." She shrugged. "Where did you see him?"

"I don't remember." I attempted to look like I was thinking. "Jenner's maybe. The grocery store. I don't know. I'm drawing a blank."

Her brows rose. "You went to the store?"

"I'm not that much of a diva, Hannah," I groaned. "Besides, I do eat. A lot."

"Obviously. I just figured you had your housekeeper do your shopping."

I crossed my hands over my phone, hiding the screen—something I probably should have done earlier. "She does, but that doesn't mean I don't run in on occasion."

"Next step: hiring Craig full-time." She smiled. "I'm sure that's in your near future."

She was waiting for a response, so I gave her an honest one. "Most likely." I paused, deciding which angle to take this. "He didn't happen to tell you that he saw me, did he?"

"No. Not a word. Why?"

Her answer had come fast.

Her expression casual, her body relaxed.

I didn't get the sense that she was trying to hide anything.

"I don't know ... just wondering." It was time to change topics. "Anyway, why do I get the feeling that you have something you want to talk to me about?"

"I do." She sighed, her head falling back, and while she gazed at the ceiling, she took several deep breaths. "Oaklyn is going to kill me."

The one person I didn't want to discuss, but it sounded like Oaklyn was the whole reason Hannah had come in here.

"Why do you say that?"

She finally looked at me, and I couldn't tell if there was emotion in her eyes or something else. "Her gift for winning President's Club was a trip, and she invited me to go with her." Her head turned, giving me more of her profile. "Did I tell you that already?"

Is this a fucking trap?

Did Hannah and I discuss this?

Shit, I can't remember.

"Vaguely familiar ... maybe. Go on."

"We've planned this whole vacation—where we're going, what trails we're hiking in Sedona, and we even booked spa treatments and excursions and dinner reservations. I'm talking the whole nine, ya know?"

"Okay ..."

"And I just found out this morning that I have to be in court, so I can't go with Oaklyn. I have to cancel my part of the trip."

Fuck.

Oaklyn was going to be crushed. As much as she hated that she was lying to her best friend, I knew she was looking forward to their vacation.

"That sucks—for the both of you," I said.

"I just feel terrible. I locked her into these dates, and she moved all her meetings around to make it work, and now, I'm bailing."

"Can you reschedule your court date?"

She shook her head. "I tried."

"Then, Hannah, you really have no choice. I'm sure she'll understand."

"But here's the thing: we prepaid for some of the specialty

spa treatments and excursions, and they have a no-cancellation policy. I don't mind losing out on the money I forked over—this is my fault after all. I can't help that work is taking precedence over play, but what about Oaklyn? She shouldn't have to lose out—moneywise or funwise—because of me."

My heart was aching for my girl. "Talk to her about it. See what she says. Maybe she'll come up with a solution."

"I hope so." She leaned forward, almost holding her stomach. "Because I'm really feeling like the worst friend ever."

TWENTY-FIVE

Oaklyn

"*Hiii*," Hannah said as I answered the phone, holding it against my ear, trying to block out the noise from the terminal.

"Hey, you."

"Are you at the airport?"

I scanned the faces of the people sitting near me at the gate. Everyone was either occupied with conversation or on their phone, the space around us so loud and busy.

I still attempted to keep my voice down as I replied, "All checked in and waiting to board."

"I can't believe I'm not sitting next to you right now."

I took a deep breath to calm the flutters in my chest, where a mix of excitement and anxiousness was swirling like the center of a storm.

This was the first time I'd ever traveled alone for pleasure. I could have taken Camden—he'd certainly offered to go in Hannah's place enough times.

It wasn't that I didn't want him here.

I did, more than anything.

I'd just worried that somehow, someway, Hannah would find out. I didn't want her to. I wanted that conversation to go exactly as I'd planned, taking place the day after I got back from this trip, when Camden and I would drive to her house and confess.

A conversation I was dreading with every ounce of me.

But for some strange reason, my conscience felt the tiniest bit lighter by not having Camden join me on this trip. That even though we were doing everything behind her back, lying and betraying her trust, this vacation was honest.

It wasn't deceitful.

It was one less thing I felt wrong about.

Oh God.

I hated myself.

For all of this.

I squinted my eyes together and said, "I know."

"You're going to have the best time. It'll be a total unplug from work, life—all the things. And even if you don't make it out for any hikes—because, girl, I'm terrified that if you go alone, you'll be kidnapped, or you'll be eaten by some wild cougar or ten-foot snake—you're going to die when you see the spa. Jenner assures me that this hotel is one of the nicest properties that the Spades have."

I wrapped my sweater tightly around myself. "I can't wait."

"I need you to check in every couple of hours—do you hear me? I'm going to be worried sick about you."

I listened to the announcement, letting me know that I was free to board, and I grabbed my oversize purse and slung it over my shoulder, making my way toward the gate agent. "I'm going to be fine. Don't worry about me. I travel all the time for work—

you know that—so I'm used to eating dinner alone and finding my way around."

"My rock star. Your independence is inspiring. But listen to me, lady. Your hot ass had better still check in at least twice a day. I need to know when you wake up and go to bed, so I don't send out a search party."

I laughed. "Hold on a sec, Hannah." I exited out of the Call screen and pulled up my boarding pass, and the gate agent scanned my phone before I headed for the jetway. "All right, I'm back. I promise you'll hear from me twice a day." Since I was one of the first to board and there was no line, I made my way straight to my seat. "Are you on your way to court?"

"I am ... sigh. It's going to be a long couple of days, I'm afraid. I'd better see you as soon as you get back."

I placed my bag down in front of me and put on my seat belt. The weight of the strap felt like a thousand pounds as it crossed my stomach. "You will, babe."

"Fly safe. Text me later—don't forget. I love you."

"Love you too," I said and hung up.

I reached for my Kindle and noise-canceling headphones, and before I tossed my phone into my bag, I wrote out a text to Camden.

> **ME**
> Taking off in a few minutes. Miss you already.

> **CAMDEN**
> Fly safe, baby. Text me when you land.

> **ME**
> I will.

> **CAMDEN**
> I love you, Oaklyn.

ME

I love you more.

TWENTY-SIX

Camden

I f Oaklyn thought she was going to Arizona by herself, she was wrong. There was no way in hell I was letting my girl go on vacation alone to enjoy one of the most gorgeous states, where she'd be hiking and going solo to the spa. I just couldn't let that happen. The advantage I had was having access to a private plane that could land directly in Sedona, whereas Oaklyn had to first fly into Phoenix and pick up her rental car and make the drive into the desert.

She texted me when she landed, and that was when I started initiating my plan.

Everything I needed was waiting for me at the hotel.

Of course, having a best friend who was the CFO of the hotel brand certainly made that easier. There were bags of rose petals to be scattered across the floor and candles that had to be lit. A bottle of champagne that was waiting to be set on ice.

I made sure the front desk alerted me when Oaklyn checked in.

The scene down there would look completely normal to her. She'd be asked for a credit card in case of incidentals and given a key, but she wouldn't be told that I'd upgraded the room to the nicest suite at the hotel or that I was waiting for her inside.

The suite was over two thousand square feet, so there were endless places for me to hide. But I didn't want to scare the shit out of her. I wanted to be in a position where I could witness her expression when she walked in the door, where I could stand subtly and then make my presence known.

So, after getting notified from the front desk, I moved into the doorway of the bedroom and leaned my back into the frame. The bedroom was off the living room, kitty-corner to the entrance, putting me away from her direct line of sight when she came through the door.

Something that would be happening any second since I heard the click of the lock and watched the door handle turn. As she stepped in with a bag hanging over her shoulder and a suitcase behind her that she rolled in, the first thing she noticed was the rose petals.

"*Awww*." A smile grew across her gorgeous face as she followed the red trail, taking in the flickering candles that were also on the floor, her gaze rising as she scanned the room, where there were more petals and dancing flames.

"My God," she whispered, her head slowly shaking, like she couldn't believe what she was seeing. The movement sent pieces of her hair into her gorgeous face.

Fuck, I was one lucky man.

Even after hours of sitting at an airport and on a plane, driving to Sedona, she was still breathtaking.

The most beautiful woman I'd ever seen in my life.

And even though I'd told her, there was no question in my mind.

No doubt.

No fear of what would happen in the future.

Oaklyn Rose was going to be my wife.

She hooked the strap of her purse over the handle of her suitcase, sitting it on top and making sure it was secure before she stepped away.

It was in that moment, her quick second glance that stretched farther across the room, that sent her eyes to me.

A few seconds passed until she realized what she was looking at.

That I was really here.

And once it hit her, an expression moved across her face, one that was filled with so much fucking love. "Camden ..."

I smiled. "Surprise."

"How did you ..." Her voice trailed off as she ran over to me, throwing her arms around my neck, burying her face against my chest, like her question no longer mattered.

I lifted her into my arms, where she wrapped her legs around me, and I gripped her with nearly all my strength.

"I flew private," I said. "That's how I was able to get here before you." My fingers dived into the back of her hair, palming her head. "I know we talked about this. I know you wanted to come alone. I know you said having me here would add to the guilt you're already feeling about Hannah, but, Oaklyn, I couldn't let you do this by yourself." She looked at me as I added, "All I want to do is protect you. I can't do that from LA. I need to be here with you and know you're safe."

She scanned my eyes. "I remember, quite fondly, all the times you told me you were no Prince Charming."

I chuckled. "Well, the circumstances were different then."

"Were they? Really?"

She was testing me.

And it was so fucking hot.

"I'm assuming, based on your reaction, you're not pissed that I went against your wishes and popped up in Arizona?"

She held my cheeks, slowly kissing me. "No." She stared into my eyes as her hands pressed into my beard, her mouth close to mine. "And what I'm assuming is, all these petals and candles are a buildup to something that's in addition to you being here." She paused, giving her lip a quick bite. "This is the most romantic gesture anyone has ever done for me—by miles. In fact, you've shown me what romance is on a level I've never experienced. You love me. Unconditionally. And now, we're here, in this amazing room, which I know isn't the same room that I reserved for Hannah and me. Tell me, Camden, what's coming next?"

I grunted, my voice low, the sound drawn out. "We're going hiking."

She chuckled. "And then?"

"We have massages booked at the spa."

Her brows rose. "And then?"

"Oaklyn ..." I exhaled against her face. "We talked about this. We decided lesson five wasn't going to happen until after we spoke to Hannah."

"I know." She took a deep breath and tilted her body back just a little but continued to look at me. "But I don't want to wait. I want this." She gazed around the room, the most honest smile pulling at her lips. "I want this to be the memory I think of when I recall my first time. How you came here to rescue my loneliness. How you booked us this big, beautiful suite. How we spent four nights in the most luxurious hotel, taking in the scenery and getting every part of our bodies rubbed and scrubbed and all the other nonsense that'll go down at the spa."

I knew she wasn't done speaking—I could tell—but as the silence resonated between us, I took the opportunity to really study her face. The brightness of her blue eyes, the small slope of her nose, the plumpness of her lips. The sprinkle of freckles under her eyes that I could only see when I was this close.

She had almost no makeup on, and her naturalness was unlike any other woman.

Because Oaklyn wasn't like any other woman.

She was fucking perfect.

I'd been with many women before her, and not a single one had had her kindness, charm, her caring nature.

They never made me feel the way she did.

They never ever made me want more.

She traced the sides of my mouth, her chest rising, emotion beginning to fill her eyes. "I don't know what's going to happen when we tell Hannah the truth. I don't know what our friendship will look like. I don't know if her opinion will affect you and me." Her voice lowered to a whisper when she said, "Oh God, I hope it doesn't." That same emotion rimmed her eyelids. "I just can't predict what will happen, nor can I control it. What I can control is this trip. What goes down while we're here." She released my face, setting her forearms on my shoulders. "And this is what I want, Camden."

I was holding the woman I loved in my arms. I'd listened to every word she said. The picture she'd painted, the request she'd all but demanded.

Since things had turned physical between Oaklyn and me, I'd experienced restraint I hadn't known I had. I forced myself not to exceed what I'd planned for each lesson. And every time she'd spent the night in my arms, we did no more than just kiss because I knew once it went further, I wouldn't be able to stop it.

It hadn't been easy.

Hell, it had been almost fucking impossible.

I'd had a mental countdown of this trip, ticking away after

each day passed, knowing once she returned, I could finally be with her the way I wanted.

But, now, after hearing this, there was no way I could deny her.

Fuck, I didn't want to.

She was right; we didn't know how hard things were going to be after we told Hannah the truth.

We didn't know how much weight that would have on our relationship.

I didn't know if Oaklyn could continue to be with me if my sister didn't approve.

The only thing I knew at this moment was that over the next four nights, she was all mine.

"Tonight," I said. "After hiking, after the spa, after dinner, we'll come back up to the room, and I'll make both of our wishes come true."

TWENTY-SEVEN

Oaklyn

As I licked the last bite of chocolate off my spoon and stared at Camden across the table, the flames from the candle flickering across his face, heat began to pour into my cheeks.

Dinner had finally come to an end.

It wasn't that we had rushed through the meal or that I wished for it to be over.

I was just anxious about what was going to happen next. I couldn't stop thinking about it, and my skin was a reflection of those thoughts.

Out of all the amazing restaurants in Sedona, we'd decided to eat at the hotel, where I'd already had a reservation. It was highly rated with an excellent menu. But most importantly, it was in the lobby of the hotel, allowing us to just go downstairs to eat after the long day we'd had. Aside from traveling, we'd hiked the Cathedral Rock Trail and observed the gorgeous landscape of the stunning desert, and then we went for a two-hour deep-tissue massage, followed by a mud scrub.

Once we got back from the spa, Camden asked if I wanted to just order room service and stay in. But I knew we'd be naked before the food got delivered and we'd never get the chance to eat, and after the hiking and spa, we had really needed food.

And I'd needed wine.

"This was delicious," I whispered and set my spoon down. "Probably the best cake I've ever had."

"Ironically, I know the pastry chef." He lifted his vodka, taking a sip, and then kept his hand wrapped around the glass when he placed it back on the table. "Macon's uncle, who is also Jenner's soon-to-be father-in-law, Walter Spade, is dating a woman who's a baker. Gloria had a bakery in Miami and then opened a second one in LA, a third in Utah inside the Spade Hotel, and now, she supplies the desserts for every Spade Hotel across the country."

"Wow." I finished the rest of my wine. "The few times I've met Walter, I've noticed one thing about him. The man is an absolute perfectionist, so if Gloria wasn't outstanding at what she does, she wouldn't have earned this role." I pointed at the plate. "I can attest, the cake is just beyond."

"She's good, I know. And it's a hell of a small world because Gloria is Brett Young's mother. I'm sure you've met Brett at one of Dominick's parties. They're best friends, and Brett and his fiancée, James, come to a lot of the Dalton functions."

"*Ummm*, James Ryne?" I laughed. "Who hasn't heard of her? She's only the most popular actress in Hollywood and also the sweetest. Yes, we've met a couple of times." I leaned into the edge of the table. "Whether you've noticed me there or not, Hannah has brought me to just about everything. I'm sorta like an extended Dalton at this point." I lifted my spoon, eating off the tiniest piece of chocolate left on there.

"I've always noticed you, Oaklyn. You're fucking impossible to miss. I just couldn't act on it."

"I know." I nodded. "For some reason, Hannah didn't mention that Gloria had opened a shop in LA. Now that I know this, things could become dangerous." I smiled.

He laughed. "Don't let Hannah know you're cheating on her with Gloria. My sister gets a little possessive when it comes to her desserts."

"If Gloria makes Nutella brownies, I might have to break up with your sister." I smiled, but inside, that thought hurt.

I wasn't going to let my brain go there tonight, to think about Hannah and our friendship and the secrets I'd been keeping from her. Today had been too magical, and seeing Camden in the suite once I'd opened the door was the surprise of a lifetime. Something I'd never have expected in a million years.

But having him here, experiencing this trip with me, the moments and memories, were just what I needed before the truth was confessed.

Probably what we both needed.

I set my spoon down once again and reached across the table, linking my fingers over his. "Let's get out of here."

His eyes narrowed, his teeth grinding his lip. "You're ready to be alone with me?"

"Camden"—I added my other hand to our pile of fingers— "I was ready the night I made the proposition. I never told you this, but early the next morning, I climbed out of bed, making sure I didn't wake Hannah, who was sleeping next to me, and I tiptoed to her room, where you'd spent the night. I was going to tell you I didn't want to wait the year. I wanted to do it now. But you were already gone."

"You saw me plenty of times after that. Why didn't you say anything on any of those occasions?"

I shrugged. "Honestly, I didn't have the nerve. It's intimidating to tell the man you've been fantasizing about for over half your life that you want him to take your virginity."

The way he stared at me was making me wet.

"And now?"

"Now," I whispered, gazing at him through my eyelashes, "I'm demanding it."

"You're so fucking sexy." His sound was similar to a growl, and he called our waiter over and requested the bill.

Once it arrived, he signed his name across the bottom, charging the meal to our room, and we were immediately on our feet, his hand on my lower back as we walked to the elevator.

Since we weren't alone, we were silent during the ride.

But Camden's hands were far from quiet as he stood behind me, holding my navel, running up and down my sides, reaching across my chest to graze my nipple.

Inconspicuous, but dominant.

Powerful.

Maybe my body was preparing for what was about to come.

Maybe I was just more than ready.

But every touch, every breath I felt him exhale, made me tingle more.

I was lit.

Electrified.

Barely able to contain myself from moaning.

With each floor we rose, more people got off, emptying the small space until we were the only ones left, the doors sliding open when we reached the penthouse.

Camden's hand found mine, and he unlocked the door and moved us inside, instantly pressing my back against the nearest wall, his hands above my head, his lips aligned with mine.

"I need to remind myself to be gentle," he hissed across my mouth. "Because all I want to do right now is fucking ravish you." He was kissing across my jaw and down my neck.

Each time he landed on a new spot, it sent more tingles through my chest and to my stomach and finally between my legs, where they settled.

Sparks ignited within my folds.

And as I tried to fill my lungs, to come up with some type of response, I was suddenly in the air.

My legs around him.

My arms resting on his shoulders.

My hair cascading across our cheeks as I bent my head and kissed him. "Camden ..." I moaned, the taste of his lips as overwhelming as the feeling in my body.

We stayed still, by the door, wrapped in each other, as he held my weight like it was nothing to him.

And when I finally felt movement, I knew we were heading toward the bedroom, and that was only confirmed when the softness of the mattress was beneath me.

"I need you naked." His hands left me, only to strip off everything that covered me—my shirt and pants peeled away, my undergarments flung to the floor.

My bareness was on display as he began to remove everything he had on.

"My God," I groaned as his clothes fell on top of mine, revealing a body I still couldn't get over, muscles I found myself obsessively touching, a dusting of hair on his chest that I liked to rake with my fingers. "Your body is—"

"Yours."

I smiled. "Yes. That too."

My eyes lowered to his hard-on.

The thickness.

The length.

I knew both well, as I'd sucked his dick, but I just didn't know how something so large was going to fit inside me.

Nerves were already flickering in my chest as he eliminated his final piece of clothing, which were his socks, and he straddled me on the edge of the bed, moving me up the mattress until my head was on a pillow.

He hovered over me, holding my face, staring into my eyes. "I want to talk to you about something. It's something I've thought a lot about." When he glanced away for just a second, that was when I realized every candle in the bedroom had been lit. There were rose petals on the nightstand and more beneath me, beside me—I was sure they were even in my hair.

"Okay ..."

His gaze returned, and he took a deep breath. "First, I need to know, are you on the pill?"

"I have been for the last couple of years. You know, just in case it happened."

"As for me, you have nothing to worry about. I've always been careful." His stare deepened, reaching the furthest part of me. "The only thing I worry about is you getting pregnant, and it sounds like that's been solved."

"Yes."

His grip tightened on my face. "I don't want to use a condom, Oaklyn. I just want to feel you—your wetness, your tightness." He paused, his thumb rubbing over my bottom lip. "I don't want anything separating us."

My eyes closed as I rested my hand over his. "I don't want to use a condom either."

In reply, his lips were on me, devouring my mouth, parting me with his tongue. I could feel the restraint in his movements, the slight shift of his hips, his tip pressed against me, sliding each time he reared back and forth.

But he wasn't at my entrance.

He was at my clit.

Teasing.

Taunting.

"*Yesss*," I moaned the second his mouth left me. The feel of him down there was only adding to the tingles, making me breathless.

"Your clit is so fucking wet."

"That's how I was all through dinner."

"*Mmm*." He looked up at me as he lowered his mouth to my chest. "That's fucking torture, Oaklyn."

"I know."

He sucked on one of my nipples, causing my back to arch, his teeth forcing my hands to grip the blanket under me.

"Oh fuck," I gasped. "That feels ..."

"You've felt nothing yet."

He moved to the other side, flicking the tight bud with his tongue, grazing the end, gently biting it.

Every time he inflicted pain, I waited for it to get worse, but it only lasted the briefest of moments before he was soothing the area. Kissing. Caressing with the pad of his fingers.

His lips crawled to my stomach.

I felt the way he inhaled, not just with air, but the way he absorbed me with his lips as well, covering my ribs, my sides, my belly button, only stopping when he reached the top of my pussy.

His nose pressed against it.

And he took his time breathing me in.

"Fuck, I've missed you."

He was talking directly to my clit.

There was literally nothing hotter.

My legs spread wider, the top of my head nudging into the pillow, my hand going to his hair.

I didn't just twirl his locks around my fingers.

I pulled them.

"Camden ..."

His name had just left me when I felt the first swipe. It was slow, calculated. He used his entire tongue, lapping me like I was a dripping dessert.

"Oh fuck." I swallowed, tearing at his hair, especially as he went faster. "*Ahhh!*"

He focused on the top, using the tip of his tongue to flick across that sensitive spot while his hand moved to my entrance. There was more than enough wetness there, but he still dragged some more down, spreading me with his finger, getting me ready for his size.

Even though he was prepping me, he was still careful.

Sensual.

The dip of his finger made me moan, "*Ohhh.*" I glanced down, his locks the only thing I could see, aside from movement, his head lifting and lowering, diving in and out. "You feel incredible."

This was the second time he'd done this to me, so it was a feeling I should have known by now. Yet every lick felt new, as did his fingering, making his way past his knuckle, halting when he was all the way in.

"So fucking tight," he grunted and licked again. "I can't wait to feel that tightness around my cock."

I couldn't reply.

Because I was in that place.

Where he licked me to the point of being completely lost.

The tingles from earlier had ignited into these fiery flames that were rising through my stomach and into my chest.

My limbs were turning numb.

My hands were clenching, drawing the blanket up into my palms.

I just needed to hold on.

To let this sensation move through me since there was nothing I could do to guide it or stop it.

Nothing I could do to slow things down.

I was gone ...

And then I was instantly back because Camden's tongue was no longer on me, his finger the only thing touching me now, lazily moving in and out of me.

Just as I looked down between my legs, I met his stare. "What—"

"I'm not letting you come."

Air panted through my lips. "I was so close."

"I know. I could feel it—that's why I stopped. You see, if I let you come, your pussy is going to be sensitive. I don't want that. I want you to be so turned on, like you are now, when I give you my dick."

And I was just about to get it because he was kissing his way up my body and positioning himself over me.

The nerves were there.

I could feel them every time I breathed out.

But there was something.

A desire that was scorching through me.

A want.

A need.

A passion that was sizzling, reminding me of how long I'd wanted this and how I'd always wanted it to be Camden.

"I'm going to go as slow as I can." He held my face, pointing my chin up so our eyes were locked. "And I'm going to do everything I can not to hurt you."

"I can handle pain."

"This is different, Oaklyn. This is something you're going

to remember for the rest of your life. I'm not going to go fucking wild on you and flip you in all these positions and promise this is the best thing you're ever going to feel." He exhaled, shaking his head just a little. "I'm going to be realistic and say it's going to hurt like hell and you're most likely going to bleed, but every time we do it after tonight, it's going to feel better."

"Maybe if you weren't so big, this would be a different scenario."

He growled, smiling, "Never going to be the case."

"Always keeping it real, aren't you, Mr. Grumpy?"

"Would you rather I lied?"

"Definitely not."

He kissed me. "I didn't think so." His finger was no longer inside me, but it was still down there as he guided his tip over my clit and past my lips to my pussy. "*Mmm*. You're still so fucking wet."

There was more movement, and by the way his fingers were stroking me and then leaving me, I assumed he was taking some of that wetness and wiping it over his shaft.

"Slow," he said as he aimed his tip to my entrance. "That was a reminder for me—not you." His forearms were on the sides of my face. "What I need you to do is kiss me, and we're going to breathe through this together."

It was finally happening.

What I'd waited twenty-five years for.

In just a few moments, I would no longer be a virgin.

A thought I wasn't sure I could wrap my head around.

As soon as his lips touched mine, I felt the first jerk of his hips, a burning that moved through me as my body began to open, widening to take in his tip.

"Are you okay?"

He couldn't have been in more than an inch, but he had

stalled, allowing me to get used to this amount before he gave me more.

I drew in some air and let that out, repeating the pattern. "I think so."

But in all actuality, it was worse than I'd imagined.

This wasn't like a finger or even two.

It wasn't the slick smoothness of the bullet he had used on me.

This was a crown that was trying to fit into a tiny opening.

And breathing through it, like he'd suggested, was all I could do.

But inside, part of me was dying from the pain.

"Are you sure?"

Breathe.

I filled my lungs, releasing that air, and did it again. "Yes." *No.* "Give me more."

His lips were back on mine, his palms on my cheeks, his tongue slipping into my mouth as he inched forward.

The burning increased.

The ache shooting into my stomach.

"Baby ..." He pecked my lips. "You're doing fucking great."

"It doesn't feel that way."

His hands tightened the moment I spoke my honesty. "When I'm all the way in and I give you a few pumps, it's going to feel better. Trust me. This is the worst part."

I believed him.

He was the expert after all.

But, my God, this was brutal.

"More," I whispered.

And that was what he gave me, finally giving me some mental relief when he said, "I'm halfway in."

Two more forward leaps, like the past two he'd just completed, and I would have all of him.

An amount I couldn't even fathom, as I already felt so filled.

"I hate to tell you how good you feel because I know you're in so much pain, but, Jesus, Oaklyn, your pussy is fucking amazing."

I didn't know whether I wanted to laugh or cry. But I knew the sooner this was over with, the faster I could find some kind of enjoyment.

"More."

He moaned against my mouth. "Damn it." His teeth ground together, his jaw flexing. "You're so tight. So wet. So fucking warm." The feral look in his eyes was a level of hunger I'd never seen in him before. "I could come right now."

When I tilted my head back, needing a break from his stare, and said softly, "More," there was a searing pain that I hadn't experienced yet.

It rocked straight through me.

And I couldn't breathe.

Tears were bubbling at the corners of my eyes.

"Oaklyn ..." He was moving my face, lowering my chin until we were eye-level. "I know, baby. Just a few more inches, and you're there."

His softness.

Tenderness.

Love.

This was when I needed it the most, and he was giving it to me.

Everything he had told me he wasn't.

But he was.

"More," I said, trying to hide the emotion from my voice, trying to stop the tears from dripping. "Give it all to me."

He was mindful of the way he was making me feel, but he did just as I'd asked.

"Breathe."

I listened to his voice, the tears soaking my skin as they dripped from the sides of my eyes.

"I'm not going to move. I'm going to stay just like this until you're ready."

I had all of him now, and I could feel myself pulsing around him.

My body wasn't used to this foreign thickness or length, so much larger than the half of a finger or tampon that it got regularly.

And even though the hot flames were still there, they didn't get worse. In fact, as the seconds passed, they lightened just the smallest bit.

"Look at you. Handling me so well. And how many times did I say you wouldn't be able to?"

I knew what he was doing, and I appreciated it.

But I couldn't laugh.

I couldn't speak.

All I could do was breathe, and I wasn't doing a very good job at that.

"Your pussy is vibrating against me."

I nodded, the final tear falling, the sound that escaped me letting him know I could feel it too. And when enough time passed, when the pain just started to subside, I said in my lowest voice, "Make me feel good, Camden. Make me somehow forget about all this pain."

He kissed across both cheeks, licking away my tears. "Baby ..."

My entire body tensed, waiting for the hurt to return as he glided back toward his tip, almost fully pulling out of me, and then he sank right back in.

It was there, a dull gnawing, a sharpness that I'd never forget, but it didn't increase like I'd anticipated.

It stayed consistent.

And it was that consistency that I began to get used to.

"Ah." The reaction that came out of me wasn't drawn out, but it was raw. "Oh fuck."

His forehead pressed against mine. "Nothing has ever felt as fucking incredible as you."

My fingers were on his shoulder.

Biting.

Stabbing as he moved out and buried back in. Each time, I held all the air in my lungs, counting down the seconds for the moment he'd promised. The one where there was even a hint of pleasure. And even though his lips were on mine and his body leaned up, his hand trickling down my navel until it landed on my clit, I was still searching for that feeling.

It didn't happen immediately.

It took multiple swipes of my clit until I finally felt it.

Maybe it was just that friction, the combination that my body desired.

Maybe I really was getting used to his size.

But the tears had dried, and my breathing wasn't nearly as labored, and I pulled my nails out of his shoulder.

"*Mmm*. Fuck yes. You're starting to feel it."

He didn't ask.

He knew.

"Yes." I swallowed. "It's getting better."

"You know, I could make this last all night, and, fuck me, I wouldn't be opposed to that at all, not with how good you feel. But you're going to be sore, and all that would do is torture you and get you to hate this. So, I'm going to make you come, and then I'm going to carry you into the shower and clean you up."

Each stroke caused my head to hit the pillow. "Make me come." I needed that passion to fill me, that release, since all of this had hurt so much. "Make me come, Camden."

His thumb was grazing my clit, like his tongue had done earlier, and there was a burst that started to kindle in my pussy.

The muscles in his chest were constricting, his abs tightening. The sight was so hot and provocative that it was almost enough to get me off.

"You're getting wetter."

I could feel it.

But his hand was giving me what I needed.

"Oh fuck," he moaned. "You're going to make me come too." He leaned up more, his other hand now on my nipple. Pinching. Flicking. "Is that what you want, Oaklyn? You want me to come? You want me to fill your fucking pussy so I drip out of you?"

My head nodded over the pillow. "Please." I sucked in more air, the fluttering strengthening, spreading. "Please, Camden."

"*Fuuuck.*" He was going faster. Harder. "A few more pumps, baby, and I'm going to be shooting my cum into you."

I wasn't sure if it was the warning, but once his words processed in my head, the thought of running out of time, not getting a chance to come before he pulled out, made me completely lose it.

Shivers exploded through my body. The shudders were next, a build that was far more intense than when he'd been licking me. And it was all driving through me, giving me that release that I desperately needed.

"Camden!" I screamed, my fingers digging into his skin. "Yes!"

"Ah, fuck me, watching you come is so hot." His caresses turned a little harder. "It's my turn." His sounds became grunts, his movements more dominant until he slowed with just heavy spikes of motion. "Oaklyn, fuck! Yes!"

As I reached the peak and began to come down, I watched

the orgasm move across his face, the pleasure morphing into the most sensual expression. I could even feel the wetness gathering inside me, his cum mixing with mine as his thrusts slowed and eventually stopped.

I ran my hands over his chest and down his stomach, my body relieved when he began to carefully pull out.

The moment his tip left me, that was when I saw all the red.

Blood.

"Camden—"

"Don't worry." His hands were back on my face. "I knew this was going to happen. That's why I said we were going to shower and I was going to clean you up." His nose pressed against mine. "You were perfect tonight, Oaklyn."

My body was still reeling from the invasion, fighting the soreness, trying to find a normalcy again.

But it had been worth every second of pain, and I knew, next time, it would feel even better.

"I love you."

"God, baby"—he tugged my lip before he kissed me—"I fucking love you too."

TWENTY-EIGHT

Camden

"Do we really have to go?" Oaklyn asked from the backseat of the SUV, where my arm was tightly wrapped around her, holding her as close as I could get her.

Her question was everything I'd been thinking about during this short drive.

Because, goddamn it, this trip had been fucking perfect. Every second of it. From the moment she walked into the suite and jumped into my arms to when we took the final ride in the elevator to the lobby, her lips pressed to mine the entire way, our last embrace before we climbed into the backseat to get a ride to the private airport.

We'd hiked every recommended trail. We ate at some incredible restaurants. We spent hours at the spa, getting treatments I'd never even heard of.

And the best part, I'd gotten to lick, taste, swallow, and fucking devour every inch of Oaklyn's body.

Not only had I taken her virginity, but every time I was

inside her, I got her a little more comfortable with my size, I got her mind off the pain, and I got her to fucking scream on every occasion.

Days and nights of uninterrupted time with my girl—everything I'd wanted.

And now, we were headed home, where we'd tell my sister the truth about us.

I kissed the side of Oaklyn's head, breathing in her fruity scent. "We can stay."

"*Mmm*," she moaned. "I work from home. I mean, I can easily extend this trip forever. But can you?"

"No."

"I know." She sighed.

"I have an idea."

I was thinking ahead. I didn't care about the outcome of our upcoming conversation with Hannah; there was no way I was letting her go.

"*Ohhh*, yeah?"

"You're going to New York in a few weeks for work, I believe. How about I go with you? We can spend a few days in Manhattan and take the shuttle to Boston and do a couple of days there. I'll meet with the Hooked guys one of the mornings, and for the rest of the time, I can show you around my old city —assuming you haven't been and you're interested in seeing it."

She turned toward me, smiling. "Camden, I would love that more than anything."

"Me too." I ducked my face into her neck, securing both arms around her, keeping her in my hold, even after the SUV pulled onto the tarmac, only feet from where the private plane was waiting.

Since I'd insisted that Oaklyn cancel her commercial flight, we had the entire ride back to LA to ourselves, but depending on my sister's schedule, we were either going to her house tonight or tomorrow.

That thought, that fucking worry, that unknown, was creating the largest hole in my chest.

I loved this woman.

I needed this woman.

I needed her more than air.

The driver opened the backseat door, and when I didn't release her, Oaklyn asked, "Are you okay?"

I exhaled into her neck, my grip tightening.

"I know, Cam." Her fingers landed on my forearm, squeezing. "I feel the same way. Trust me. But I love you, and that's all that matters right now."

I growled at her words, holding them in my chest, hoping they would fill that gaping hole.

And I didn't release her, not until after our bags were loaded onto the plane. Once she got out of the SUV, I followed directly behind her, my hand going to her lower back as she walked toward the stairs.

As soon as her feet hit the carpet below the first step, she turned toward me and circled her arms around my waist. "I know I've said this a million times already, but thank you for surprising me. You turned this trip into the most amazing dream."

I held her cheeks, aiming her face up at me. "I'm so fucking in love with you, Oaklyn Rose." I kissed her softly and gently, and when I pulled my lips away, I reached down and grasped her ass. "Get up those steps. I need a drink before I text my sister and find out her plans for tonight."

Her eyes widened as she nodded. "That makes two of us."

She climbed the stairs, and I followed a pace behind, noticing that when she got to the top, standing on the landing, she didn't enter the plane. She just stayed there.

Frozen.

An odd feeling came across me as I looked at her back. From this angle, that was all I could see. "Oaklyn ..." I couldn't imagine what had caused her to halt, why she wasn't making her way onto the plane. If she was suddenly hit with anxiety or wasn't feeling well.

Hell, maybe she was about to tell me that she didn't want us to confess to my sister tonight.

I had no fucking idea.

But since she still hadn't responded, I tried again. "Oaklyn?" When a few seconds passed and I still didn't get a reaction from her, I moved in behind her, joining her on the landing. "Baby, what's wrong?" My arm slipped around her stomach, and I pulled her against my chest, staring at the back of her head, waiting for her to face me.

It was that movement, pulling her toward me, gripping her stomach, that earned me a reaction.

Her body turned rigid, like fucking stone, and she pushed my hand away, slowly looking at me from over her shoulder.

"Camden," she whispered, the fear in her eyes making me want to protect her. "Fuck."

Fuck?

Why ... fuck?

What is she talking about?

Where is this fear and worry coming from?

I didn't know what caused me to look over her head and into the belly of the plane, but when I saw who was waiting for us inside, when it was supposed to be just the two of us, I knew why Oaklyn was on the verge of a panic attack.

Hannah sat in one of the center seats with her arms folded across her chest.

Anger filled her expression, a glare mounting in her eyes.

Her lips were pulled into a thin, hard line.

I was positive she had witnessed the kiss Oaklyn and I had just shared outside—any of the four windows to Hannah's left would have given her the perfect view.

Not that it fucking mattered.

My presence in Sedona, along with the fact that we were boarding The Dalton Group's private jet rather than the commercial flight Oaklyn was supposed to be on, proved we'd spent the last four nights together.

That we were more than just friends.

Fuck.

Me.

"Hey, lovebugs," Hannah said, her voice carrying across to where we stood, causing Oaklyn to turn toward my sister. "How was your little vacay? Did you enjoy the desert together?" Her eyes narrowed. "What, you really thought I wasn't going to find out?" She shook her head, like a teacher scolding a student. "Come on. You guys know me way better than that." She nodded toward the seat next to her. "Why don't you come in? You have a whole flight to explain to me how long this relationship has been going on for and why the hell I had to find out like this."

My hand moved back to Oaklyn's stomach.

There was zero need for her to push it away at this point.

"I guess it's time to tell her," I whispered. "Jesus Christ."

Oaklyn clung to my hand. "This is the last thing I wanted. Damn it, Camden."

"I know. Me too."

She made her way onto the plane and took a seat across from Hannah, setting her purse on the floor. I took the spot beside my girlfriend, immediately calling over the flight attendant.

"Vodka. Rocks. And keep them coming," I told her.

"I'll have the same, thank you," Oaklyn said to her.

When it was just the three of us, I studied my sister's expression. It hadn't faded even a little, her edges harder than before.

I dug for the right words. Where to start. How to make her understand that betraying her trust and lying had been so fucked up of us, but that it was the only way we had known how to do it.

"I don't know if you're going to believe me when I tell you this, but we had every intention of coming to you tonight and telling you about us." I glanced at Oaklyn, worried that she was on the verge of falling apart. With the way her eyes were filling and her chin was quivering and her posture was sinking even deeper into the chair, I could tell she was seconds from losing it. "As soon as we got on the plane, I was going to text you and find out if you were free this evening. If you weren't, we were going to tell you tomorrow."

Hannah tucked her legs beneath her, resting her arms on the armrests. "Sure you were."

"He's telling the truth, Han." Oaklyn's voice was so soft. "I swear."

"And what were you going to tell me exactly?" Her eyes penetrated mine. "That you've been fucking my best friend behind my back for, what, months now, and you're going to dump her, just like you do every other woman? Camden"—her head dropped, her arms moving back to her stomach—"I can't handle you hurting her and treating her like you do all the other women you've been with."

"I'm in love with Oaklyn." I let that settle in, watching as my sister slowly looked up at me. "Yes, you heard me correctly. I love Oaklyn. She's nothing like all the other women. She's the only woman. And the only woman who will ever be in my life again."

She stared at me, blinking, processing, her gaze gradually

moving to Oaklyn. "Why didn't you tell me? You tell me every-thing—that's who we are. We share every single part of our lives with each other. Yet this is the biggest thing that's ever happened to you, and you wouldn't name him. You would barely even talk about him. Why?"

The first tear fell down Oaklyn's cheek, and I released her hand to catch it.

That simple graze of her skin caused her to look at me, love exploding from her eyes before she glanced back at my sister.

"Because you wouldn't have understood." Her answer was honest, raw. And the emotion in her voice and face showed just how hard it was for her to admit that. "Because if I'd told you I was in love with your brother, you would have said to me every-thing you just said to him. I didn't want to hear it. If it was a mistake, I didn't care; I still wanted to make it." Another tear dripped, but I let that one fall. "Because Camden is the only man I've ever wanted to be with. The man I've thought about since the day we met as kids. The man I wanted to take my virginity." She paused to breathe. "If I had said those things to you, you would have looked at me like you're looking at me right now. You would have tried to stop me. You would have listed every reason why I shouldn't have those thoughts." She looked at me one more time and said, "I didn't want to hear it, and I didn't want to be stopped."

"This was a better alternative?" Hannah shot back. "To lie? To do it all behind my back? Knowing I would eventually find out?"

"Hannah," I barked, "be careful how you speak to Oaklyn. She might be your best friend, but she's the love of my life, and you might not like how things went down, but know this: best friends or not, you will not make her feel worse than she already does." My teeth ground together. "And you won't make her feel ashamed of what we did."

While my sister stewed on those words, I returned to her line of questioning and said, "To answer you, I didn't think you'd find out. I thought we'd been fairly careful. I was sure that tonight or tomorrow would be the first time you heard or thought of any of this."

Hannah laughed. "You're kidding, right?"

"No," I voiced.

She grabbed her drink from the table beside her, holding it with both hands, and she leaned forward. "I've been watching. I've known for a while. And then all the little nuggets you two were dropping just confirmed my suspicions. Exhibit A, when Oaklyn wouldn't mention who Mystery Man was. Exhibit B, when Craig and I were alone in Ford's kitchen and he accidentally mentioned your name and the dinner he'd thrown for you two. At your new house, which you hadn't even told me about yet." She rolled her eyes. "Exhibit C, when we were all together last and you"—she focused her attention on me— "wouldn't take your eyes off my best friend. Exhibit D, when you"—she then shifted to Oaklyn—"turned into the heart-eyes emoji whenever I mentioned Camden's name."

"Hannah—"

"Oh, I'm not done, brother," she said, interrupting me. "Exhibit E, what about the last-minute trip to Boston you supposedly took this week, but you booked the private jet to Sedona?" She took a sip and placed her drink down. "That took me all of two seconds to confirm, by the way. If you were really trying to be sneaky, you would have taken a commercial flight. At least, I wouldn't have access to those flight logs."

I'd told Craig not to say anything to my cousins, but I'd never mentioned keeping that secret from my sister.

But that was only a small part of the truth that she'd unveiled.

She'd known for a while.

Probably close to the very beginning.

She'd certainly outsmarted me.

Goddamn it.

She crossed her hands in her lap and smiled. "The plaintiff rests." Her grin was so fucking sly.

"Just like Oaklyn said, if she had told you when things first started between us, you would have tried to stop us. Our beginning was a little unconventional"—I lifted my hand and cupped Oaklyn's cheek, brushing my thumb over the corner of her lips —"but it was what we needed. Things had to move at our speed, on our timeline. If things had gone down differently, I don't know if we'd be here now. Together."

I concentrated on my sister again. "Yes, we did it all behind your back. That's fucked up. We know that. Oaklyn has been a goddamn wreck over it. It's made me feel sick because, like my girl, I don't keep anything from you. And every day, we've talked about telling you and what that'd look like and what that'd feel like. Being in a relationship is all we want, but the thing we want equally as much is for you to support us." I nodded toward Oaklyn. "If she doesn't have that ..." My voice trailed off. "I don't know what'll happen to us."

Before Hannah could respond, Oaklyn said, "You've been my sister for more than half of my life, and for just as long, I've been crushing on your brother. I can't imagine how that makes you feel. To know that every time I'm around him, I'm growing more in love with him. That I give him something I've never given to another man."

More tears were dripping, and I didn't stop them. I didn't even catch the ones that rounded her lips.

"It's horrible; it's wrong. I despise myself for not telling you. Camden has one half of my heart, and you have the other, and to know that this was going to hurt you has completely shattered me." She reached for one of the napkins that had been placed by the tray of food under the windows and dabbed at her eyes. "I know what you're going to say. You're going to say if it shattered me that badly, why did I do it? Why did I continue to do it? Why didn't I come clean earlier?" She put her hand on top of mine and continued, "I couldn't stop it. He's everything I want, everything I've always wanted, and I followed that half of my heart, knowing how much it was going to destroy the other half. I should have told you sooner—I know that—but I couldn't. And I'm sorry. I'm so, so fucking sorry, Hannah."

The flight attendant returned with a tray of drinks, placing two glasses beside me and another two next to Oaklyn. "I'll check back after takeoff. We should be leaving any second."

I raised the glass to my mouth and swallowed down several gulps, keeping my eyes on my sister.

She was glancing between Oaklyn and me.

Back and forth.

With such an unreadable expression.

"You two had quite a lot of assumptions going into this, didn't you?" She crossed her legs, moving her hands to one knee. "You assumed I would be dead set against your relation-ship. You assumed you wouldn't get my support. Oaklyn, I know you're assuming this is going to be the end of our friend-ship. Why?" Her tone lightened, and so did her expression.

Even her questioning was peculiar, given that Oaklyn and I were guilty as hell.

"Do I need to remind you of the conversation we had our sophomore year in high school when I came into your room after the hot tub party? You know, when you told me to stay the hell away from Oaklyn and the rest of your friends and we pinkie swore on it?"

She licked across her lips, almost like she was trying to hide her grin. "Camden, that was ten years ago."

With my hand back on top of Oaklyn's, the other around

my vodka, I locked my grip on both and replied, "And? That was the ultimate promise between us. I didn't think it had an expiration date."

"And, even at that age, you were on a mission to sleep with every girl you laid eyes on. I wasn't going to let one of my besties become the topic of any locker room. So, yeah, I banned your ass from dating any of them. But we're not kids anymore."

I pounded the rest of the booze, set down the glass, and reached for the full one. "What the fuck are you saying, Hannah?"

"I'm saying that once the bachelor found the right woman, I knew you'd be consumed with her. I knew you would love her. And I knew she would become the one."

I shook my head, trying to make sense of this. "Okay ..."

"For you to be happy and in love, that's all I want." A smile tugged at her lips. "And to hear that the person you've chosen is the girl I love more than anyone in this world, I couldn't be more excited."

"Hannah," Oaklyn cried out, "oh my God, I love you—"

"Hold on." Before my girl turned mushy and threw herself out of her seat and hugged my sister, I needed to make sure I understood what I'd just heard. "Are you saying you're all right with this?"

"That's exactly what I'm saying." She pointed at me. "That doesn't mean I'm happy about the lies—I'm not." Her finger moved to Oaklyn. "And I don't appreciate not being told and having to fake a trial just so I could bust you two this way"—she winked, an expression that told me she was so pleased with herself—"but I hear the reasons you gave me, and after talking with you two, I can understand them much more even if I don't like them."

All this built-up anxiety.
All this worry.

Was really for nothing?

"You sneaky fucking bastard," I groaned. "You really didn't have to be in court?"

"Camden," my sister sighed, "this is one of the many reasons why I'll always be a better litigator than you."

I drove my hand through my hair, tearing at the strands. "I can't believe what I'm hearing right now."

Oaklyn was out of her chair in seconds, closing the distance between her and Hannah, and their arms wrapped around each other.

And as my sister looked at me from over Oaklyn's shoulder, she said, "You hurt her, and I will kill you. I don't care that we shared a womb; this girl means everything to me."

"I know." I nodded, finally giving her a smile. "You have nothing to worry about. I promise."

TWENTY-NINE

Oaklyn

"To date night," I said to Hannah, holding my glass of champagne in the air and clinking it against my best friend's flute.

"To date night," she repeated, smiling.

I then turned to Camden and tapped my drink against his tumbler of vodka. I did the same to Declan's scotch before taking a sip.

Thursdays had become the night the four of us went out every week, hitting our favorite bar for after-work drinks, which usually extended well past midnight. This was our eighth Thursday in a row, and following our first outing, I'd set one major rule, making the three of them promise not to break it.

No lawyer talk.

They'd been good so far and upheld that rule. But I could tell since the moment we'd arrived here tonight, Declan and Camden were dying to discuss Hooked. The trial was coming up very soon, and they'd been incredibly stressed, spending up to eighteen hours a day at the office, flying back and forth to Boston to meet with Easton, Grayson, and Holden—the partners.

So, during those long hours he was away from home, I'd not only been spending lots of time with Hannah, but I'd also been working with the interior designer and redoing our new house, choosing fabrics and finishes and designs that fit our style. And now that my lease was up, I was fully moved into the house.

A move that I loved.

That Camden loved.

And that Hannah loved so much.

She reached across the table and clasped her fingers around my arm. "Have you told Camden your idea for the bathtub?"

"She has," Camden growled, running his hand up and down my back. That was a conversation we'd had a few days ago when I explained how I wanted a bigger standing tub in our en suite, a size we could fit in together rather than the solo tub we currently had. "And she knows she can do anything she wants."

"But I've decided not to do it," I told her, glancing between Camden and Hannah, grinning. "Because I think I have a much better idea."

"Oh?" Hannah questioned.

"Instead of allocating the money toward a new bathroom design, I've decided we should put it toward a condo that I found. A super-charming two-bedroom, two-bathroom in West Hollywood. It's in the perfect neighborhood, where rental prices are currently exploding, and it'll get scooped up and rented in seconds."

Declan loosened his tie, pulling it several inches down from his throat. "Your second investment property. Big moves. I like it."

I looked at Camden again. "Except this one would be ours."

Camden slipped his arm around my shoulders and gave me a light kiss. "The first of many that'll be ours."

"If you guys keep it up, you're going to have more than a side hustle on your hands; you're going to have a full-time gig," Declan informed us.

"That's the plan," Camden responded. "And if Oaklyn doesn't want to manage it, we'll hire someone."

With Hannah's hand still on my arm, she squeezed. "You'd give up your job?"

I nodded. "I really think I would."

"But I thought you loved it?" she asked. "And you're their President's Club winner year after year. Would they even let you leave?"

I laughed. "Well, they'd have no choice, and you're right; I do really enjoy my job, but I'm starting to dig property management, too, now that I'm managing Camden's condo. I think, for a while, I'll still do both. But if we continue to add more condos to our portfolio, which is our goal, I might make the switch."

"And she's so fucking good at it," Camden added. "Dealing with the tenant, scheduling repairs, handling the rent, and bookkeeping. Shit, I haven't found anything she's not good at."

"Because she's a badass bitch," Hannah joked, gazing into my eyes when she continued, "But, for real, you are."

She was just about to release my arm, and I stopped her. "We both are."

"You're absolutely fucking right about that," Declan declared, swallowing the rest of his scotch. "You badass women need to keep yourselves occupied for a second while I steal Camden away."

I shook my head, smiling. "I knew it. I can see it on both of your faces. You just can't help yourselves, can you? Unplugging is virtually impossible."

Declan stood, pointing at his chest. "Hey, I made it how many weeks without breaking your rule?"

"You can talk shop at the table, you know," Hannah said to Declan. "Oaklyn won't spank you if you do."

Declan shook his head and clasped Camden's shoulder. "I'll spare her the details and leave the spanking for Camden."

"There's only one ass that gets spanked in this relationship," Camden roared in my ear, quickly kissing my cheek.

As I watched the guys disappear, I giggled, eventually turning my attention back toward Hannah, who had the biggest smile on her face. "What's making you so happy right now?"

"Everything. This. Us. The four of us." She lifted her flute. "This is what I've always wanted—my brother and my best friend to be completely in love, not necessarily in love with each other, but I'm all for it, and I can barely contain myself." She sipped and then sipped again.

After Camden and I had purged our truth on the flight back from Sedona, there hadn't even been a pause in my friendship with Hannah. Hannah and I got together the following evening to talk again, that time without Camden, and I went into detail about the proposition and a little about the lessons—something I knew Camden wouldn't tell his sister. I didn't unload every bit of it, but just enough so Hannah knew how it all had gone down and the baby steps we had taken. I wanted her to know that it wasn't her brother who had pursued me, that I was the one who had made the first move, so if she was going to be angry with anyone, it should be me.

But she wasn't.

And despite being upset that she had been lied to and kept in the dark, Hannah had understood where Camden and I were coming from and why we had made those decisions.

I wasn't sure it was even possible, but our friendship felt stronger because of what had happened.

Because of our new bond.

Because of the way our future was now intertwined more than the two of us had ever expected.

I laughed at my best friend, whose smile hadn't faded even a little. "You know, this is our eighth date night, which means you've known about us for over two months. This isn't exactly new anymore, girl, and you're all giddy like you just found out."

"Maybe not new, but it's perfect, and it just keeps getting better."

I lifted my glass and gently touched it against hers. "Cheers to that."

She took a drink and adjusted herself on the chair, fixing her hair before she said, "Now, I just need Jenner and Jo to tie the knot. Sydney and Ford to have a little one. And Dominick and Kendall to set a date."

"Isn't most of that in the works?"

Her smile grew. I wasn't even sure how, considering it was already so big. "Yes, thank God. As you know, Jenner and Jo's wedding is in a month. Sydney and Ford are trying to get pregnant and haven't set a wedding date—which I'm not supposed to know about, so vault—and Kendall and Dom are narrowing down dates; they just have to decide if they're going to have the wedding in LA or if they're going to wait another year and do it at the new Spade Hotel in Hawaii."

"Hawaii—not that I have a vote, but Hawaii."

"*Saaame.*"

I glanced toward the boys. I couldn't hear what they were saying—they were too far away—but their faces didn't have the serious expressions they normally wore when they discussed work.

"And you and Declan?" I asked, turning to my best friend again.

She put her hand on her heart. "What about us?"

"Something tells me you're on the verge of taking the next step with him."

Her eyes widened. "Why do you think that? Has Camden mentioned something?"

I shook my head. "No, nothing like that. It's just a feeling I have. He's obsessed with you."

"I'm more than obsessed with him, but I'm not going to rush him. Declan has to move at his own speed. The fact that we're even in a relationship is somewhat of a miracle—I mean, you know his reputation prior to me." Her hand dropped, but her grin remained intact. "Things are so good. I'm more than fine with that."

"Really? You're *fine* with it?" My brows rose. "*Fine* is a woman's least favorite word in the dictionary."

She snorted. "Listen, if he got down on one knee, I would scream yes. But I'm not giving him any pressure. I'm not even sending him hints."

"Like leaving wedding magazines on your coffee table? Or accidentally texting him engagement rings and telling him you meant to send them to me?"

"I would never."

I laughed so hard that my head tilted back. "*Mmhmm.*"

"Okay, I totally would, but I haven't. I've been good." She held up her hand like she was swearing in a witness. "We have tons and tons of time for an engagement to happen, and I really am the happiest I've ever been."

"I'm just teasing you." I winked and glanced at the boys again. "What do you think they're talking about?"

"Not Hooked—I can tell you that. Declan's wearing the wrong expression for that conversation."

"I swear, I was thinking the same thing."

"Who knows?" She shrugged as I gazed back at her, but she

was still focused on the guys. "Quick, talk about something other than them; they're headed right for us."

"Oh, I know. I forgot to tell you that I picked up some cake from Gloria's bakery yesterday afternoon, and I ran into Macon. He said he was heading back to Hawaii and wasn't sure if he could make it to our housewarming party. I told him Camden would be gutted if his best friend wasn't there."

"I hope you gave him all the shit. Because he has to be there."

"I did, and he's going to surprise him and fly back for it. And—"

"And who are we talking about?" Camden said, his hands on my waist, his face in my neck.

"Macon." As I eyed Hannah, the feel of Camden caused goose bumps to rise across my whole body, his heat spreading right into me. "I was telling her how upset Macon is about missing our housewarming party."

"I'm sure he's really upset," Camden said, chuckling, looking up from my neck, his hands moving to my navel. "That motherfucker is banging every chick in Hawaii."

"Here's what I don't get," Hannah said as Declan took a seat beside her. "Macon has all the money in the world. Access to the Spades' fleet of jets whenever he wants them. And he can't come back for your housewarming party? That's fucked up."

"It's the women, baby." Declan turned her face toward him. "He can't leave the women."

Her eyes rolled as she turned toward her brother. "That's really why?"

"Who the fuck knows?" Camden muttered.

But I knew he was no longer paying attention.

He was too busy nuzzling my neck.

"He's going to get the wrath of me the next time I see him," Hannah said.

I had to give it to my best friend; she was the queen of playing everything off.

Not that her brother was even focused on her at this point.

He was far too infatuated with me.

His hands circled toward my ass, his lips lifting to my ear, where he whispered, "We need to go."

I moved my mouth toward him. "Now?"

"Yes." His voice was a heavy, deep growl.

I slowly looked at Hannah. "We're going to call it a night." I sucked in a breath as his hand dipped beneath the table to rub between my legs. He was testing me, in front of his sister—my God, he was ruthless. "The guys, as you know, have to be in early, and I have a project I have to finish when I get home."

"*Suuure* you do, babe." She smiled. "But I have to be in court in the morning, so early is probably not a bad thing."

"Finally," Camden hissed as Declan and Hannah climbed off their stools, "I get you all to myself."

I clenched his fingers and gently pushed them away so I could stand, and I went over to Hannah, hugging my best friend good-bye before I moved on to Declan.

"You two be good," Declan said, stretching his arm across Hannah's shoulders.

Camden nodded at him. "I'll see you in the morning."

"Aren't you following us out?" Hannah asked.

"In a minute," Camden replied. "I'm going to use the restroom first."

She smiled at us and waved, and when they were gone, his hands immediately went to my waist, and he turned me toward him, holding me close to his body.

I licked across my lips, taking in the handsome sight of my

delicious boyfriend. "I thought you were going to eat me at the table."

"I was about to."

I traced my finger down his chest. "Insatiable. That's what you are."

"*Mmm.*" His gaze deepened and darkened. "I don't think I can wait until I get home."

My head tilted. "You mean ... to be with me?"

He nodded.

"Camden, we live only fifteen minutes from here."

"And?"

I laughed, but my voice instantly quieted when he took my hand and held it against his pocket, rubbing my palm over the hardness that was tucked inside there.

"Do you feel that?"

Based on the location in his pocket, the size, the texture that I could feel through his suit pants, I knew it wasn't his dick.

And the moment I realized what it was, my cheeks reddened.

"Yes"—I drew in more air—"I feel that."

"It's about to be inside you."

Wetness was already between my legs, but it began to pool. "Here?"

"Here," he grunted. "And right now."

THIRTY

Camden

When I wanted my girl, I refused to wait. I didn't care where we were. I didn't care what time it was. All I knew was that I had no desire to get in my car, drive us home, knowing full well there was a good chance we'd hit LA traffic on the way.

What I wanted was her taste.

Her pussy pulsing around my cock.

And her fucking screams in my ears.

We came here every week, sometimes more. I was already familiar with the unlit alley that was between the bar and the building next to it, completely hidden from the street. It was where Oaklyn had given me a blow job.

And it was where I was taking her now.

With her hand locked in mine, I led her toward the restrooms and out the back door, taking her toward the narrow opening.

"I remember this spot all too well," she said softly. "The night when everything changed."

Once we were several paces into the darkness, I turned around and pulled her body against mine. "Physically, yes, since it's the evening I took your mouth without it being a lesson. But mentally ..." I ravished her lips, and when I pulled away, I finished, "You had me long before that night, baby."

The moment my tongue entered, her sounds filled the quiet space around us. Oaklyn's moan was light, needy, consuming. And every time I heard it, it made me go fucking wild.

I felt the air for the wall and pressed her back against it, holding her cheeks for just a second, locking our faces, while her hands gripped my shirt, like I was about to let her fall.

She knew better.

Her grasp just showed me how much she wanted me.

"I'm going to fucking devour you," I roared.

I didn't care how loud we were—the street out front would drown out all our noise.

I reached down, tracing the sides of her thighs, searching for the bottom of her dress. Once I was underneath it, I hissed as I touched her bare cunt. "No panties." I gave her my lips again. "Did you know I was going to fuck you in this alley?" I swiped my thumb across her clit.

"I didn't know it was going to happen here, but I knew there was a possibility. With you, there's always a possibility."

I ground my thumb into the same spot, where she was already so fucking wet. "Someone's turned on."

She held my arm, trying to push me deeper between her legs. "I need you."

"Is that what you were thinking about at the table? How badly your pussy needs me? How good it's going to feel when I fuck you?"

She leaned her head back, and my mouth immediately

went to her throat. "As soon as you started touching me, I couldn't get the wetness to go away."

I traveled a little lower, her clit already hardening. "Where did it start ... here?"

"*Yesss.*"

I reached into my pocket and took out the butt plug that I'd brought with me. I fucking loved her ass. Whether I was giving her a finger or a plug or the tip of my cock—all of it was sexy.

All of it turned me on.

All of it made her come so goddamn hard.

"And did it drip all the way down to here?" I was now at her pussy, teasing it with the top of my finger, not going in more than my nail before I pulled back out.

She gripped my arm even harder, trying to drive me in deeper. "More."

"Tell me." My lips vibrated against her throat. "Tell me you want me to fuck you, Oaklyn."

"Please." Her voice sounded like a gasp. "Camden, I need you. Please."

I was so hard that my cock ached.

Every whine, every breath that came out of her, just made me want to unzip my pants and bury myself inside her.

"I've already heard that you need me," I growled. "I need to know why. I need to know how fucking badly."

Her hands were on my belt, button, zipper. She was reaching inside the space she'd just undone, through the hole of my boxer briefs, where she fisted my cock. "I'm going to show you instead, so you can feel just how much I need you."

Before I could respond, before I could demand an order out of her, her lips were surrounding my tip, sucking the bead of pre-cum from my head, swallowing it.

"*Fuuuck,*" I exhaled, my balls tightening, my entire body reeling as she pumped her mouth down my shaft. "That's it." I held her hair in my fist. I didn't even need to direct her—she knew just how I liked it. "Is this how hard you want me to fuck you?"

Her suction increased.

"And is this how fast?"

Her hand was working around the bottom of my dick while her mouth could only handle the top. But what she did there, the way she swiveled her tongue and mashed her lips against me, even using her cheeks, was one of the best fucking feelings in the world.

And the way she was going at it, I could easily blow my load down her throat.

I wasn't going to do that.

I was going to save it for her cunt.

But this tease was fucking everything, and it showed me exactly what she wanted.

While she was down there with her mouth open, I was going to give her one more thing to suck.

I popped my cock out from her lips and fed her the butt plug. "Suck this. Get it so fucking wet that it'll slide right into you."

I couldn't see her face, her eyes, the hunger or need, but as I held the base of the plug, I felt the saliva from each bob of her lips. I heard the sounds it made as she used the same suction as she had on me. And when the metal was just the way I wanted it, dripping and lubed, I brought her back up to her feet, my hand instantly returning to her pussy.

It was even wetter than before.

"*Mmm.*" I flicked her clit before cupping her pussy, two fingers going straight inside her. "Oh, yes, you're so fucking ready for me." I twisted my hand, giving her friction from every angle. "You like having me in your mouth. I can feel how much it turns you on."

She was against the wall again, the shadow of her body telling me she was spread across it.

Waiting.

Taking everything I was giving her.

"It's one of my favorite things to do to you."

"Yeah?" I lifted her leg and wrapped it around my waist, this position giving me much more access, and I ran the plug around that tight, forbidden hole. "What are the others?"

Her breathing was heavier now. It always turned more labored when I got close to this spot.

"Riding you." She sighed and drew in more air. "When I take away your control and you become vulnerable and I get to watch you come inside me."

Goddamn it, that was one of my favorites too.

"I fucking love when you talk dirty to me, Oaklyn."

I also loved to see her bounce over my cock when she was in the position she'd just described, her tits in my face, each drive pulling the cum out of me.

"Fuck yes." I pushed the tip into her, feeling her body tense even though she was used to this by now. "What's another?"

Her hand returned to my shaft, the slickness still there from her mouth, her fingers stroking my length. "When I kiss every inch of your body."

"Yes"—my lips were right above her mouth, smelling the tangerine and blueberry coming off her skin—"that."

She winced for just a second while I gently steered it the rest of the way into her ass, her noise then changing to moans. "Ah! Fuck!"

My girl liked this as much as I did.

When I filled every crevice on her body.

I held the base until I was positive it was secure before I released it to go to her clit, brushing that spot from top to bottom, back and forth.

"Oh God, yes." She arched into me, her leg latching on to the back of mine. "And you know what else I love about kissing your body? When I get on my hands and knees and I get to tease you with my body. When I put my ass in your face and kiss down your legs. When I drag my breasts over your dick and kiss up your stomach."

"Oaklyn ..."

Her fingers were moving faster, holding me harder, her other hand on my sac.

Tickling.

Urging.

"Fuck me, Camden. Don't make me wait ... I need you."

My fist pounded the brick above her head, and I took her mouth again, needing to taste the dirtiness of her words. Needing to feel the tongue that had just made my cock feel so fucking good.

I couldn't taunt us anymore.

I needed her just as much as she needed me.

"Take it," I told her. "Put my dick where you want it."

She lifted her hips, sliding my crown down her clit, stopping when she reached her pussy. "*Yesss.*" It wasn't even in yet; she was just anticipating the way it was going to feel.

"You love that dick, baby."

Her heat was already surrounding me. It was coming out just like her wetness, coating me as she pushed me in.

"*Ohhh* shit." I held her waist. "You're so tight." I thrust all the way in and stayed fully submerged while she pulsed around me, gripping me from the inside.

"Camden ..." There was so much pleasure in her voice. "More."

There was nothing hotter than hearing her beg for me.

I grabbed her hands and held them above her head. "I want to fucking pound your pussy."

323

"Please. I need it ... hard."

Jesus Christ.

There was no woman more perfect for me than Oaklyn Rose.

I didn't hesitate.

I just lifted her into my arms, wrapping her other leg around my waist, and I slammed my dick into her tiny little body, pulling out and doing it all over again. "Goddamn, you feel amazing."

She was almost weightless, and every time I reared my hips up, I held her higher in the air and drove her toward me, meeting in the middle.

"Don't stop," she cried. "I need it harder."

Harder would make me come.

I didn't want to do that yet.

I wanted to enjoy every second of this.

So, I turned us around and leaned the top of my back against the wall, extending my legs out so she was almost straddling me. "Show me how hard you want it."

She circled her arms around my neck and used my shoulders to rock herself over me, grinding against my cock. "*Ahhh!*" She filled her lungs. "Camden, yes!"

She was close.

I could tell by her movements, the way she was getting wetter.

I reached down and touched her clit. It was like a fucking button; the moment I pressed it, she began to buck, rotating, sliding, my shaft now hitting every angle inside her.

Even her G-spot.

"Oaklyn," I grunted, trying to hold off my orgasm, the intensity in my balls becoming dangerously close to releasing. "Come. Now."

I flicked her clit, and within a few more swipes, she was lost.

Screaming throughout the alley.

The combination of the butt plug and her clit and the stroking into her pussy was like an explosion. The tingles owned her, so much so that her rhythm faded, and that was when I took over the movements.

"*Fuuuck!*"

I swore I shouted the same word, but it was her voice that I heard in my ears, her breath that I tasted across my lips.

Her stomach shuddered, her arms loosened, her cum made me slide in even easier. I turned her around, putting her back on the wall, and I started my sharp climb.

"How did that feel?" I propelled forward, twisted my hips, and released back, using that pattern, but my power built with each plunge.

"It's still not over." She couldn't catch her breath. "It's as relentless as you."

"It needs to hurry. I'm about to give you another."

"No—"

"You know better than to say that word to me." I aligned my nose with hers. "You're going to come with me. And you're going to fucking scream when it happens."

"Camden!"

There were no surprises when it came to her body.

I knew it better than she did.

What steps it took to get her where I needed her.

What she desired.

What motion brought her there the fastest.

That was why I used the wall to hold her weight and slipped a hand down the front of her, playing with her clit at the same time.

Just when I did, the spark was back in my balls, trickling into my stomach. "You'd better fucking come."

Her face moved into my neck, and she lifted herself higher. "I'm so close."

"I know. That's why I'm telling you. Come. Now." With the pad of my finger, I gave her clit a harder spank and picked up my speed, pushing through her tightness. "There it is," I moaned the second I felt her tighten around me. "Just what I wanted."

"Oh! Fuck!"

She was shaking over my dick, her navel a mess of shudders, and I sank myself all the way in, that stillness everything that I needed because what was happening inside her was so fucking strong.

"You're milking me, Oaklyn."

Just like her mouth every time it was around my tip.

Now, it was her pussy, demanding my orgasm, pulling it from me.

And I gave it to her, shooting my first load into her cunt, tilting my hips back and thrusting forward when a second shot came out of me and a third.

"Fuck!" I exhaled, inhaled. "Fuck!" I yelled again, emptying myself, draining every goddamn drop until there was nothing left.

For either of us.

Just calmness and breaths.

"Fuck me, you're amazing," I whispered against her lips.

I didn't let go of her.

I didn't pull out.

I didn't set her on her feet.

I stayed frozen, wrapped in her.

Exactly where I wanted to be.

"Stop taking my words," she replied. "You know I love you more than anything."

I kissed her.

Hard.

My lips, the feel of them, the way I held them against her—it was stronger than any response I could ever say.

And when I pulled away, I was quiet for a moment. "Is it time to go home?"

"We don't have to. I'm sure there're plenty of other alleys on this street you can take me into."

I smiled at her answer, which only reconfirmed how perfect she was for me. "You know what that means?"

"No?"

I reached around and touched the plug that was still inside her. Tapping the base. Turning it just a little. "I'm keeping this right here until I replace it with my cock."

EPILOGUE

Camden

The house was fucking perfect. Oaklyn had worked with our interior designer, replacing all the art and furniture that had come with the home, many of the finishes that existed, the wall paint and wallpaper, creating a feel and mood that was everything we had been looking for.

The most important part was that she was here, living with me, and I got to wake up next to her every morning and hold her in my arms when I went to bed.

She was the best thing in my life.

The sunshine to my goddamn grumpiness.

The one thing I never let go of, no matter what happened, no matter how hard things got, no matter what highs and lows we faced.

I would fight for her.

Protect her.

Love her for eternity.

Oaklyn Rose was the woman of my dreams.

And, as I stood with my cousins—Dominick, Jenner, and Ford—along with Declan in the living room, I watched her walk around the open floor plan of our home, making sure everyone attending our housewarming party had something to eat and drink, ensuring there was nothing they wanted for.

My girl was always worried about the happiness of those around her before she considered herself.

Fuck, I loved that about her.

Because that meant I could focus solely on her happiness, giving her everything I thought she needed.

And all the things I just wanted to spoil her with.

"Get over here," I growled as she passed me, wrapping my arms around her waist, pulling her back against my chest, burying my face in her neck. "I've missed you."

"Could you be any cuter, my love?"

"*Mmm.*" I kissed her cheek, inhaling that fruity scent I still couldn't get enough of. "Are you having fun?"

She'd organized the entire party, down to the food that Craig was serving to the booze that would be poured. She'd worked with a party planner to set up all the tables and chairs, coordinating the servers and bartenders, the flower arrangements, and music.

There was nothing she'd forgotten.

"It looks like everyone is having a blast," she said, scanning the crowd, "so, yes, I'm having fun."

"Oaklyn ... Oaklyn," I groaned. "This party is for us, baby, not everyone else."

"You know how I am."

She winked as she turned around to face me, and just as I was about to reply, Dominick and Kendall popped into our conversation.

Dominick casually draped his arm across Oaklyn's shoulders. "Amazing party," he told her. "Top-notch. And what you've done to the house? Shit, I'm impressed."

"Thank you," Oaklyn replied, beaming from his compliment.

"Girl, you're incredible at party planning," Kendall said to her. "Maybe, if you're feeling up to it, you could help plan our wedding?"

"Honestly, I would love that," Oaklyn replied, and then she grabbed Hannah as my sister was about to walk by. "I'm going to help plan this one's wedding too." Oaklyn raised Hannah's hand to her face. "My God, this ring is stunning." She smiled as she looked at my twin. "My bestie is engaged. I still can't get over it."

"Neither can I, girl," Hannah responded. "Declan did good, and he planned the best weekend of my life. Maui, sand, sun, and cocktails. It couldn't have been more perfect. And if it wasn't for this party, we'd still be there."

"Happy you made your way back for us," Oaklyn said to her.

"How about the three of us meet for wine next week?" Kendall said to Hannah and Oaklyn. "We can talk about all of our wedding ideas." Kendall then looked at Dominick and grinned. "We've finally picked a location for ours." When she glanced back at Oaklyn, she said, "It's going to be in Hawaii."

"*Yesss!*" Oaklyn sang. "Hannah and I were hoping you would go that route. Macon says it's going to be the most unbelievable hotel and the views will be magnificent."

"What did Macon promise?" my best friend said as he joined us.

Of course, the motherfucker had come back to LA to surprise me for the party—a move that I'd semi-expected. I had known he wouldn't miss it.

Macon didn't play that way.

Not when it came to me.

"Just that your new hotel in Hawaii is going to host the biggest, most luxurious wedding the first month it's open," Dominick said to Macon.

"No pressure, my friend," Macon said, laughing. "It's a good thing I'm only in charge of the build-out. The GM, who my brothers and Jo and Walter are going to hire, will handle all those details."

"What are you chirping about?" Jo asked as she heard her name mentioned, which dragged her and Jenner into our circle. "And what exactly am I handling?"

"Our wedding," Kendall said to her. "I mean, the GM you employ will hire all the staff to support the extravaganza that my future husband insists on having." Kendall placed one of her hands on Dominick's chest. "This one wants the wedding of a lifetime. If it were up to me, we'd elope."

"Babe," James Ryne said, now that she and Brett had joined our group, "you're about to be a Dalton. There's no eloping. There's only party after party to celebrate your special day, and I cannot wait to be there."

Kendall looped her arm through James's, and the two of them smiled.

"Guys," James said, "I have news."

"News?" Jo said to her.

"It'd better be a wedding date," Jenner said to Brett. "This has been the longest engagement ever."

"Hold on, hold on," Sydney said as she walked in our circle with Ford. "Don't leave us out. We want to hear the news."

James looked at Brett like he was the only person at this goddamn party. "We don't exactly have a wedding date to announce, but we have something just as good."

Oaklyn gasped, and my hands tightened on her stomach. "Is it what I think it is?"

James nodded and rubbed her belly. "We just hit our second trimester."

Brett looked at his soon-to-be wife, his hand on top of hers, cradling her stomach. "And we're having a girl."

"A girl!" all the ladies in our group screamed, and they reached for James, hugging her, coddling her, stroking her stomach.

"And we're having a boy," Ford told us once everyone quieted.

"Wait," I said across the circle. "You and Sydney are also pregnant?"

Sydney touched her belly, which was hidden behind a baggy dress. "We're just in our second trimester too. I'm at fourteen weeks."

"Oh my God," James said to her. "Our babies are going to be future husband and wife." She wrapped her arms around Sydney, and they hugged.

"There's way too much marriage and baby shit going on here," Macon said.

His brothers, Brady and Cooper, were standing behind him, the playboys that I once had been.

Before her.

Before my entire life changed.

Before all I could think about was making Oaklyn my wife.

"Trust me, you bastard, you're going to get tied down one day, and when that happens, we're going to throw one hell of a fucking bachelor party," I told Macon.

"Bullshit," Macon replied. "I don't believe I'll ever be tied down."

"No?" Jenner said to him. "You think you'll be single forever?"

Macon nodded.

"Let me tell you something," Jenner said to him while the entire group listened. "Declan Shaw believed the same thing. He told me endless times that he would never wed. That no woman would ever be enough for him." Jenner nodded toward the patio, where Declan and Hannah were now standing. The two of them had escaped our circle and were having a moment alone to themselves. "Yet look at him. Engaged as fuck."

"And very much in love," Oaklyn added, but she was gazing at me.

Oaklyn hadn't known that Declan was planning to propose to Hannah during their trip to Maui, but I had. I'd kept it to myself just in case my girl got too excited and somehow hinted at it when she was speaking to Hannah.

I knew because Declan had talked to me about it several weeks back during one of our double dates at the bar, where he'd asked for my permission to marry my sister. Hell, that was a question he needed to ask my father, and that was what I told him. But Declan said that he'd already cleared it with Pops and he wanted my approval as well.

I'd sure as shit given it to him.

Declan was meant to wed my twin. She'd never loved anyone more in her life. The two of them were perfect for each other.

And as they stood all by themselves on our patio, surrounded by a view of the Hills, I couldn't hear what they were talking about, but I could see their expressions.

Their happiness.

Their fucking love.

The rock on Hannah's finger that glistened all the way over here.

My sister wasn't the only one feeling completely content.

I was too.

And since Oaklyn was facing the group, I turned her around, and she wrapped her arms around my neck and kissed me.

"My God, this family has a lot going on. Four weddings—Dominick, Jenner, Ford, and now Hannah—and with Brett and James and Ford and Sydney, that makes two babies on the way."

She was going to get proposed to soon—she just didn't know it.

"Yes," I growled, and I cupped her cheek with one hand and slid my other hand into my pocket. "And you know what I have for you?" I found the button on the small remote and hit it.

Her face turned red when she felt the sensation in her ass.

My favorite color, aside from emerald green.

"You put on the vibration?" she whispered, her eyes widening. "Come on, really?"

"And I'm going to leave it on."

"Camden, you have to pull this thing out of me soon. I have a party to manage. You can't keep it in me *alll* night."

"You're going to keep it in all night," I grunted, "and when you least expect it, I'm going to find you. I'm going to drag you into our room. I'm going to lick your pussy. And I'm going to make you come so hard that you fucking scream."

Interested in reading the other books in the Dalton Family
Series ...
The Lawyer
The Billionaire
The Single Dad
The Intern
Or check out Signed, which stars Brett Young

The Playboy, which stars Macon Spade
Mr. Hook-up, which stars Easton, Grayson, and Holden from
Hooked

ACKNOWLEDGMENTS

My Bella, this is the first *The End* I've ever typed without you by my side. Thirty-plus books, and you were there for every one. Your face was always somewhere near my keyboard or on my lap or looking at me from over my screen. I miss those days more than anything. I would do anything to have one of those moments again. I love you.

Nina Grinstead, I remember like it was yesterday when the idea for this series was born and each of the conversations that followed. Just a simple idea that turned into this. A dream. A family that changed so much—for both of us. I never believed—I just couldn't fathom—but you did. You envisioned. You manifested. And you turned my dreams into a reality. Your belief in me is something I will cherish for the rest of my life, something I'll never take for granted. I promise I'll never let you down. Team B forever.

Jovana Shirley, I appreciate you more than words can say—even my words. When I email you at the last minute, you squeeze me in. When I throw unexpected projects your way, you find time. What that means to me, what that shows me—I tear up, just thinking about it. We've been at this a long time together, and I feel like we're just getting started. As I always say, I'm never doing this without you. Never ever. Love you so, so hard.

Hang Le, my unicorn, you are just incredible in every way.

Judy Zweifel, as always, thank you for being so wonderful to work with and for taking such good care of my words. <3

Chanpreet Singh, thank you for constantly holding me together, for being someone I can always count on, and for helping me in every single way. Adore you, lady. XO.

Nikki Terrill, my soul sister. Every tear, vent, virtual hug, life chaos, workout—you've been there through it all. I could never do this without you, and I would never want to. Love you hard.

Pang and Jan, I love you both so much.

Sarah Symonds, thank you for everything that you do, for being one of the most thoughtful and generous people in my life, for pushing my words and endlessly having my back. LY.

Logan Chisholm, girl, what would I do without you? You saved my butt on the last book, and you saved my butt again on this one. Thank you for being amazing, for your incredible insight, and for giving these Daltons—and me—all the love. XO.

Ratula Roy, I live for you. When you call me and lay it all out, when you compare the current situation to a book I wrote a million years ago—because you know, you remember, and you never forget. You found the hole in *The Intern*, and you found the hole in this one, and like always, you knew just how to fix it. I love you more than love—and I'll never stop saying that to you.

Kimmi Street, my sister from another mister. Thank you from the bottom of my heart. You saved me. You inspired me. You kept me standing in so many different ways. I love you more than love.

Extra-special love goes to Valentine PR, my ARC team, my Bookstagram team, Kelley Beckham, Sarah Norris, Kim Cermak, Kayti McGee, Tracey Waggaman, Elizabeth Kelley, Jennifer Porpora, Valentine Grinstead, Monica Murphy, and

Devney Perry, whom I love more than anything. I'm so grateful for all of you.

Mom and Dad, thanks for your unwavering belief in me and your constant encouragement. It means more than you'll ever know.

Brian, my words could never dent the love I feel for you. Trust me when I say, I love you more.

My Midnighters, you are such a supportive, loving, motivating group. Thanks for being such an inspiration, for holding my hand when I need it, and for always begging for more words. I love you all.

To all the influencers who read, review, share, post, TikTok —Thank you, thank you, thank you will never be enough. You do so much for our writing community, and we're so appreciative.

To my readers—I cherish each and every one of you. I'm so grateful for all the love you show my books, for taking the time to reach out to me, and for your passion and enthusiasm. I love, love, love you.

NEWSLETTER

Would you like a free book? To qualify for exclusive giveaways, be notified of new releases, and sales? Then, click <u>HERE</u> to sign up for my newsletter. I promise not to spam you.

MARNI'S MIDNIGHTERS

Getting to know my readers is one of my favorite parts about being an author. In Marni's Midnighters, my private Facebook group, I post covers before they're revealed to the public and excerpts of the projects I'm currently working on, and team members qualify for exclusive giveaways.

To join Marni's Midnighters, click HERE.

ABOUT THE AUTHOR

USA Today best-selling author Marni Mann knew she was going to be a writer since middle school. While other girls her age were daydreaming about teenage pop stars, Marni was fantasizing about penning her first novel. She crafts unique stories that weave together her love of darkness, mystery, passion, and human emotions. A New Englander at heart, she now lives with her husband in Sarasota, Florida. When she's not nose deep in her laptop, she's scouring for chocolate, sipping wine, traveling, boating, or devouring fabulous books.

Want to get in touch? Visit Marni at ...
www.marnismann.com
MarniMannBooks@gmail.com

MR. HOOKUP

Camden and Declan's clients, Easton, Grayson, and Holden—the founders of Hooked, a dating app—have their own book coming out. *Mr. Hookup*, which is Easton's story, is a steamy, forbidden, billionaire, office romance that's releasing on October 3, 2023.
Here's a sneak peek ...

———

CHAPTER ONE

A 100 percent match.

That was what the screen showed as I stared at it, silently, my mouth so wide, my jaws hurt.

How in the hell had I achieved that percentage?

As one of the founders of Hooked, a hook-up app my best friends and I had launched just today, I knew that number was nearly impossible to achieve. I knew that because while we were in beta testing, we'd run every possible scenario through Harvard's database, trying to configure an average percentage among our future users. We learned 100 percent was statistically equivalent to the odds of winning the lottery.

The average would be in the eighties. An overly impressive number would be in the low nineties.

But 100 percent?

Shit, that almost couldn't exist.

But it had.

With me.

And I was gazing at that number as it flashed in the center of my phone in twenty-eight-point green, Garamond font—a font, size, and color my best friends and I had debated over for weeks—and underneath was the user I'd matched with.

SaarasLove.

All right, Love, who are you? And are you going to rock my whole world?

That was the reason we'd developed this app in the first place.

To be rocked.

And rocked hard.

With my friends and I nearing the end of our final semester of grad school at Harvard, we lacked two very important things —time and money. We didn't want to spend hours at the bar every night, fishing for women, buying drinks, when we were only after one thing.

Hooking up.

After a late-night session of the three of us bitching about how tired we were of the relentless pattern of time, money, and courting, Hooked was born.

But never did any of us anticipate a perfect match.

If I logged into the mainframe and checked the users who had already signed up, I was positive there wouldn't be another with a number so high.

Unless . . .

My heart began to pound, my throat tightening as I pushed myself off my bed and peeked out into what used to be our living room and was now our makeshift office. My best friends, who also happened to be my roommates, were on the couch. Grayson had his laptop resting on his legs, a beer in one hand, his phone in the other.

"Easton, you look like you just swallowed a fucking goat," he said. "You all right, buddy?" His backward hat gave just enough slack that he could furrow his brows.

"Is there a glitch in the system?" I nodded toward his lap. "Check right now and make sure couples are matching at all different percentages."

He dropped his phone and began to type one-handed. "We're all good." He took his hat off and ran his hand through his dark, untamed mop. "Jesus, you just scared the shit out of me."

Holden was in the same position, but double-fisting two mugs with a set of headphones stretched across his head, cupping both ears. As though he could sense my fear, he glanced up from his screen, using his shoulder to free up his ear. "What'd I miss?"

"Just Easton taking ten years off my life, that's all," Grayson barked. He held the bottle to his lips, guzzling until it was gone. "He thought there was a glitch."

Holden shot up straight, setting both mugs down and knocking the other headphone off his ear, the headband crashing to the couch as he began to type. "Was there?"

"No," I told him.

Satisfied with my answer, Holden lifted both drinks off the table, taking a sip from one and then the other.

"What do you have there?" I asked. "Two different kinds of coffee?"

"Coffee in this one"—he held up his right hand—"and

349

water over here"—he held up his left hand. "You see, I've got to chase the caffeine with something neutral or I'll be climbing the walls soon."

It wasn't even ten in the morning. One was already drinking beer and one had enough energy to run the Boston Marathon.

And we all had class in an hour.

Holden placed one of the mugs down and rubbed his dark blue eyes. "What made you think there was a glitch?"

I took a seat on the chair next to the couch. "I matched with someone at a hundred percent."

Grayson reached into the six-pack that was sitting on the floor and took out a full beer. "Impossible." He twisted off the cap and tossed it toward the kitchen, missing by several feet. "I don't believe you."

I held the phone out so both could see the screen.

"I still don't believe it." Grayson used his free hand to type, pecking the keys much harder than he needed to. "I'm reaching out to David and Brennon to make sure something else isn't going wrong, or maybe there's some weird shit with your account."

David and Brennon were our coders and good friends who were finishing up their master's degrees at MIT and had developed our entire app. It was amazing what an unlimited supply of weed and beer had bought us, an arrangement we wouldn't have gotten from anyone but them.

"Well, I believe it," Holden said as he crossed his legs over the coffee table. "Think of how perfect you and this girl will be if you're already this compatible."

"He's not looking for perfect, he's just looking to get his dick wet," Grayson replied.

Holden wiped off the creamer that had stuck to his golden-brown mustache. "Regardless, it'll still be pretty wild if you're hooking up with someone you have that much in common with."

"Shit." Grayson slowly looked up from his laptop. "David said nothing is wrong. You really are the fucking unicorn of this app, my friend."

"I can't believe it." I shook my head. "We know the chances of this happening. How did it happen to me?"

Grayson turned his tall frame, positioning himself into the corner of the couch, and crossed his long legs. "I'm just glad it didn't happen to me. I have zero interest in anything perfect, permanent, or pouty—all potential possibilities when you match at one hundred percent."

Grayson, the forever antiromance spokesman, would rather be castrated than settle down.

Holden laughed. "Well, I think it's phenomenal"—he winked at our grumpy friend—"and maybe this was the whole reason why you came up with the concept of Hooked: fate matched you with the one."

Even though I didn't agree, Holden had an interesting take on it, which didn't surprise me given that he was the romantic one of our trio.

Hooked, initially, was my idea. I'd been the one to lead the bitching session.

But this couldn't be why.

I was sure of that.

Grayson rolled his eyes. "It's a good thing we have Mr. Romance over here, creating happily ever afters for us."

"What's her username?" Holden asked me, ignoring Grayson. "You know, so I know what to call your future wife."

I waved away that thought, but still replied, "SaarasLove."

Grayson snorted. "She better not turn into your wife. I need a sidekick while I continue sleeping my way through this

city, and we know this dude"—he pointed his thumb at Holden
—"is getting hitched the first opportunity he gets."

"Have you matched yet?" I asked Grayson.

"Eighty-one percent," he replied.

"Who would have thought there were women in Boston
who would have anything in common with you," Holden said
to him.

"Miracles happen," Grayson shot back.

"What did you end up scoring?" I asked Holden.

He flipped on ESPN, waiting to hear the score of last
night's Sox game, before he replied, "Eighty-nine percent." His
smile was so polished and white and straight, he could score
himself a toothpaste commercial. "I'm seeing her tonight."

Grayson took another long drink of his beer. "This motherfucker will show up with roses and wine, I'll bet my dinner
on it."

"So?" Holden scratched his two-week-old beard. "I
consider that kind of stuff foreplay and there's nothing wrong
with it."

"Except the app wasn't created for that reason," Grayson
said. "Why don't you save the money you don't have and just
focus on pus—"

"I'm going to let you two hash out whatever this is," I
chimed in, interrupting Grayson. "I have to go message Love."

"Love," Grayson roared as I got up from the chair. "Good
luck with that."

I flipped him off and returned to my bedroom, adjusting
the pillows behind my back as I loaded the app, pulling up
SaarasLove's profile. What set our app apart from our competitors was that instead of using first or last names along with
photos of the user's face, we only allowed usernames and body
shots or icons to protect everyone's identities. Within the
private chat feature, users could exchange whatever informa-

tion they wanted—pictures, names, phone numbers—but that was at their discretion.

What I could gather from SaarasLove's profile was that she lived within a sixty-mile radius of the zip code I'd provided—a distance she couldn't exceed, or we wouldn't have matched— and her picture was a long-range, out-of-focus shot of her sitting on a rocky beach, fully clothed.

I needed to know more about her.

I opened the chat feature under my BostonLifer account, a name that had come to me when we'd gotten closer to launch, and typed out a message.

ME

> Hey you, my 100% match. I've got to say, that's an impressive number. I'm pretty sure it means we're supposed to meet up.

SAARASLOVE

> Hiii! Honestly, that number kinda shocked me too. So, who are you, Mr. Boston? Tell me everything, don't leave out a single detail. :)

ME

> Getting right to the point, I like it. I'm in my last year of grad school, I just started a business with my best friends, I'm an avid Pats and Red Sox fan, I'm pretty athletic myself, and I'm into all things outdoors. Your turn.

SAARASLOVE

> Just finishing up my undergrad and working, like you, but for someone else, not myself. I wouldn't call myself athletic, but I love to walk. If I could turn traveling into a career, that would be my ultimate dream job—which I do a lot anyway for my employer. I love bad reality TV and ice cream, the chocolate-ier, the better. In fact, if frozen Hershey syrup becomes a thing, I'll be their top customer.

ME

And it looks like you enjoy the beach, according to your pic.

SAARASLOVE

I do. I love it.

Is that scotch in your pic? Whiskey? Are those the same—forgive me, I'm a simple drinker and just stick with wine.

ME

Scotch, yes. When I feel like indulging, that's my drink of choice.

SAARASLOVE

Except you're on a college budget, like me, and drowning in student loans, so you wait until the pub has $2 drafts, amiright?

ME

Lol. You're definitely not wrong about that.

What are your plans for this weekend?

SAARASLOVE

I'm actually headed home. I've got some things to tie up there.

ME

Is home far?

SAARASLOVE

It'll feel like a totally different world from here.

ME

I was going to ask you if you wanted to meet up.

SAARASLOVE

> Mr. Boston, what I love about this new app is that not every student I go to school with knows I'm on it since they can't see my name or my pic. What I hate about this app is that I have no idea what you look like. Show me something, anything, just so I can have a feel of you to know if there's any chemistry.

I laughed as I read her message.

If she only knew she was speaking to a co-owner, something I wouldn't tell her.

The guys and I had decided not to tell anyone until we absolutely had to. We just didn't know how that would go over when we were meeting up with women we'd matched with.

I certainly wasn't going to ask one of my roommates to come in and snap a picture of me. The amount of shit I'd get for it, especially from Grayson, would be endless. So, I slipped off my T-shirt and moved in front of my full-length mirror, aiming the camera at my chest and abs, areas I worked hard at when I was at the gym, and I turned my face to make sure it wasn't included when I took the shot.

Pleased with the result, I attached the photo to the message and sent it.

ME

Love, your wish is my command.

SAARASLOVE

> Hold a sec. I need to process THAT. And maybe wipe the drool from my lip.

ME

Lol.

SAARASLOVE

> Mr. Boston, wow. WOW. Wow.

> **ME**
>
> I'm glad you like what you see.

> **SAARASLOVE**
>
> You're freaking chiseled. Like, no. Love, yes.

Several seconds later, a picture of her came through. It looked like she was at the same beach as in her profile shot, but in this one, she was in a bikini. Her knees were bent, and she was holding them against her chest with her arms wrapped around them. She was looking away from the camera, the angle showing her long dark hair and toned arms, her thin frame, the tiny ball her body was tucked into.

> **ME**
>
> Love, you're gorgeous . . . and that body, damn.

> **SAARASLOVE**
>
> Thank you. :) But it's not exactly a close-up shot like yours, so you're not seeing everything, ya know?

> **ME**
>
> I've seen enough to know you're beautiful.
>
> How about that date when you get back from home?

> **SAARASLOVE**
>
> I'd really love that.

Click HERE to purchase Mr. Hookup.

THE PLAYBOY

Would you like to read Macon Spade's story? *The Playboy* is book one in The Spade Hotel Series, where the ultimate playboy heads to Hawaii to build the family's most elaborate hotel. But construction isn't the only thing that goes down on that island. Macon's book is pure steam and scorching chemistry, and it's releasing December 7, 2023.

Click HERE to purchase The Playboy.

ALSO BY MARNI MANN

SPADE HOTEL SERIES—EROTIC ROMANCE

The Playboy (December 2023)

Book 2 (Winter 2024)

Book 3 (Spring 2024)

HOOKED SERIES—CONTEMPORARY ROMANCE

Mr. Hook-up (October 2023)

Book 2 (Spring 2024)

THE DALTON FAMILY SERIES—EROTIC ROMANCE

The Lawyer

The Billionaire

The Single Dad

The Intern

The Bachelor

THE AGENCY SERIES—EROTIC ROMANCE

Signed

Endorsed

Contracted

Negotiated

Dominated

STAND-ALONE NOVELS

Even If It Hurts (Contemporary Romance)

Before You (Contemporary Romance)

The Better Version of Me (Psychological Thriller)

Lover (Erotic Romance)

Drowning (Contemporary Romance)

THE BEARDED SAVAGES SERIES—EROTIC ROMANCE

The Unblocked Collection

Wild Aces

MOMENTS IN BOSTON SERIES—CONTEMPORARY ROMANCE

When Ashes Fall

When We Met

When Darkness Ends

THE PRISONED SERIES—DARK EROTIC THRILLER

Prisoned

Animal

Monster

THE SHADOWS DUET—EROTIC ROMANCE

Seductive Shadows

Seductive Secrecy

THE BAR HARBOR DUET—NEW ADULT

Pulled Beneath

Pulled Within

THE MEMOIR SERIES—DARK MAINSTREAM FICTION

Memoirs Aren't Fairytales

Scars from a Memoir